"Thea Sutton's prose combines Gothic relish with a surgical, lancing
precision. Compelling, original and brilliantly disturbing."
—Kate Weinberg, author of *The Truants*, one of *New York Times*'
10 Best Crime Novels of 2020

"The writing is elegant and powerful. No word wasted
and each sentence adding one more brush stroke to this dark,
gaslit painting. *The Women of Blackmouth Street* pulses with
dread and foreboding, with a devious ending that is just
one more turn of the screw. Boldly impressive."
—Anthony Atanasio, director and filmmaker,
The Persistence of Memory

"*The Women of Blackmouth Street* submerges the reader into a heady,
brutal past with uncompromising mind doctor Georgia Buchanan
and her fierce desire to save the most vulnerable."
—Jenna Kalinsky

The
Women of
Blackmouth
Street

The
Women of
Blackmouth
Street

THEA SUTTON

Encircle Publications
Farmington, Maine, U.S.A.

The Women of Blackmouth Street © 2021 Thea Sutton

Paperback ISBN 13: 978-1-64599-263-9
Hardcover ISBN 13: 978-1-64599-264-6
E-book ISBN 13: 978-1-64599-265-3
Kindle ISBN 13: 978-1-64599-266-0

Encircle editor: Michael Piekny
Cover design by Deirdre Wait
Cover images © Getty Images

Published by:

Encircle Publications
PO Box 187
Farmington, ME 04938

info@encirclepub.com
http://encirclepub.com

"It is wrong, always, everywhere, and for everyone, to believe anything upon insufficient evidence."
—William James

PROLOGUE

"Hysteria." The doctor drew out the syllables. "From the Greek, *hysterikos. Of the womb.* Or rather, *suffering* from the womb, as the meaning has evolved in our time."

He turned, bearded chin tilting to his audience, from the young woman strapped to the metal table beside him. The bowl of the theater pulsed a dazzling white in contrast to the wooden church-like pews where the medical students sat, eyes locked on the creature before them.

She could be a corpse but for the rise and fall of her chest, the sliver of lids over fixed eyes.

"What you will witness today are the four stages of hysteria." On a tray behind the doctor lay a leather-covered box with red-velvet lining in which nestled a cranial drill, silver-plated with a shiny round topknot handle. "You will see that at the beginning of an attack, the patient's mouth is wide as if she is screaming." The doctor ambled around the table taking a leisurely stroll but, like the best of impresarios, never losing eye contact with his audience, as though daring them to turn away from his spectacle.

"Then you will observe the epileptoid phase or tonic rigidity where the young lady's muscles will contract, her neck twist, her legs thrash in counter rhythm to the gyration of her fists outwards."

A few men in the front row shifted in their seats, pens targeting notebooks, faces reflecting the yellow-green cast of the encircling walls.

The doctor smiled his satisfaction. "I don't suppose any of you has ever witnessed this progression?" A rhetorical question. "The chronic spasms are followed by extreme emotional states such as lust, hate and fear. What we can expect is for our patient to slip into delirium or a hallucinatory state. She may plead, choke, howl her pain."

Presenting his back to his disciples for the first time, the doctor picked up the cranial drill from its pocket of red velvet. Holding it up like a chalice to the light buzzing overhead. The bare leg—a gleaming white ankle manacled by a black strap—twitched.

Vision blurring, I turned away. When I looked up again, the dimensions of the lecture hall stretched and contracted. To the rear of the theater, a flight of stairs and a row of doors, blistered paint chipping from the frames. I rose and began the climb, each step lengthy and impossible. Until I reached the first door, slightly ajar.

In the slant of light, a woman with greying hair waited, it seemed, just for me, yellow bed jacket over her shoulders. Her lips crooked upwards in a relieved smile at my entrance, features patrician save for the nose eaten away by the pox. Behind her sat a girl on a faded pink divan. Her pale fingers played with the long tassels of a scarf on her lap until, as though coming to a decision, she lifted the fabric to her head like a crown before slipping, then looping, then tightening it around her neck.

The world spun. My mouth swamped with the taste of metal, dull and bitter, an instant before vision narrowed to a pinpoint of black.

CHAPTER 1

"Apologies for disturbing, ma'am. I'm afraid the matter can't wait."

I bolted awake. Sunlight saturated the room through a dusty window and for a moment I was back in Boston, far away from the gloom that usually gripped London and its environs. In the doorway stood the squared-off shape of a caretaker. His eyes, rheumy and pale, leaked a rare sympathy.

The drip of last night's cocaine lozenge lingered in the back of my throat, along with the sensation of a nail screwing itself into the back of my head. "I'm sorry, what can't wait?" Impatience mixed with dread, my voice was thick from lack of sleep, my hands smoothing cobwebs of hair from my face. Ignoring the stiffness in my limbs, the pinch in my lower vertebra, I straightened in the spare wooden chair where I'd collapsed in the early hours of the morning.

I recalled entering the gates of Bethlem Royal Hospital late last evening, the fires that had broken out in the London docks reddening the sky with angry welts. Running alongside Lambeth Road, *Bedlam*, as the asylum was known to me and my colleagues in America and Europe, consisted of a squat central block with two vulture-like wings comprising three stories on either side. The last place I wanted to be.

I'd escaped Boston to leave my work behind, though perhaps *escape* was too strong a word. I was searching for a type of recalibration, a place of quiet and far enough away from scandal. This summons to Bedlam was both unwelcome and unsettling.

I was more than familiar with asylums, although I'd only had an abbreviated tour of Bedlam one year previously under the watchful eye and bulbous nose of Mr. Pond. I cast the caretaker a quick glance. Last evening he'd needlessly pointed out that female patients occupied the west wing and males the east before we'd headed off in a westward direction, finishing with a warren of wards and rooms located off the galleries, each one containing a single toilet, a sink and cold baths.

Endless corridors of mental ruin, it was rumored that it would take five hours to walk all the wards of Bethlem Royal Hospital. And I'd done my best last night.

The small library where I'd surrendered after my useless search was empty except for rows of mildewing books, spines cracked and worn, exposed by the sepia filtering through a grimed window. Morel's *Traité des Maladies Mentales*. Prichard's *A Treatise on Insanity and Other Disorders Affecting the Mind*. Charcot's *Les Névroses Traumatiques*. The hallmarks of my profession.

With a pronounced stoop, the caretaker stared at me. He executed a series of meaningless steps, one back and one forward on the threshold, each annoying in its own way. I recalled that a handful of silver, readily received, had made my unsanctioned visit last evening possible, that and the keys on Pond's belt opening the locks on two dozen ward doors.

Ignoring his expectant gaze, I squinted across the room to the scarred desk where my reticule and, more significantly, the note I'd received twenty-four hours earlier at Roxbury Park waited like a lesion that demanded an immediate excision. An anonymous summons that had lured me to Bedlam, its meaning obscured. An echo of my failure back in Boston? Or something else entirely?

Another woman soon will die;
Unless Georgia Buchanan arrives in time.
Bedlam, September 7, 1891

The words repeated in my head, taking me back to Boston. At the thought, my father's image bloomed like a rash in my mind's eye, standing on the balcony off the bloated conservatory that he had built to exacting specifications for his summer home in Rhode Island, each slab of marble imported from Perrugia and each leaded glass panel judged with an eye grown accustomed to lashings of money.

I pictured him waiting outside the rooms of my practice in Boston, a man still in his prime with an outrageous fortune already behind him. His face in profile, limned in shadow and disapproval, watching from the window as my patient, veil pulled across her face, disappeared into the darkness of an anonymous carriage.

When he finally turned around, mouth folding into a frown, I knew what he saw, a daughter to whom he'd given everything and who was tossing it back at him with both hands.

Diseased minds were my interest—how could George Buchanan ever accept that fact? I spent my time with haunted widows, scullery maids, and nervous girls, along with professors and cadavers, rather than with the set to which my father had spent most of his life acquiring access. People like Archibald Rivington, the next American ambassador to Britain, and his recently deceased daughter, Sophie. The experiment that I didn't want to think about right now. The colossal failure that undid my life.

The ocean between us was a good thing.

The caretaker cleared his throat. "There's a gentleman to see you."

I pretended not to hear, thinking that coffee, or better still, a dose of Dover's powder, or at the very least a lozenge would have done.

Smoothed the nerves, dulled the aches. My lips were dry and a cigarette would serve, but none was at hand. If there was one element I'd learned in pursuit of my peculiar profession, it was that physiology was a curious thing—we were nothing if not an alchemical soup.

I settled back down on the hard chair. "Before you show him in, a question, Mr. Pond."

"Will do my utmost, ma'am."

"The patients. In the women's wing. Any unusual disturbances this past night?"

He scratched his cheek. "Depends what you're meaning."

"Anything serious." Anything fatal was what I really wanted to ask. *Anyone dangling from a noose?* Someone I could possibly save from killing herself? From slashing her wrists? Isn't that what my summons, the childish rhyme, was all about, a gruesome taunt calling me back to my dead Sophie?

"Worst was a fit. A choking fit. Though she's one that's prone to them."

My eyes closed in gratitude.

"The gentleman waiting, ma'am."

My eyes drifted open. "Tell him another time." Keeping men waiting was a prerogative I'd made my own.

"Major Arthur Griffith." As if that was all the explanation needed. Before I could object, the caretaker shuffled aside to allow London's Assistant Commissioner of Police to enter the library.

CHAPTER 2

"Miss Buchanan, good to see you again, despite the unusual hour and circumstances." Griffith grasped for normalcy where there was none, holding the rim of his black bowler, a signet ring winking. "Your man told me of your whereabouts."

The chair creaked beneath me. The last thing I needed right now was a functionary who presumed acquaintanceship after the briefest of contacts. "You might find your time better spent apprehending murderers and thieves than inquiring after my whereabouts."

"Noted, Miss Buchanan, and the very reason I happen to find myself here at Bethlem." Griffith claimed the only other chair in the room, hat balanced on his knees, a royal purple waistcoat straining in protest. He was one of those luckless men whose head was too small for his body, lost beneath a profuse moustache and outsized mutton chops.

"Next I suppose you will tell me why I was summoned to meet you here under such mysterious circumstances. You might as well have simply signed the rather threatening note, Commissioner."

"I'm not certain I take your meaning."

"And I'm not certain I take yours. You are being deliberately obscure. If you had wanted to meet with me here, you might well have asked directly." Although both of us knew, I would have declined his invitation. "Regardless, I'm on sabbatical and hadn't anticipated acquainting myself with patients here at the asylum."

He looked at me, eyebrows lifted. "I suppose I should address you as *doctor*."

"Not sure where you learned that piece of information. I'm not a physician."

"Forgive me if I'm not entirely clear on that point." He paused, elbows on the arms of the chair, touching his fingertips together. "Nevertheless, our discussion at Roxbury House this past weekend led me to believe, given your unusual expertise, that you might be interested in assisting us."

The Denby's country house, an invitation for a weekend that I'd reluctantly accepted, where I'd paid little enough attention to Griffith sitting at the opposite end of the dining table that seated twenty-two. Until later, dragooned into a corner by Lady Denby, I'd listened to the Assistant Police Commissioner's lurid and self-important accounting of recent murders in the nether regions of London. "Helping whom?" I asked.

Bitterness inhabited the slack jowls of his face, despite the pale eyes and the regard that couldn't quite hide an innate and personal dislike—of me, specifically—and whose origins weren't clear. I was convinced I'd never met him before but whether he knew my father or had heard of my work in Boston or abroad was entirely possible. Smiling at the question. "The Metropolitan Police and more precisely, a particular investigation. One that grows increasingly urgent."

"The matter you were forced to attend to, cutting short your weekend at Roxbury House?"

"Not unlike the urgency of your situation?" He repeated my words back to me. "The matter you were forced to attend to here at the asylum?"

"Of a scholarly nature." I'd concede that at least, but the demureness rang false, an attribute that didn't come naturally to me.

"In the middle of the night?" The signet ring on his little finger flashed gold. "But then that is the nature of crises, isn't it?"

A moaning in the background began in the hallway outside, arced and then ceased, the lament stifled into silence. I was accustomed to pauper lunatics like the ones here at Bethlem, scientific experiments at the Salpêtrière and hysterics at Boston's Nervine Sanitorium. But now I had an Assistant Commissioner, one leg crossed and one black leather shoe rocking, chin angled in a pose of superiority, looking for someone or something here in this madhouse.

There was a hint of accusation in Griffith's gaze, as though we'd met somewhere else, in disagreeable circumstances, before the Denbys, although I couldn't think when. The Denbys were peripheral friends of my father's, and who knew where Griffith's connection to them began or ended.

I'd encountered Griffith's type before, the careful mannerisms, finely rounded vowels. No doubt landed gentry, reduced to earning a living in the civil service and stinging from the insult. Perhaps with a father cursed with a penchant but not a talent for gambling. I saw a mosquito-infested plantation moldering somewhere in the far-flung reaches of the empire. And an older brother who had inherited the wreckage. Primogeniture in motion.

Griffith interrupted my thoughts. "I should think you might be interested in this case, Miss Buchanan."

"And why might that be?"

"We are dealing with *a series* of murders here in London. At least three of which we know are connected."

I was pulled along, reluctantly. "Yes, the ones you'd referred to at Roxbury House, after dinner." The series of murdered women. In the ward nearby, a door clanked shut, iron hinges creaking. I shook my head. "You must be mistaken. Surely you have plenty of investigators at your disposal. I've no experience with murderers."

"Of course, you don't, Miss Buchanan. But you do have experience that we lack, in related matters."

"I'm not sure I follow you."

"Then let me be blunt, if you insist." He paused for effect. "We are dealing with a madman, a brutal assailant, a deranged killer."

"Distressing, but I don't see how I can help."

"What you mean to say is that you decline to be of assistance." Griffith sighed extravagantly to show his disappointment. "You are a reputed alienist, Miss Buchanan. Frankly, the surgeons we have at our disposal are journeymen at best, drunkards at worst. Whereas your association with Dr. William James at Harvard and Professor Jean-Martin Charcot in Paris would bring a certain credibility to our investigation."

He let the statement stand before adding. "Your knowledge of the workings of the human mind, of the workings of insanity, could prove of value in the apprehension and conviction of this murderer. We are combatting more than just an assailant here, Miss Buchanan. Anarchists and social reformers are using these killings for their own ends. The entire city is about to go over the edge."

My stomach coiled, which I told myself was from a lack of breakfast rather than a sense that Griffith was about to move from persuasion to something stronger. It had started with his anonymous summons, the one he wouldn't admit to sending, knowing full well it was a lure that someone with my professional instincts couldn't resist.

Griffith nodded, as though listening to another conversation altogether. He slanted away to peer out the lone window where, other than a brick courtyard, there was nothing to see, a finality without a horizon. He didn't look at me when he said. "Another body, butchered and bloody, was discovered this past weekend in Shoreditch—and you're quite right. It is the reason for my having to leave Roxbury House so quickly. Another actress or prostitute or whatever we are to call them, behind one of the music halls. Perpetrated by the same hand."

I didn't share Griffith's casual disregard for these victims: I saw them, as a woman of science, as equal flesh and bone to the Assistant Commissioner and myself, our bodies and our minds formed by the miracle of nature and the rules of nurture. After a pause that was long enough, I said, "I've no particular insights into the mind of a killer."

"I had hoped you would be agreeable, Miss Buchanan." Griffith turned away from the window, back toward me. There was a new sternness in the tone, the headmaster with a recalcitrant student. His aristocratic diffidence had disappeared.

I suddenly recalled something that Alice James had once said, in the glowing green of the garden in Beacon Hill, after her stay at the sanatorium over that cold, wet spring. *How sick I am of being good and how much I should respect myself if I could burst out and make everyone wretched for twenty-four hours.* In my experience, women were taught not to want what they wanted. It had never done Alice James much good.

My voice sharpened. "Although our previous meeting was short, I didn't expect you to come away with the impression that I'm interested in pursuing a practice on Harley Street. I'm here in London on sabbatical, to follow some research, and therefore not inclined to take part in one of your investigations, Assistant Commissioner."

"You have no care for those wretched women?"

"Your newspapers tell of the wretchedness of the poor every day and little enough is done about it," I rose from the chair, my shoulders tightening like bolts. I blocked out the images from last evening and from the last seven years of my life. The suffering, the misery, the acute psychic pain etched on the faces of those swept away by madness.

Griffith cocked his head at the outlandish opinion and at the suspicion that I was perhaps a socialist. Concern for the poor was suspect, particularly for the only daughter of one of America's wealthiest men of industry. His pointed glance took in the superb tailoring of my long, fitted jacket with its three-quarter length sleeves and matching striped skirt, gleaming with newness and, frankly, money. He rose to stand behind his chair, gripping the rails.

We faced each other like pugilists in a ring. It occurred to me suddenly that he must have some experience with interrogation and, worse still, that we weren't so different after all. We both had gruesome tales to tell.

Griffith cleared his throat. "I am not a man without sensitivity or refinement, and it pains me to allude to your recent difficulties, the reason for your fleeing Boston and leaving behind your medical practice, if I might call it such. I value discretion as do you, surely."

I stepped toward the table to collect my reticule. "Fleeing? I don't run from anything, Assistant Commissioner. You've a dramatic turn of mind." I paced to the door, one hand already on the cold ivory knob, the contact momentarily throwing me back into my dream, to the doctor in the operating theater, and another row of doors. Griffith circled behind me, the smooth movements belying his considerable size.

"Dare I say that I feel it unbearably rude to even mention the scandal." The Assistant Police Commissioner lowered his voice and I could feel his breath on the nape of my neck, hot and wet, scented with his morning's sausage and coffee. "And even less inclined to utter the name of that poor young girl. A child, really. Of such an illustrious family. I'm sure your father's largesse and influence did much to lessen the rumormongering, although," Griffith stepped back and, producing a pocket watch from his waistcoat, eyeing it, said "there are those who might see fit to exploit the tragedy."

A rush of white noise in my ears. "Don't think to coerce me."

Griffith clucked, his eyes bright. "This time it is you who is being dramatic, surely. I merely suggest that you keep an open mind and meet a colleague, a publisher who, if he is not delayed, has asked to meet with us here shortly." He pocketed his watch. "His arguments will prove more persuasive than mine."

CHAPTER 3

The doorknob twisted under my hand.

The stranger entered the library. He was taller than average, with thick hair cropped to his head, clean-shaven. An air of confidence in the set of his shoulders and the tilt of his jaw. Under his arm a leather satchel, the hide like a worn saddle in contrast to a jacket of fine herringbone.

Interesting how threat focused the attention. The newcomer and the room faded away and all I saw was the brocade swag tightening against Sophie Rivington's skin, her silk slippers kicking at the air in sweet, agonized release. William's voice echoed in my head. *The world is all the richer for having a devil in it, dear Georgia, so long as we keep our foot upon his neck.*

And when I looked up again, the specter of Sophie Rivington hanging from a noose was gone.

The stranger closed the door behind him, backing me into the center of the room.

"Punctual as always, Knight." The statement landed as a kind of criticism. Griffith patted his waistcoat. "Miss Buchanan, I should like to introduce Mr. Charles Knight, publisher of *The Illustrated London News*. And Knight, Miss Buchanan, freshly arrived from Boston."

"I was just leaving."

"I've come at the right time, then." Knight inserted himself into the breach, face unreadable, a tightness around the eyes.

"I was saying to Miss Buchanan that I'd hoped you might prove much more persuasive than I in engaging her to our shared cause. I have apprised her of the current circumstances, the murder of another actress, possibly the fifth by this madman, impressing upon her how much we require her particular expertise."

Knight adjusted the satchel under his arm. "You understand insanity, I'm led to believe, Miss Buchanan?"

"The Assistant Commissioner's assumption. I never claimed expertise."

A trolley outside the door, the clatter of dishes indicating that breakfast would soon be served in the dining hall. I knew it would be thin gruel for most and more robust porridge for those whose families could afford to slip a few coins to the orderlies who roamed the unending hallways; Bethlem Hospital was constructed with an Italianate design in mind, in itself a kind of madness

Knight's glance was speculative. I sensed the man knew more about me than was good and if I required a reminder, it was in the note in my reticule hanging from my wrist. A reminder that either of the two men could have sent it. The thought didn't sit well.

He gestured toward me with a replica of a smile. "Whatever definition we may agree upon with regards to your *expertise*, you are reputed to be an alienist, a mind doctor, from what I understand. Griffith here," he turned to the Assistant Commissioner, "would like to involve you in his most recent cause, and for what reason, I'm not entirely sure." He paused, sliding his satchel onto the desk, sending dust motes scattering into the air. "In any case, we have a matter that requires immediate attention. Your attention, Griffith. There's been another woman found. Killed. Murdered last night, it appears."

Several flies had risen from their death throes to bat the window. Griffith swatted one with his hat, muttering under his breath. "Nothing I don't already know, Knight. And the reason I've chased down Miss Buchanan here." Jowls flushed with irritation. "You sound positively delighted. Your runners and their detective cameras got there first and I won't ask how."

"It makes me wonder why your men don't spend more time protecting the citizenry in the East End. The resolution of this unending crisis is in your hands. You're the Assistant Commissioner, after all."

"We had an agreement, Knight."

"Your assumption, not mine."

Griffith sniffed. "These broadsheet wars you're determined to win—you win them at my discretion, Knight. Don't overplay your hand. You have nothing to gain but everything to lose if you fail to time this perfectly."

"Bloody hell, Griffith. Your career hangs in the balance each time the murderer slips from your grasp." Glaring, Knight rolled his shoulders under the fine suiting of his jacket before slipping the satchel from the table and back under his arm. "And let's not forget, I have something else that *you* might find of use."

I studied Griffith, his bulk filling the window. A sullen silence before he picked up his bowler hat. "We'll get to that, I promise you." He motioned towards the door, a sideways glance at me. "I should like for you to join us, Miss Buchanan."

Not the words I was hoping for. I turned away and looked at the row of books, their crooked spines with their gold and black lettering, mocking me. I was often accused of arrogance, of pride and of self-indulgence. What of it? Our lives were the stories that we told ourselves, stories that I helped patients construct, making patterns and finding shapes where none existed. Creating order from painful chaos. Playing God? Perhaps. Someone had to. Otherwise our time on this earth was comprised only of random events, revealing no moral arc, no heroic theme, and most often just a tragic refrain. On rare days, I helped make reason where there was none.

I remembered the dead woman. The dead *women*, according to Griffith and Knight. What order-out-of-chaos was owed them, I thought, a pang hitting my chest.

They waited at the library door, each with his own purpose in mind. Griffith, radiating a strange animosity. Knight, the publisher, with anger coarsening his features.

Against my better instincts, I left with them.

We spilled from Knight's carriage at Haggerston Street, somewhere off Drury Lane, heavy clouds threatening overhead. A crust of poverty pockmarked the low buildings, forsaken in the early morning. The ever-present film of coal laced the air, coating my tongue and watering my eyes. Walking in single file, following Knight's lead, past shuttered gin dens and scarred doss houses, we stopped after a few minutes when our path narrowed to nothing. A dead end.

It was hard to miss. A macabre still life on the ground in front of us. The woman's skirts arranged above the knee, striped woolen socks catching the milky light from an unknown source in the alley. Her mottled skin was the color of stained linen. As though she was straining to hear a question, her head was posed to the left, sightless eyes fixed on a crack of sky.

A corpse in first bloom. I sank to my knees. She gave off the aroma of spirits, a combination of offal and musk, her mouth open in a rictus of surprise. Mere anticlimax because, I knew, with a clean cut across the jugular, bleeding lasted, at most, three minutes. A slice from the right to the left side of her throat proved the point and would have produced only a neat spurt of blood. No uncontrollable geyser.

I looked up to see Griffith crossing his arms over his uniformed chest. He scanned the environs, eyes darting. "An untidy business. Let's have her removed." His words left a mist in the cool morning air. "Where is the patrol? They must be nearby. They should have left a man here to ensure no one tampers with the remains."

A dove cooed in the distance, like a mourner at a wake, a peaceful sound in contrast to the sacrilege at our feet. I waited for Knight to recoil but he'd clearly already seen the photographs his runners had taken. "The last thing you want is a crowd to gather round, I'd wager." He strung out each word to make his point, a grin aimed at Griffith, boots gleaming in the mud.

Griffith scowled. "You've already taken your damned photographs. To add to your collection." He lowered his voice. "You find it in your best interest to publish sensational details despite the fact the public, not to say the rabble, is roused to a fever pitch. To boost your circulation, nothing more."

Knight's brow shot up. "Why not publish photographs as evidence of these killings? We're pioneers, Griffith, modernizers. Photography can be a tool not only for newspapers but also for the law. Our cameras can help the police in apprehending and prosecuting the perpetrator of these crimes. You should be delighted."

Griffith's pause was significant. "We hold off publishing the photos until the killer is caught. Not before. If you wish to have continued access, Knight."

The narrow alley was still, holding its breath.

Although it was morning, the little daylight that was allowed to penetrate this corner of hell seemed to fall on the corpse. Intestines had been draped over the dead woman's shoulders, a shawl glistening in the gloom. It was no secret in our enlightened scientific age that there were many anatomical routes to the body cavity and to the abdominal area with its nest of female organs. With her skirts around her waist, it was simple to ease the knife into the abdomen and pull the entrails through the opening. One sweep of the blade, no more, had exposed the two almonds and the pear, the decorous nomenclature for the female organs, to public view.

I rose, leaning away from the body, from the woman that once was.

"We should get her to the morgue." Miraculously, we were still alone, shuttered windows, leaning crazily, the only witnesses so far. I ignored Knight, looking to Griffith to summon one of his patrols.

Knight shrugged his shoulders, then stared down at the dead woman, his expression contemplative, as though we had all the time in the world. "No surprise that such a person would end up here, in such a state, attacked by a madman."

Griffith expelled a breath, fixing his hat more firmly to his head. "Your pronouncements are of no use to us here, Knight, or anywhere, much less in your damn broadsheet."

"*Attacked by a madman.*" Knight nodding as if to himself. "What is madness if not an aggressive response to poverty, then?"

I watched him adjust his cravat, eyes lowered, as though he were composing his next editorial. He seemed detached, curiously unmoved. My breath billowed in the damp air. "Madness is having this discussion in an alley while a dead woman lies at our feet."

Knight smoothed the pristine linen at his throat. "I can't help that reformists like Charles Booth are unearthing the truth about the poor and destitute in the East End. And choosing to make the knowledge public."

With a glower for the publisher, Griffith expelled a breath, then paced around the corpse, glancing at the low-slung buildings, like broken, pitted faces surrounding us. "Take a look, if you dare, Knight. The East End has only ever been disreputable. It's said one in four of these houses doubles as a gin shop, for God's sake. As a publisher and a gentleman, you should know where your loyalties lie and it's not with the rabble." The level of enmity was thick. "And as London's Assistant Commissioner of Police, I shall put an end to this."

"You're doing a fine job thus far." Knight's arms folded across his chest.

"Careful, Knight."

Something passed over the publisher's face so quickly I might have imagined it. A contraction of his jaw, a thinning of his lips. The white crispness of his shirt against the dark of his jacket was a sudden assault in the damp of the alley.

I swung away from the woman whose frozen eyes stared up at us. "If you won't call for the patrol, I will."

Griffith jammed his hat lower onto his head, glancing at Knight then back at me. I was the third person in this duel. I doubted the Assistant Commissioner carried a whistle in his jacket to summon the constabulary. Adjusting the brim over his forehead, Griffith looked away from us and stared down at the corpse as if for the last time before turning without a word and walking in the direction of Drury Lane.

Resisting the urge to cover the body with my cloak, I took a breath, noticing for the first time a faint rain dampening my face. Wiping at the moisture with a gloved hand, I watched Knight adjust the satchel under his arm with precision, as though a treasure lodged there. We stood apart and silent, until he walked around the dead woman to stand so close to me, I was forced to look up at him.

He didn't hide the sudden intensity of his gaze. "Griffith asked you to assist him in building his case against Tarski." Rain glistened on the lapels of his jacket. "As the Shoreditch Savage. Correct?"

Knight was two steps ahead of me, and at least one ahead of Griffith, and I didn't like it. I leaned toward him, deliberately taking up what was left of the space between us. "I don't know what you're talking about. The name means nothing to me."

Knight slid a hand in a pocket, looking nothing like the London publisher I'd met an hour earlier. "Aaron Tarski, a Polish immigrant, a madman and a Jew."

"An immigrant, a madman and a Jew. The one doesn't follow the other." There was no argument here. "Your logic confounds me."

"It shouldn't." The publisher paced back, away from me. His eyes were hard. "I suggest that you don't involve yourself with Griffith or this investigation."

I said nothing, nor for a moment did he. Above us, somebody

opened a window, then wisely closed it again. "I don't take kindly to direction or threats, Mr. Knight. Not at all."

"That's unwise, Miss Buchanan. And you strike me as an intelligent woman, or so I've been led to understand." Again, the sense that he knew more about me than he should. "You must learn to take better care of yourself. And of those close to you." He let the statement float between us before adding, "I'm not sure that you're aware, but we have acquaintances in common."

Every muscle in my body tensed at the same time. Someone, somewhere, banged on a door with the percussive obsession of a lunatic, breaking the spell. Then voices as Griffith and three men with a stretcher squeezed themselves into the alley.

Like so much rubbish at the bottom of a bin, the body was removed, transformed into a bundle of heaped rags, a few brown curls escaping from the burlap. Hoisted onto a stretcher with little enough care, the men jostled their burden toward the alley's exit, a haphazard procession. In a few moments, nothing left to show on the ground except a jumble of mud and stones. I didn't allow myself to think about who she'd been, the life she'd lived.

Around us signs of life, a troupe of rag pickers fanning out like rats released from a trap. The distant sounds of wagon wheels crunching over flagstones. The doves replaced by black crows cawing in our ears. Moisture dripped from Griffith's hat, clinging to his beard. "Now that's done, we shall return to the station on Commercial Street." The police station. He made the announcement as if from a podium.

Knight trapped Griffith with a stare. "Where you will ask Miss Buchanan to build a case against an innocent man."

The Assistant Commissioner took aim. "Knight, for the second time this morning, I am advising you to tread carefully."

A flicker of emotion in Knight's eyes like he was remembering something else, something he wanted to forget. I glanced at the satchel he still held under his arm. And watched Griffith do the same.

"Your photographs," Griffith said, the words heavy with distaste.

"There in your satchel, captured no doubt by your bloody cameras." He turned to me. "Please let me explain, Miss Buchanan. Once we have the killer condemned and put away, with your help of course, Knight may publish the photographs of these Shoreditch victims to commemorate the victory of justice done." And in case the publisher hadn't understood. "Once I've *won*, Knight, just to be clear."

Knight grunted a laugh. "I *may publish*, Griffith? As though I'll be waiting for your permission? A reminder—I have other photographs in which you've expressed a particular interest." He trained a razored gaze on me.

Griffith pretended he wasn't listening. "Miss Buchanan, you will find all of these photographs of Knight's, *all of them*, of interest. Particularly, if you persist in your reluctance to assist us in this investigation."

From damp to suddenly cold, it was as though my body sensed something my mind couldn't grasp. Griffith continued. "There is little I can do, you understand, should *The Illustrated London News* choose to publish photographs and divulge the details of the life and death of a fragile girl from Boston, from such a good family with political aspirations yet. Terrible to have her splayed like a pinned butterfly in a curio cabinet for all the world to see."

Knight glanced at the satchel before his eyes travelled back to my face. I forced a swallow, throat dry. *I suggest you don't involve yourself with Griffith or this investigation.* The threat echoed in my mind and in the alleyway.

CHAPTER 4

Avoidance was a curious thing. How well I knew of the absurd concealment families engaged in, secreting away their loved ones in barbarous conditions, often strait-coated, shackled in attics and dank basements. The punishment of bed rest and constant feeding for the nervous patient who had already taken willingly to darkened rooms. Circuitous conversations, whispered asides, blank-faced denial, everything and anything to hide the truth. It appeared that I was scarcely immune.

For a moment, Sophie Rivington's pale profile and unseeing eyes hovered into view and then dissolved.

The drizzle had become a steady rain. We were once again the three of us, more precisely two men arrayed against me, in the grubby square, puddles forming at our feet. I took stock of Knight's set expression and waited because I'd learned that silence often served a purpose, a void few could resist. Knight proved no exception. The sober suiting, the neatly barbered hair, the face unfashionably clean-shaven, Knight presented masculine coherence at its disciplined best.

"Are you not aware of what is at risk, Miss Buchanan?" The question entirely unnecessary.

I wanted to ask him how he obtained not only an image of the dead girl in Boston but also the unfortunate details around her death, but the question lodged like a small bone in my throat. How much did he know about Alice James, William James, and me? "You have a photograph of the corpse of Sophie Rivington in your possession and would use it. To answer your question, I'm aware of what's at risk." It didn't take much to imagine what would spill from Knight's hands, the mortified flesh denied seclusion of the grave, captured in linotype forever.

Knight and Griffith exchanged another look I didn't like. How many women and men had I encountered, shut away in asylums and worse for hearing voices, speaking to the dead, refusing their husbands' counsel, being poor or holding strange beliefs? "These unfortunate women about whom you profess concern, the prostitutes or actresses, *whatever we're to call them*, you would illustrate their images, their last moments in extremis, Knight, for your own commercial purposes. And you," I turned to Griffith, "intend to suppress the public frenzy by crucifying this immigrant and Jew with evidence provided by my attesting to his madness. Whether he is guilty or not. To assure your position as London's future commissioner."

I refused to look away from them. Without offering a word, Knight hooked his finger under my arm, gesturing to a portico hanging unevenly across the alley over a boarded-up shop and a faded sign. Out of the rain, at least. Griffith, hat drooping with moisture, followed. We stopped, huddled under a dilapidated entry, water sluicing down alongside through a patchwork of troughs.

I shook myself free. Knight's eyes narrowed. "You're unbelievably arrogant, Miss Buchanan. You dare cast the first stone? A young heiress under your care *hangs* herself. It's said that the young girl's family wanted to have her committed to a sanitarium, but you advised otherwise. One wonders why?"

Griffith mopped moisture from his face, scarf sagging around his neck. "Arrogant is correct, one thing we agree upon, Knight, and a particularly unappealing characteristic for a woman."

I swung my gaze between them. For the moment, I was flanked by the two of them, buttressed into a corner.

"Should the full facts emerge," Griffith relishing each word, "one might wonder if you, personally and professionally, could bear the scrutiny. Archibald Rivington, soon to be appointed the ambassador to Britain and close friend and colleague of your father's." He left off, letting the words sink in before adding. "Little wonder you fled Boston for London, Miss Buchanan. *Anything* to bury the scandal, yes?"

Both Knight and Griffith, for different reasons, must have considered my father's reach, but even I recognized that while George Buchanan's influence could be ruinous in America, England might well exceed his grasp. Knight's eyes locked me in place. "Self-slaughter isn't that what they call it? Although the official cause of death is cited as fever. Understandably." Knight failed to mention that Sophie Rivington had slit her wrists before hanging herself. Or *gouged* them, more accurately. With a dull, pearl-handled letter opener.

Knight took a step back, one booted foot landing in a puddle, the faint rain like a scrim separating us. "Your involvement in the affair, and some might say culpability, would also come to light. The girl might be alive today had you advised that she be sent to an asylum, or should we call it a sanatorium, for her own protection."

I wondered how he knew. My neck tightened. I thought of the note that summoned me to Bethlem, the taunting cruelty of it, the childish rhythm.

> *Another woman soon will die.*
> *Unless Georgia Buchanan arrives in time.*

The alley was silent as though all madness has been cesspooled from the world, leaving me staggering in its wake. I was guilty. Griffith and Knight had that right. As did whomever had sent me that note.

My mind swam, drowning in the possibilities, none of them good. Griffith, using Sophie Rivington to coerce me into sending a plausibly innocent man to prison. Knight, using Sophie Rivington to threaten me if I involved myself in Griffith's plans. What did I really know? That Knight had the photographs, of both the Shoreditch victims and of Sophie. That Griffith had neither; his only chance to manipulate me was through the publisher. And that here we were, fighting over corpses like our lives depended on it.

"I will meet you at the morgue at noon," I said.

"The mortuary?" Griffith looked as though I spoke a foreign language. "I should prefer that you meet with Tarski whom we can bring into custody by day's end."

"I prefer to deal in fact not conjecture. If I examined the latest victim and learned more of her circumstances, perhaps from the attending surgeon—"

Griffith threw up his hands. "Surely, a consultation with the murderer would prove more valuable. What might you learn about a madman from a corpse?"

Knight looked about to say something and then seemed to decide that silence would serve him better.

"More than what I might learn from a man who is probably behind bars for nothing more than being poor and coming from foreign soil."

Griffith's arms fell to his side. "You are making the situation more complicated than it need be, Miss Buchanan. We will have the suspect in custody and require that you simply meet with him and affirm his madness. Quite straightforward. Some documentation is required, of course, for the judiciary. Then we close the case. Monster and mayhem removed from the streets. And Knight's photographs of the dead prostitutes and actresses," he gestured to the publisher, rolling on his heels, mouth set in a grim line, "serve as a fitting coda."

"I choose not to go to the police station on Commercial Street." I gathered my skirts now heavy with rain. "I will go to the morgue. In exchange, I have your word that whatever photographs and information either of you has regarding the Rivingtons remain private."

I stepped out from under the portico but not fast enough. Knight was behind me, gripping my shoulder. He spun me around, my sodden cloak slowing me down, close enough that our breaths combined. "You are in no position to demand anything. I've been a gentleman this morning." A hardening of his features that made him look nothing like a publisher.

I pretended to consider his words for a moment. "And you've fooled no one." I wrenched my shoulder from his grasp.

Griffith surveyed the alley, above it all for the moment, ignoring Knight and me, as though excavating for new possibilities. *We had an agreement, Knight.* A finely balanced one. A repellent alliance of greed and ambition. Then lowering his head, he watched my eyes fall to the satchel under Knight's arm. "Very well, then." A change in tone, suddenly congenial, making the nerves beneath my skin tighten. "For the moment, Tarski and Commercial Street can wait. Until Montague Street. The workhouse mortuary. At noon."

My eyes left the satchel to lock on Knight, his eyes blank and hard. He looked away, moved aside and let me pass.

CHAPTER 5

The Whitechapel mortuary was nothing more than a shed, growing out of the workhouse like an angry wart. It lacked proper facilities other than an old keeper, a pauper inmate, whom I met scuttling like a beetle about the back entranceway. As he led me to one of the small autopsy rooms, the stench of putrefaction was like a blow to the stomach, even for a stalwart like me.

I was unwilling to give in to the urge to hold a handkerchief to my face. My first dissection years ago, now recalled to me with uncanny detail, had a similar unexpected gaseous assault when old Dr. Marlowe had edged his scalpel along the abdominal wall of a bloated corpse. This scene was not much improved now. Narrow walls leaning inwards, two overhead gas torches lighting Dr. Phillips' post-mortem handiwork. Tall and balding, he wiped his hands on his apron like an exhausted cook as the inmate made a hasty introduction before bolting out the door.

"Meddling women," Phillips grunted at me. "Two nurses from the Union Infirmary had already stripped and partially washed the corpse to ready it for me, unaware that they were stripping away evidence. I've done the best with the tampered remains." At his elbow, a wooden case with its fitted velvet interior held his instruments, the bowel scissors, amputation knives, a small saw, two hook and chain retractors, three scalpels, and needles and threads. "Savaged woman, about eight hours' dead, found not by a constable on his nightly rounds but by a runner in a backstreet off Drury Lane."

One of Knight's men. "Do we know her name?"

"Annie Childs, if that's her real name. But what does it matter with these sorts?"

His disgruntlement showed as he bowed over the corpse. "You're here for Griffith, you say?"

I couldn't answer the question for myself, let alone Phillips. I'd been summoned to Bedlam with threatening language and emerged ten hours later with no answers and two men who sought to blackmail me, for different reasons that were scarcely beginning to emerge.

Glancing up, scowling, Dr. Phillips prepared to pull the apron over his head then decided against it. "At least you were spared the bone and gristle tempo of actual dissection. You're not a relation, are you?"

It was far from possible that I could be a relative of the woman lying on the table in front of us. A thin sheet covered the corpse to the shoulders exposing only the greying face with its sightless eyes. She could be of another species entirely. Slack jaw displaying crooked, caramelized teeth, cheeks and nostrils streaked with broken veins, the outlines of shins beneath the sheet bowed from malnutrition. I discovered later from Phillips's notes that her clothes, now in a sad bundle in the room's corner, consisted of a faded jacket, found hooked at the top and buttoned down the front, with bloodstains about the neck, both inside and out. And a black skirt, the fabric thin from wear, covering two stained petticoats and a large pocket, tied around her waist with strings. Although torn, both down the front and at the side, the pocket had been empty.

I swayed forward despite myself, death always the great equalizer. There was a bruise over her right temple and two bruises, each the size of a man's thumb, on the top of her chest. Neither appeared to be recent.

I had no choice but to address Phillips's backside. A flask of gin jutting out of a pocket as he put away his instruments. "Griffith has asked for my assistance, Dr. Phillips. He believes that I may bring some useful knowledge to this ill-fated business."

Phillips straightened, swallowed a grunt of pain, either at the mention of Griffith or the tightness in his back. "Griffith is an impatient man. He's unwilling to wait until I deliver my post-mortem notes to the inquest mid-month?"

"I should have sent word—but there was no time." Best explanation I could muster. "I'm a colleague of Griffith's, you could say, a student of mental illness."

Phillips startled. I might have declared myself from the moon.

"*A nerve doctor?*"

"Of a sort—a mind doctor, an alienist, or some might say a student of the mind."

He shook his head. "I'm dimly aware of practitioners calling themselves alienists and neurologists. Preoccupying themselves with the intricacies of the human brain." He rearranged some of his instruments in the wooden case, holding a retractor up to the light, frowning. "Although I give it all scant credence. If you were to ask me, insanity walks in lockstep with the onward march of heredity, a type of bacterium handed down from one generation to the next." He was silent for a moment. "In any case, how is that of help here?"

A question I'd heard asked too many times. "There are those who believe that patients with mental illnesses are individuals with brain and nerve diseases, much like any others burdened with physical afflictions such as gout or tuberculosis."

He gave me a look, inspecting my face, in case I might be mad myself. "Again, how can any of this possibly serve the dead woman on the examination table?"

"Griffith hopes I can learn something of the victim's circumstances that will help us understand the workings of her assailant's mind. To assist in his apprehension and conviction. By examining the evidence, we can get a glimpse as to the possible motives of the perpetrator, draw a profile or an outline of the type of individual we should be looking for. "

"The victim's circumstances were as to be expected," he shrugged, wiping a smudge from the retractor with a large thumb. "Poverty, drink, and a paucity of good judgment. Perhaps work at a music hall, in the chorus from time to time. I'm afraid that there is nothing that I might tell you other than the very physical circumstances of the victim's death. As to peering into the workings of her assailant's mind—" he trailed off.

"I'm not without experience in these matters, Dr. Phillips. I've spent a number of years analyzing psychological behavioral patterns among violent patients."

"You have some knowledge of dissection, then? Of a neurological nature?" He rubbed a hand on his apron.

I nodded, although I guessed at what he was thinking. That there was the odd woman, a few recent graduate physicians who wisely kept to the field of reproduction and female matters. Alienism was foreign enough without adding a female component to the discipline. I owed no one an explanation regarding my attraction to this nascent field. Nor an account of my father who had been disinclined to allow his sole offspring into the world without the proper armature of reason and science, along with several foreign languages. Although George Buchanan would be the first to admit that the educational experiment had gone further than he'd intended.

"I didn't think to examine Miss Childs's brain matter for evidence of disease," Phillips's brow furrowed.

I removed a small notebook and gold pen from my reticule. "That may not be necessary. At this moment, I'm more interested in learning about the mental state of her murderer."

"You are quite certain?"

"I am." Being asked to explain myself or having my skills and experience ignored, which did I detest more?

Seemingly satisfied that I had the stamina to withstand the details he would supply, he wiped his palms on his apron again before beginning. He told me what I already knew. "The deceased was discovered lying in Haggerston Yard, near Drury Lane, on her back, on the left-hand side of the steps that lead from the alleyway. The head was approximately six inches in front of the level of a bottom step, and her feet were pointed toward a shed at the end of the yard. The left arm was across the left breast, and the legs were drawn up, the feet resting on the ground, and the knees turned outwards."

Blue ink bled on the page of my notebook.

"The face was swollen and turned on the right side with the tongue protruding between the front teeth, but not beyond the lips as it was much swollen. Are you certain that you wish me to continue?"

Without looking up. "Continue."

Phillips moved to stand at the head of the corpse. "There were no signs of a struggle."

"No sign."

"Where her head had lain, there were six spots of blood, the coppers informed me, varying in size from that of a sixpenny piece to that of a small point. There were also patches and smears of well-clotted blood on the wooden palings. There was no blood in the passageway which leads us to believe Miss Childs was murdered in the yard."

For only the second time since entering the room, I stepped closer to the table. "She is older than one might believe."

Another grunt escaped him. "Not all prostitutes or actresses are young, Miss Buchanan."

My breath sieved through the aroma of death. "There was no sign of struggle," I repeated.

"The bruises on her right temple and on the top of the chest are not recent." I detected the sin of omission, but he anticipated my question. "You will ask me next exactly how I believe Miss Childs died." His gaze turned direct. "I did find more marks, however, on the face and about the sides of the jaw."

"I can see that."

"I am of the opinion that the person who cut the deceased's throat took hold of her by the chin, and then commenced the incision from left to right."

"I wonder if she had the time to cry out."

"By pressure on the throat no doubt it would be possible. Although I also believe that the thickening of the tongue would be one of the signs of suffocation. In other words, Miss Childs was partially strangled."

Behind us, the door opened.

CHAPTER 6

Graveyard miasma. Griffith huffed in the entrance, bringing along a rush of fetid air from the alleyway where, I'd noted earlier, scratched and dirty shells of coffins were pressed into service like exhausted workhorses.

"If you lean in more closely, Miss Buchanan, I am certain you can see the wounds despite the doctor's post-mortem work." Griffith pointed at the corpse.

"The doctor was just apprising me of the facts of the murder."

Phillips snorted his assent, acknowledging that niceties and introductions had been dispensed with sometime earlier.

"You understand, Phillips," Griffith said fully entering the room, not bothering to remove his hat, as though he had no intention of staying long. "Miss Buchanan graciously declined to meet with the murderer we will soon have in custody until she had the opportunity to visit with you. As such, she needs to know of what he is capable. Or so she has advised." Griffith looked at me with the now familiar distaste.

I ignored him. "Continue, doctor." I waved a gloved hand over the deceased's face. "But if I may suggest, these incisions along the skin appear as though there they are two cuts, one along the line of the jaw and completely encircling the throat, the other starting at the front of the neck and finishing on the right side between the lower jaw and the breast bone." My gold pen traced the air.

Phillips sucked in his lower lip. "You have a good eye, madam." Noted with a grudging respect that was also familiar. "Two distinct cuts on the left side of the spine, parallel to each other and under an inch apart," Phillips stated.

"And what of it, doctor?" Griffith shoved his hands into his coat pockets.

"The muscular structures between the sides of the vertebrae," Phillips said without looking at the corpse, "had an appearance like an attempt had been made to separate the bones of the neck."

"What is it you're meaning to say?" I asked.

"Yes, Phillips. Out with it. You will be required to report your findings to the inquiry as it is."

"I believe," I watched Griffith's fingers worry the insides of his pockets, "that the doctor concludes the murderer attempted and failed to sever the victim's head."

The men looked at me simultaneously, as though I'd just uttered a blasphemy.

Attempted decapitation.

The Assistant Commissioner muttered under his breath.

Outside the workhouse mortuary came a customary cadence. A draft horse dragging yet another wagon laden with a corpse. Death was a brisk business here in London as elsewhere. There were so many Annie Childs that the provision of houses for the immediate reception of the dead—funeral homes as they were known in America—was still enough of a rarity to cause concern. I knew well enough that emanations from human remains were believed to cause sickness and death, although little enough was done about it.

"You are correct in your assumption." Gaslight bounced off Phillips's head. "We can only hope the ravenous press will not soon feast on the death of this miserable worn-out little actress."

Griffith fished a handkerchief from his coat, holding it up to his face, mopping his brow.

The doctor returned to the head of the table. "There were... are abdominal injuries. The abdomen had been entirely laid open, the intestines severed from their mesenteric attachments, lifted out of the body, and placed by the shoulder of the corpse." Phillips continued in the same even tones. "The uterus and its appendages, along with the upper portion of the vagina and the posterior two-thirds of the bladder had been entirely removed."

"How was this... damage inflicted?" I asked.

Griffith exhaled loudly. "With great violence, presumably, Miss Buchanan. This is not an attack by a man but by a wild fiend. An animal. A crazed animal."

"I'm not certain I would agree," Phillips said. "The injuries to the abdomen particularly—there is a skill in their execution."

"Could you elaborate, doctor? What type of skill?" I rolled the pen between my fingers.

"That of a butcher, no doubt," Griffith interrupted.

Phillips looked down the length of the body draped in the sheet, a caul covering the worst of it. "All I can say with any certainty is that the wounds to the throat and abdomen were made with the same knife, a very sharp weapon, with a thin, narrow blade at least six to eight inches long. Not a knife common to cobblers or footpads."

"So more of a knife used in..." I prompted.

Phillips offered a shrug. "Perhaps used in amputations." He glanced up from the body. "I would also say that my own impression is that anatomical knowledge and surgical skill were used in extracting the viscera."

Griffith drew in a breath. "Your distinction is baffling, doctor. What difference does it make how the viscera were extracted?"

"If truth be told, sir, I myself could not have performed all the injuries, even without a struggle, in under a quarter of an hour. If I had done it in a deliberate way, such as would fall to the duties of a surgeon, it would probably have taken me the best part of an hour."

I added a note in my book and without looking up said, "It makes every bit of difference, giving us an insight into the temperament of the perpetrator as well as an indication of his background and state of mind. For example, this Mr. Tarski you hold in custody—a madman in a frenzy of violence would not have been able to inflict precise wounds such as the ones Dr. Phillips describes."

Griffith's small head momentarily blocked one of the light fixtures, throwing a looming shadow on the wall close behind. "You have yet to encounter the man. How can you possibly know?"

I turned back to Phillips. "And what of the entrails?"

"The missing organs? The whole inference seems to me that the operation was performed to enable the perpetrator to obtain possession of these parts of the body."

"What other evidence do you need to convince you of the perpetrator's insanity?" Griffith asked. He shoved his handkerchief back into his pocket.

I snapped shut my notebook. "It all depends upon your definition of sanity."

"Dear Lord, madam. You are speaking nonsense now," Griffith looked as though he wanted to push his bulk further into the room to make his point if only there were space. "A lunatic is a lunatic."

"You asked for my cooperation and I'm giving it to you. A preliminary profile of the killer."

Phillips no doubt wondered what grand bargain we'd struck. The gas light sputtered. "I have been a police surgeon for twenty-three years and it is my opinion that the injuries have been made by someone who had considerable anatomical skills and knowledge. In other words, there are no meaningless cuts. It was done by one who knew where to find what he wanted, what difficulties he would have to contend against, and how he should use his knife so as to abstract the organs without injury and excess bloodletting. And all of it accomplished in the early hours of the morning."

I'd heard enough. "Thank you, doctor. Assistant Commissioner, I understand that an autopsy has already been performed on the other victims. Is it possible to see the surgeon's notes or perhaps I might speak with him directly?"

"The surgeon who performed the autopsy on Jane Douglas and Mary Holland is Dr. Llewellyn. I can secure the notes for you, Miss Buchanan." Phillips said, already stripping off his apron.

Griffith's tone was clipped. "Entirely unnecessary given that we are clear the murders have been committed by a single madman. In each case the victim has been a woman of abandoned character, each crime committed in the dark hours of the morning and, more important still, this man is a maniac given each murder has been accompanied by hideous mutilation. Further, the crimes were committed within a very small radius, in the neighborhood of Shoreditch. Ergo, Miss Buchanan, the fact that these tragedies were committed in proximity of the other and are so strangely alike in detail, we can only conclude that they were the deeds of a single man with a mania for murder."

"I appreciate your summary." I closed the top button of my jacket, ready to leave.

"I will forward Llewellyn's notes," Phillips tossed his apron into a bin by the door before exiting the autopsy room without a backward glance. Leaving Griffith and me with the corpse of Annie Childs.

Griffith crossed his arms over his chest. "Now that we've concluded this business, you will meet with Tarski, Miss Buchanan." Delivered with a level of threat that set my teeth on edge.

I glanced at the dead woman, then just as quickly back at Griffith. "One meeting offers insufficient time to arrive at a definitive conclusion regarding the sanity of an individual much less produce an assessment of his culpability in a series of murders."

Griffith's expression was of exaggerated puzzlement, like he was trying to decipher the nonsense words of a child. "Time? Have you taken the *time* to review any of the broadsheets? The *Guardian* or *The Illustrated London News*? I fervently wish we had the luxury of time. But this tide of hysteria to which you are somehow inured is impervious to any due process or order. Do you wish to be responsible not only for more killings but also for revolution on the streets of London?" The last question was thrown at me like a brick.

A tightness in my chest shifted. "You need a scapegoat." I meted out each word. "You're a desperate man."

Griffith's jowls reddened. "Who is the desperate one? A young girl, the daughter of the future ambassador to Great Britain, would still be alive had your assumption, or rather, supposition proven correct. Not precisely a story you'd like told."

An accusation not far off the mark.

"We have two days before Tarski becomes once again a free man. Unless I can furnish credible evidence that he is the murderer we seek."

"I can't," I began.

Griffith's grimace turned to a thin smile. There was nothing in his expression that he'd even heard me. He took a step closer. "This isn't intimidation, Miss Buchanan, but an order. After your assessment of Tarski, proceed to write a document that I will find of use to present to the Police Commissioner and, in turn, to the judiciary. Borrow freely from your mentors, Dr. James and Professor Charcot, with whom you studied and have affiliation. They will lend great credibility to your case. And to mine." Griffith's high color receded, his face tight with something close to hatred. "Did you see the body, Sophie Rivington's, after it was cut down?"

My head hummed, my chest catching the pressure of each heartbeat.

"The flesh and blood of it tells the story, one that I wouldn't hesitate to have told. Two days," he said. "You have two days." He glared from the low doorway, eager to present his monster if only to prove that he existed. Gods and monsters—our own anxieties given shape—

although in my experience, it was humankind from which we had more to fear.

I was prepared to war with Knight and Griffith's demon. For Sophie Rivington and for Annie Childs. No more women would die, by their own hand or by others, if I could help it.

Arrogant of me—I know.

CHAPTER 7

The letters fanned out on the side table in the hallway of Berkeley Square like a game of roulette. Roulette revolvers, not dice, a dangerous variation on the theme a handsome Russian émigré had explained to me some weeks ago at a shooting party in Cumbria. My fingertips hovered over the envelopes in the likelihood that one might hold a charge. Or another summons.

Berkeley Square was a palace of gold leaf and marble. Heavy velvet curtains shifted in stolid breezes above crammed glass cases groaning with porcelain and ivory. Everywhere silk wallpaper, an explosion of blooms, alongside Chinese vases swarming with creeping vines. Not to my taste at all.

Despite the glaze of beeswax on every surface of the townhouse, the scent of decay smeared the air, as though I hadn't bathed and disposed of my clothes immediately upon the return from the Montague Street morgue hours earlier.

Berkeley Square was my home for the duration of my stay, the owners having decamped to the country, and my privacy was complete as good servants were said to have neither eyes nor ears. The townhouse was empty, the help below stairs. My solitude and relative anonymity should have been complete. If not for the intrusion of Griffith and Knight.

My mind returned to the foul-smelling charnel house presided over by the competent Dr. Phillips—competent even though I'd detected spirits on his breath and the flask beneath his coat. Not to claim moral high ground but I registered the tick like a crack in a mirror.

Sawbones and drunkards, according to Griffith.

I was aware of the ripple of rage spreading across cities like London, Birmingham, and Manchester. But it didn't take much to see that neither Griffith nor Knight had concern for the welfare of the women in Shoreditch. Less still for Sophie Rivington.

I thought again of Annie Childs, sensed her pulling me towards her. I listened to the pulse of the clock in the hall and nothing else. No answers. No footsteps. No one at the door to come drag me away to Griffith and the police.

The correspondence waited as did my cigarette.

The letter opener slid against my open palm, envelopes examined and then discarded. An invitation to a gala, a lecture at the Royal Geographic Society, then a bill from the dressmaker on Bond Street. I recalled the kaleidoscope of fabrics and patterns sprawled in my dressing room this past August, the trunks and wardrobes overflowing with gowns and shawls, more than I could ever wear over several lifetimes.

An addiction of another sort but one I was willing to indulge.

Numerous calling cards, friends of my father like the Denbys at Roxbury House, who would wish to welcome me to London and to fill time, which could be endless when one was burdened by the privilege of too many hours. I pushed them to the side.

I thought of the anonymous note, its message printed in block letters and now buried in the nacre-lined snuff box at the bottom of my wardrobe.

Another woman soon will die.
Unless Georgia Buchanan arrives in time.

With the address of Bethlem Royal Hospital. Bedlam—as though, somehow, I could have found answers there. Answers to what, the source of my own guilt? Answers to my great, infernal quandary, Sophie Rivington? Somehow this made me responsible for some nameless woman in a London asylum prepared to slip a noose around her neck or slide a knife across her wrist?

There had been no other Sophie to be found in the wards of Bedlam. The summons was intended to goad me, I was convinced, perhaps to remind me of my hubris. The weapon forcing me to involve myself in Griffith and Knight's plans.

Pacing wasn't helping. A longed-for cigarette tugged at my lips. The tobacconist off Bond Street would top the list for tomorrow. William's manuscript, on the chair by the cold grate of my rooms, could wait a few moments longer. I craved reading his manuscript almost as much as I craved tobacco on my tongue.

Instead, I convened in my mind all the girls and women who had filed through my waiting room on Mount Vernon Street in Beacon Hill. The constellations marking the sad and the mad, the thin lines running between each. I could detect lies with the accuracy of a tuning fork. Only Sophie Rivington had escaped detection.

What had I overlooked? A young girl, on the threshold of adolescence, Miss Rivington had been outwardly healthy with good color and constitution. Save for her sudden descents into a kind of mania, first reported by her concerned mother. Beautiful, sensitive and refined, indulged every day of her young life, the child had been a cipher.

I'd witnessed it myself, the extravagant behavior that had transformed a normally docile girl into a virago, talking to herself, jumping about, tearing off her clothes and throwing them into the fireplace. On her weekly visits, she would weep for no reason or turn somber and taciturn. Soon there had been a loss of speech, spasmodic choking.

Time had been required, silences and exchanges, the transformation of hysterical symptoms into a delicate set of negotiations. A gradual return to health, six months of normalcy until—

I blinked as the memory emerged of that last good day with Sophie in Beacon Hill. She leaned toward me in the wingback chair and out of the not-so-distant past.

"*Do you know what I do when I first meet a person?*" she asked. The voice high and childish.

"*What do you do, Sophie?*" I was standing behind the piano, my late-mother's piano, the silent participant in the room. It had been a gift from my father to his new bride, a discordant fact in that my father had no use for music that I knew of.

Sophie's face tilted up, nostrils flared, the blue of her eyes alive with humor. "*I think of an animal... or should I say that a specific animal immediately comes to mind. The animal the person most resembles—to me at least.*"

"*So give me an example.*" The wood of the piano lid where I had left my pen and paper was cool beneath my palms.

"*Well, my mother is a giraffe.*" A sly laugh. "*With her long neck and slender face. And her rather sturdy hips.*"

"And your father?"

"*A squirrel—wouldn't you agree? Small and industrious. And my brother—rather like a Clydesdale.*" She leaned further into the divan with a slight laugh.

"*Anyone else?*" A faint freckle marked her left cheekbone, glowing through translucent skin.

"*There's you, of course, Miss Buchanan.*" She ventured a slow smile. "*A jungle cat. Sleek and mysterious.*"

The memory dissolved and I was alone again in London. Boston far away. Where Sophie Rivington had been laid to rest, six feet beneath the ground and *would remain so*. Despite Griffith and Knight's and even my own attempts at a resurrection.

The wide hallway was airless, the snaking logic of my deliberations exhausting. I listened to the pulse of the house, imagining heavy footfalls at the front door. Pictured Griffith and Knight. My face burned with sudden anger and I raised my head, took a step back and wrenched open the door to the cooling night air.

Although a far larger city than Boston, London was quiet, stifled here on Berkeley Square, a continent removed from the savagery of Shoreditch.

I took another moment to absorb the city at dusk. The square was deserted, elegant and subdued, neat hedges stitching the townhouse in place. Flickering lampposts lit the steep stone stairs and cast shadows on the handsome urns flanking the door.

A flash of white, something I hadn't noticed before. Balanced between the lip of the urn to my right and the leaves of a green palm sat an envelope sealed with wax, startling in its purity save for my name in block letters. It was identical to the one I'd received exactly two days ago at Roxbury House.

With stiff fingers I snatched the note from its thicket. This time I didn't wait for the letters to swim before my eyes before I tore the square open, the red wax crumbling like a scab into my palm. There was just enough light to make out the words. I gripped the note so hard that the paper puckered under my fingers.

> *Every man is guilty of the good he did not do.*
> *The Saracen Head, Blackmouth Street, September 9, 1892*

The quote, I believed, was Voltaire. Another address this time, not an asylum, not Bethlem. Tomorrow. Resisting the urge to crumple the note, I stared at the block letters, upright as soldiers. Willing the simple black strokes to reveal their meaning. Who was playing with me?

I no longer wished for a pall of smoke to blanket my lungs. I craved the reassuring recklessness that came from a dose of Dover's powder. The envelope and its contents were night-cool in my hands, a summons to the depths of my own conscience. The last place I wanted to go.

CHAPTER 8

The man sat on the low bench, a burlap bag of skin and bones. He didn't acknowledge my entry into his cell nor did he respond when the two wardens slammed the door behind them. None too pleased, were Griffith's men, when I insisted on seeing the prisoner without them. Better this way, I thought, time alone with the alleged monster. The Shoreditch savage, as Griffith had promised.

"Mr. Tarski, my name is Georgia Buchanan and I'm an alienist, a mind doctor. I'd like for us to have a brief conversation."

The scent of old sweat and unwashed linen pinched my nostrils. One hand lay at Tarski's side, the other on his lap, the palms turned upward, nails crescented with dirt. Face slack and without expression.

I dragged the stool that the wardens had provided closer to the center of the narrow cell, no window except the grilled square on the door. We were a few feet apart, yet Tarski's age was difficult to determine. A trickle of drool escaped the side of his mouth, his eyes as unfocused as a newborn's. The man heard voices, Dr. Leaside, the prison doctor, had told me just inside the prison courtyard, mouth pursed sourly, as he'd sorted through Tarski's symptoms like rubbish at the bottom of a bin.

Nothing unusual in the pantheon of hysterics or mediums conversing with the devil, as some still like to believe. Apoplexy, brain disease, who's to know? I'm a doctor, not an asylum keeper.

Tarski, I'd learned, was being kept separate from the general prison population. Griffith safeguarding his scapegoat.

I hadn't waited for the Assistant Commissioner's men to come and collect me at Berkley Square like a trunk or a piece of hand luggage. My own carriage had taken me here to Millbank Prison.

Breathing shallowly, head turned to the wall, Tarski hardly appeared a well man with his curious lack of affect, a sign of dementia praecox, I considered, and its attendant degeneration. It was not unusual for beggars, vagabonds, lunatics living in the streets to demonstrate a remarkable lack of concern for what could happen to them.

We sat in silence, the minutes marked by the drip of water condensing on a pipe overhead. A familiar setting for those in my profession, the dead air, the heaviness that a diseased mind exuded, a contagion that I had immunized myself against like smallpox. Or so I liked to believe.

Every man is guilty of the good he did not do. The words hadn't left me since the previous evening, a repetition, slowly carving out a trough in my stomach. And the address, the Saracen, the environs where Aaron Tarski allegedly roamed like the feral animal he was made out to be, by Griffith at least. I didn't know whether to open or close my mind to that fact.

"Mr. Tarski, perhaps you could tell me how you came to be here at Millbank? Do you recall? Anything at all?" And then, "You live in Shoreditch, am I right? Do you have family there?"

No reply, only a shifting on the bench, the hand on his lap clutching air like a sea creature. I was here to bring down the curtain, determine Tarski's fate, but I felt myself withdrawing, a dispassionate yet keenly aware observer. Tarski's breathing was even, his reactions nonexistent.

There was no inventive side of the hysteric here, no erratic nature to this man's affliction.

I thought of William's manuscript, the first fifty pages I'd reviewed into the early hours because I knew I would be unable to sleep. The latest summons with its block lettering keeping me dry-eyed and on edge.

William wrote brilliantly, fearlessly, and with a clarity that had conjured his voice in my London sitting room. I was familiar with his theory of emotions, revised from an earlier paper he had composed and which we had discussed at length, spinning the ideas around like a globe on its axis. I'd sifted through the ideas, his acceptance of the close relationship between action and the expressive and physiological accompaniments of emotion. How had he explained it?

Objects of rage, love, fear not only prompt a man to outward deeds, but provoke characteristic alterations in his attitude and visage, and affect his breathing, circulation and organic functions in specific ways.

The conversation reemerged with the exactness of a photograph. We had spent that June afternoon in his study alone, his wife having taken the children with her to her parents in Connecticut for the summer. The humidity lay heavy, making a hot house of William's library, oversized peonies drooping blowsily in their vase, the linen curtains still. The casement was open, a hopeful gesture for a breeze that would not come. The cambric of my blouse stuck between my shoulder blades.

A neural definition of emotion, I remembered saying, putting his thoughts into my own words. *The physical preceding, or better still, inviting the mental state.*

He'd shaken his head. *What I mean, my dear, is we feel sorry because we cry, angry because we strike, afraid because we tremble, and not that we cry, strike, or tremble because we are sorry, angry or fearful, as the case may be.*

So simple, so startling, and so very different from what I'd learned with Professor Charcot in Paris. This shift away from elementalism toward a functional, process-oriented account of mind and behavior.

I recalled one of my first patients, Mrs. Celia Sorenson, Bostonian mother of two, whose experiences of violent sensation and melodrama played itself out in my practice on Mount Vernon Street. Mrs. Sorenson who, when resting in her darkened room, would tell of a green-eyed cat coming toward her from the shadows. She would scream, suffer a convulsive attack punctuated by trills of maniacal laughter. Did the internal precipitating event cause the physiological change, the hysteria?

I forced my attention back to Tarski. Was that what I was looking at in front of me? An example of a man whose actions, or lack thereof, had created this attendant mental state?

"Mr. Tarski," I leaned forward, "tell me about your family, your friends, those you are close to. You are from Poland." Not for the first time, I wondered how well he understood English. There was a flicker in his eyes but still no change in his expression.

"Poland," he repeated, the voice sounding like water emerging from a rusty tap. "Poland." Then the voice drained away.

"Do you miss your home? Your country? Your family?" Family in a ghetto perhaps, outside Warsaw or Krakow? Tarski was one of thousands, the boatloads of immigrants disgorged from vessels in port towns like Belgrade and Montenegro to find themselves in Shoreditch and Bishopsgate, emblems of poverty and vice. The papers reminded me daily that East London was awash in overcrowded tenements conducive to disease, violence and immorality.

Boston, too, was a city of immigrants, the Italians in the north, the Irish and Jews in the south. I thought of my long-dead mother. My father had never chosen to explain himself to me, how he had found in the hills of Calabria a bride with coiled Titian hair and grey eyes. I knew her from a cameo, her image flanked by another little girl, who had succumbed from the same tubercular fever passed like a poisoned chalice from mother to child. At the thought, a vague memory stirred, of sitting at the end of a bed, arms reaching for me, then whispers to keep away. A nanny carrying me from the room, far from my mother's hazardous embrace.

The image faded like it always did.

I asked Tarski about his siblings, wife and children. He mumbled, eyes cast to the ceiling. His age, his religion, the date and the year. He couldn't tell me about Poland, London, where he had lived, whom he had loved, what he had done to earn a living. When I asked him to describe the cell we were in, he was confused at the question. Seeking a bridge of rapport, I found none.

I resisted looking at the watch pinned beneath my jacket. *The Saracen Head, Blackmouth Street.* Allowed myself to remain alert in the silence, to allow Tarski to reveal himself. The pulsing of the overhead pipe, then something else. Not so much a noise as a feeling, that we were no longer alone. I looked over my shoulder.

An eye, glaucous and greedy, pressed against the grilled square of the door. Watching.

CHAPTER 9

I was at the door in an instant, my palm pressed against the metal jamb, locked in. And the eye pressed against the grill—gone.

I wavered. Had I imagined it a moment ago? My ears burned, straining to hear receding footsteps outside the cell. Imagining that Griffith would like nothing more than to observe me with Tarski. The heavy latches on the prison door, the heavy bolts whining into place. Imprisoning me here.

I shook off the feeling and returned to Tarski, who flinched before settling himself back into his half-slumber. Exhaling, I sat on the stool but this time with my body slanted toward the door.

After a few moments, I lowered my gaze to the notebook on my lap. Phillips, as promised, had given me Dr. Llewellyn's autopsy notes. I'd read them after setting aside William's manuscript before breakfast. The details of the deaths and autopsies of the Shoreditch women did little to connect this man, this skeleton with the mind of an infant, to the crimes for which he stood accused. The particulars, if they could be trusted, didn't yield much.

Mary Holland had met her end at the entrance to the stable yard at

Great Wild Street, a poorly lighted, narrow and tenanted enclave on one side with warehouses dominating the other. In short, the perfect haunt of prostitutes and actresses. A patrolman had been about his business at three in the morning, reporting nothing unusual, only to come upon Holland's body a scant twenty minutes later. There had been several side notes about Holland having been seen earlier in the evening, well in her cups and in search of her "doss money" along Blackmouth Street. With hips swaying, she'd soon spied her mark. Her killer, Aaron Tarski?

My eyes had lingered on the address. *The Saracen Head, Blackmouth Street.* I filed the detail away for another time.

Llewellyn's comments regarding Holland's injuries were grim. There were two gashes to the throat, cut ear-to-ear right back to the spinal column. Further ferocious abdominal mutilations that had laid the stomach open from a point just below the breastbone to the lower abdomen, most probably the cause of death. Once again, the viscera were missing, the uterus, the fallopian tubes. No signs of struggle. It didn't take much to imagine the murderer attacking Holland from the front, pushing her head back, his thumb bruising her right lower jaw and his fingers her left cheek as he cut her throat.

And as with Annie Childs, there was little blood to tell the full story. If she'd been alive when her throat was cut, blood would have baptized the front of her clothing rather than forming a small pool on the pavement beneath her neck. Which had led Llewellyn to conclude that Holland was strangled before she was mutilated, dead before she was savaged.

Her face discolored and her tongue lacerated, blood flow constrained, Holland was sacrificed in timely fashion, the mutilations quickly, deftly and skillfully performed, according to Llewellyn, by a long-bladed and moderately sharp knife. In no fewer than ten minutes, allowing the murderer to merge unseen back into the shadows of the theater district. Jane Douglas's story was a similar one, having unfolded a few alleys to the south of Great Wild Street. Again, the female genitalia missing, I noted.

I glanced up at Tarski. Not the work of a raving lunatic. Not the actions of a man who could hardly sit upright.

"Mr. Tarski," I began again, leaning forward, my expression neutral, my voice calm. "Dr. Leaside here at the prison has reported that you have told him that you sometimes hear voices. Can you tell me about when that happens and what the voices say to you?"

Tarski slumped lower onto the bench, both hands now resting in his lap. The dripping water from the overhead pipe seemed louder. My thoughts scattered. I weighed the lives of Mary Holland and Annie Childs on an imaginary scale. Lives and deaths that hadn't counted. Until now.

I'd read the broadsheets. Knight's *Illustrated London News* wasn't the only one. Suddenly, newspapers were taking notice with sharp headlines condensing a contagious mix of rage and fear about the ghastly crimes of a maniac and about which nothing was being done, by the police or the politicians.

If what Griffith believed to be true, then the conviction of the man who sat across from me could staunch the killings and serve as a salve to my conscience. Or was it pride? My stopping these deaths where I had failed to stop another.

I focused again on Tarski, a carapace, like a beetle's discarded shell. The man was also Jew, I'd been told repeatedly, and the crimes he stood accused of unprecedented in British experience, bearing the exotic stamp of immigrants and foreigners. No Englishman could have perpetrated such a heinous sin as evidenced in the alleys of Drury Lane, the pundits said. The papers were all too eager to report that the murders smacked of Hebraic ritual killings, of primitive superstition.

My notebook and pen still rested on my knees. I'd hesitated reviewing the notes from other doctors that Leaside had given me prior to my meeting with Tarski, not wishing to prejudice my own perceptions. I opened the leather-bound book and extracted a sheaf of papers. Small and cramped, loose and erratic, the scrawl of individual opinions blighted several pages now piled upon my notebook.

Dr. Houchin's opinion of Tarski. *"Mr. Tarski declares that he is guided and his movement altogether controlled by an instinct that informs his mind; he says that he knows the movements of all mankind; he refuses food from others because he is told to do so and eats out of the gutter for the same reason. He says that he is ill and his cure consists in refusing food. He is melancholic, practices self-abuse. He is very dirty and will not be washed. He has not attempted any kind of work for years."*

Maurice Whitfield, the relieving officer for the Mile End Old Town— the poor house where Tarski had been briefly housed—gave a statement explicitly asserting that the Jew was neither prone to self-slaughter nor dangerous to other people.

An unsigned report. *"Incoherent; at times excited & violent—a few days ago he took up a chair, and attempted to strike the charge attendant; apathetic as a rule, and refuses to occupy himself in any way."* From a Dr. Smithens. *"A chronic harmless lunatic; idiot or imbecile."* And then another jotting, in a different hand this time. *"Individual is morose in manner. No sensible reply can be got by questions. He mutters incoherently."*

I gathered the papers, replacing them in the pages of my book adding a few scattered sentences of my own. Then I shifted in my seat. Still no response, no reaction from Tarski, his face blank. There was neither the intelligence nor the motivation there—to murder and vivisect two women and vanish in the roil of Shoreditch without a trace.

The conclusion was not reassuring, would do nothing for me, nor for the dead women most recently lying on slabs at the mortuary on Montague Street. Not for the first time in my life, I wished I believed in God, in a benign hand that would come out of the clouds as if in a child's picture book, to right the world.

Instead, I said, "Thank you for your time, Mr. Tarski." He had yet to acknowledge my presence, except to turn his head to the wall. The sweating pipe overhead sighed, releasing three beads of water onto the ground. The hands that rested on Tarski's lap began a slow and measured beat; his left hand clutching his genitals.

At the Salpêtrière, there had been a young woman who could not sit at a dining table without thinking of defecation while she was eating nor, she confessed, could she see a man's hands without feeling sexual excitement. I now looked at the ground and at Tarski's shoes, the cracked seams like a dirty riverbed. The sawing sound increased, the rhythm registering like the protesting springs of a bed.

I rose from the stool, a part of me still watching, at once repelled and transfixed. He emitted a choking sound, strangled, more like muffled grief than sexual release. The door opened behind me, then the footsteps of a warden, followed by shouts, and Tarski was grabbed and thrown from the bench. He didn't seem to notice. He didn't protest.

Onanism was hardly murder. Masturbation did not fall within the category of mania but instead was thought to cause mental and physical deterioration. I'd witnessed attempted cures involving mechanical restraints, surgery, and moral discipline, most often delivered in clinical settings. None of which had probably been offered Mr. Tarski.

I'd entered the cell expecting a monster. I left having met a simpleton. Tarski was clearly not the Shoreditch killer.

CHAPTER 10

M oments later I was on the corner of Mission Street, in a jumble of hackney cabs and wagons. Night had fallen and with it my mood. A boy in a newspaper cap trotted by, his vest as frayed as his voice, hoarse from squawking the day's news. I didn't need to see more headlines. Bad enough hearing them.

I tried to shut down the dread threading my veins, the sensation that I'd been snagged into a web I didn't understand. I could send an innocent man to the gallows. Or, I could find the true murderer and, in turn, have my life and Sophie Rivington's death exposed. I clenched my fists, nails gouging the inside of my gloves.

My carriage waited a few steps to the north to take me to the Saracen Head. *A man is guilty of the good he did not do.* I considered preparing a document for the Commissioner, one based on the findings of the autopsies, extrapolating from the details a possible profile of the Shoreditch killer. Giving Griffith, if not exactly exonerating Tarski, another avenue of investigation. There were many texts I'd consulted in the past to better understand the deviant mind. Most recently Cesare Lomboro's work in the field of criminology, a treatise that had established the hereditary nature of deviance, of the born criminal whose degeneracy was thought to be clearly identifiable through physical features—fleshy lips, large jaw, pitcher-shaped ears and high cheekbones. Based on my own experiences working with diseased minds, the treatise was overly simplistic and divorced from the more nuanced understanding of the human psyche.

Centered around the autopsy reports and my visit with Dr. Phillips, I inferred the murderer was intelligent, highly self-controlled with a basic knowledge of human anatomy. He killed his victims swiftly before removing their viscera, specifically their reproductive organs, demonstrating a reluctance to torture them. I sensed not only an underlying anger but also a compulsion to repeat, to serially strike out at a certain kind of woman. *Why* was the question that needed an answer.

Blackmouth Street was in Shoreditch, I reminded myself. Along with the possibility I might learn something more of use.

I spotted a woman hovering close to my carriage, a small wavering figure. As I moved closer, I noticed her eyes were wet with cold or tears, impossible to tell. I shifted past her with a nod to the coachman sitting on his roost. But she seized my sleeve just as he was about to clamber from his post and swing open the door.

"Please forgive me… I'm terribly sorry, Miss Buchanan. They said I might find you here." Pale face with the taut delineation of youth and something else. Her fingers in worn gloves dug deeper into my arm.

"We've met?" Hatless, as though she'd left home in a hurry, with shoots of hair escaping neat plaits, the young woman looked like she might fly apart. Her distress immediate, I scrolled quickly through the possibilities. "Perhaps we can find a place to sit down." I cast a glance back at the hulking prison silhouetted against the night skies. "Or my carriage?" It was all I could think to offer.

"I am—my name is—the governess." She seemed to be attempting to sort out a clouded memory. "For the Knights, Charles and Constance Knight. For Master Charlie and Miss Violet, their children. They said

I might find you here by the prison. That you could help."

I took her arm which was as fixed as a porcelain doll's. *The Knights?* Her foot sank into a puddle, and she stepped aside suddenly, as though a fresh thought occurred to her. Her eyes fluttered shut, then opened wide.

Deranged, unbalanced or something else? I noted her pupils, the sheen of sweat on her forehead, the worn but costly hunter-green wool of her three-quarters jacket, the clean but scuffed boots.

"There is no time… the children." Her voice was hesitant. "They are not in the nursery. Where I put them down to sleep after their tea. I was sitting right by their beds. I swear it. And when I awakened, they were," she inhaled, "gone."

⚜

Together in the coach we made our way to Mayfair, the governess who had managed to give me her name and Knight's address on Curzon Street, still holding fast to my hand. The pieces of her jagged thoughts began to make some sort of sense. The Knight children were missing and she stood accused. That much I could tell. Either or both Knights had intimated that I might be of assistance. While I had no experience in finding children, I did have some in helping mad women.

Victoria Trevyn was now quietly weeping, her silver blonde hair and pale complexion giving her an otherworldly cast in the dim light of the carriage. "I fall asleep. I don't remember, and then Mrs. Knight accuses me of all manner of things."

"Of what things?"

"She says she finds me in the garden at night. Walking in Marylebone after midnight. All the while the children are unattended. But nothing ever like tonight." She wiped at her eyes.

A somnambulist, I thought. Miss Trevyn walked in her sleep.

"Miss Trevyn. We have little time and your powers of observation, your recollection of details, these are important. I have every confidence that you are capable of calmly and logically telling me what happened earlier today, so we might know where to look for the children."

She raised her head and her eyes were clear, the shimmer gone, the pupils eating up the darkness in the carriage. "I remember nothing."

"Tell me what you do know. Nothing is too insignificant. What's the last thing you do remember?"

She drew a breath, then another, before beginning her recital. They, Charlie and Violet, had finished their lessons in the early afternoon. A walk in the park to tire them out. Charlie was an imp, full of mischief, intent on launching his sailboat in every puddle. Violet playing one of her silly make-believe games involving her dolls, two sisters lost in the woods, happened upon by witches. Charlie got his trousers wet and they had to roll them up. Then they returned home for their tea, mutton, toast, milk and a boiled pudding. Their regular bedtime after a bath and prayers.

I looked out the carriage window to see Park Lane, close to Mayfair, and thought of Knight, arrogant and demanding, in the alley off Drury Lane. The controlled expression, the impeccably pressed shirt and watered-silk waistcoat, and then his hand on my shoulder, outrageous and insistent. Knight knew I'd been making an assessment of Tarski at Millbank Prison. Though why he and his wife would involve me in their domestic affair escaped me, unless they didn't have much faith in the quiddity of our Assistant Commissioner.

"I so wish I remembered something… anything." The governess wiped at her cheeks with her free hand, the other one still clasping mine.

"Nothing unusual, in terms of the children's routine?"

"What do you mean?"

"Did they go right to sleep? Visitors to the nursery? Cook, a maid perhaps, or their mother?"

Miss Trevyn resumed shaking her head. "No one. Although she comes to say good night most often."

"Who does?"

"My cousin." She corrected herself with another shake of her head, a shimmer of silver in the shadows of the carriage. "Or I should say, Constance, that is, Mrs. Knight." Not entirely unusual, a poor relation, I thought, pressed into service as governess. "She didn't come into the nursery this evening."

The carriage rounded a corner and she told me that she'd left the children sleeping to go to her own room off the nursery, as was her habit, then to return at nine o'clock to ensure all was well.

"Then it happened," she slid down slightly on the upholstered seat, letting go of my hand.

I sat up straighter. "What happened?"

The governess looked around the carriage as though someone might overhear, fingers tight on the upholstered squabs. "I fell asleep, in the nursery. Again." And when she'd been awakened hours later from her death-like slumber, she was being shaken by the housekeeper, Mrs. Branksome, until her teeth had chattered. She had heard nothing. She hadn't left their sides and so how could it be possible that the children were gone. Without her knowledge?

"This has happened before?"

"No. Not exactly." She stopped as the carriage slowed to a halt, a sudden darkening under her eyes, like she might begin crying again. "The children have always been safe, in their beds." Her face disappeared behind her hands. "But this time is different."

CHAPTER 11

The Knight household was ablaze, every torch, taper and gaslight raging. The residence, tall and stately, sat in the center of a ring of elegant townhouses. In the entranceway after a short flight of marble steps, Knight waited, a figure etched by the shards of crystal slanting from the chandelier.

"Miss Buchanan." His voice was rough, the vowels sharp, the careful enunciation blunted. He stood over Trevyn, hands knuckled at his sides. I slipped an arm around the governess's shoulders, all but holding her up. The black-and-white checkered marble floor beneath us felt soft as a sunken grave. "Charlie, Violet," he invoked the names of his children. "You must remember something, Trevyn." He swore foully under his breath. "Miss Buchanan—*make* her remember."

Trevyn stood mute, lashes lowered over her eyes, breaths short and agitated. I led her over to a chair in the corner where she collapsed in a heap.

When I looked up, a tall woman in a redingote coat, the merino flaring around her, appeared at Knight's side. Her gaze slid away from Trevyn and locked on me. "My children," were her only words, stark and inflamed. Constance Knight held her arms tightly around her waist as though she would come undone. Her voice was scarcely audible, and I could tell she was trying to maintain a semblance of calm. "If you can help us…"

Imagination is a terrible thing. Even I could barely hold the images in my head, a line of perspiration snaking against my skin and down my back. The children could be dead. They could be bundled into a barrel and on their way to a country in the east to become young slaves. They could be serving illicit appetites in a sweat-drenched bordello in London. They could have been suffocated in their sleep and slipped into the brown current of the Thames.

Constance Knight's eyes never left mine, dark and burning despite the attempted decorum of her words. "Miss Buchanan, to have you so rudely summoned, I can't apologize enough." Drawing her arms more tightly around her waist. "Alice James has told me so much about you and I didn't know where else to turn. And my husband, Mr. Knight, knew of your whereabouts. So, I sent Trevyn as it was all I could think to do."

My mind absorbed the information. *Alice James.* They were acquainted somehow? I pictured Alice telling her newfound friend about her illness, her talking cures with Georgia Buchanan. Someone who might help Trevyn remember something for these children.

A clock struck, a dozen peals that multiplied in my head.

"I've been everywhere, looking." Constance Knight continued with stifled dread, then forced her voice to grow stronger, to break through her panic. "I will go anywhere no matter what the hour or whatever the place. To find them."

"Have you summoned the police?" It was the logical place to begin.

"No police." Two words from Knight that might have been a stone wall.

Constance Knight's arms dropped to her sides and it looked as though she was about to say something, but the sound died in her throat.

Knight's stare jerked to mine. "We've always found them before, without the police." An explanation, wanting and threadbare.

Undoing the clasps on my cloak, I shrugged off the garment, tossing it to the side, along with my doubts about Knight. They would have to wait. "May I see the nursery?" I had nowhere else to begin.

"Of course, the nursery." Constance Knight swayed back a step, "although we thought you might wish to speak further with Miss Trevyn. To see if she remembers…" She broke off, catching herself. The governess sat in her chair like a chastened child, unable or unwilling to look away from the hands clasped on her lap. "Of course, absolutely, whatever you think best, although we've searched thoroughly." Constance Knight's eyes glazed over, hands clenching at her side as though she was squeezing an amulet that had the power to bring back her children. Then, talking to herself more than to us, gathering her coat around her. "I can't stand to wait here any longer. I will take to the park down by Park Lane. Charlie loves to play there."

She swung away, the polish of her dark hair caught from the light overhead, the wide hem of her skirts sweeping across her riding boots. Knight looked up sharply from the governess who still sat rooted to the spot, but his wife had already gone, disappearing down the stairs and into the night.

The house was of stately proportions demanding of respect, a querulous dowager with creaking bones. We showed little deference, our strides eating the long hallway, past a series of anodyne landscapes in sepia colors, leading to the stairs spiraling upwards. Knight grabbed the newel post slick with beeswax and took three steps at a time.

On the second floor the gaslight burned too brightly as though recalling a child's fear of the dark.

At the far end of the corridor, Knight pushed open the double doors of the nursery. It was warm and dark with the scent of sweetened milk. A slice of moonlight bleached the outline of the two small beds, a rocking chair, a grammar and scribbler, lying carelessly on the floor. A screen set before a small stove chugged out heat, the atmosphere more hothouse than children's room. A quick glance told us that the casements were locked shut, secure, impervious to entry from the outside.

I was an intruder, unfamiliar in so many ways with nurseries and all things domestic, and yet even I didn't dare conjure the monster that would boldly take children. The bedclothes were mounded high. To make it seem as though little ones still slumbered there?

Knight stood aside while I moved quickly into the nursery, stopping at the first bed. I bent closer and then straightened to walk to the second bed, the air scented with a suggestion of crushed almonds. Laudanum, tincture of opium. Children were often dosed with the remedy, Mother Bailey's Quieting Syrup, to make them more compliant or to sleep more soundly. A routine in many households.

A low door, partially ajar, to the right of where we stood. With the crook of my elbow, I pushed it open. A narrow cot, probably for Trevyn, neatly made, sat a few feet from a modest wardrobe. I felt a momentary stab at what I might find inside. Then stepping forward, I pulled the knob on one of the door panels. The scent of lemon verbena rushed over me while I took in a row of cotton shirtwaists and two skirts which I thrust aside. Except for a jumble of shoes, the bottom of the wardrobe was empty.

Back in the nursery, Knight and I stood rooted to the ground. Victoria Trevyn and Constance Knight hadn't followed us. With a finger and a thumb, Knight rubbed his eyes, face open and raw. While I imagined his wife in the darkening streets, fearless as only a mother could be against whatever devastation the night held. Her head tilted down, eyes red-rimmed, and with no logical plan. The stirring behind a mulberry bush, a door cracking open. A sign, any sign, that her children may be near.

I closed my eyes, picturing the Knight's house from the street, having had only a glimpse upon my rushed arrival with Trevyn in tow. Narrow and tall, an iron gate girded by shrubs, its shuttered windows a kind of reproof to those who would pass by. Elegant lines that soared four floors high to a tower room, not unlike the widow's walks that I was familiar with in Boston. But shorter, squatter. This tower was ornamented with a circular oriel, perhaps eight feet across, looking down on the small green patch of a garden and the dome of a compact conservatory. Those windows, customarily painted shut, as if they were never meant to be unbolted.

My eyes opened. They would have ransacked the entire house, the servants looking in every room, in every wardrobe and under every bed. The back of my head began to pound, the skin of my scalp prickling. "Knight," I pointed to the ceiling. "The tower room."

We were back in the hallway through a narrow corridor bordered on either side by what I took to be servants' rooms, plain with either fading wallpaper or whitewashed walls and sparse furnishings. Knight fumbled with the latch on a low door leading to an even narrower spiral staircase. The tower was more of a crawl space than a room with a round window overlooking a steep slate roof.

The garden glowed phosphorescent, moisture beading on the roof of the conservatory to the east. An oak bench with curved legs blocked the window but Knight moved it with one swipe. I already had a hand on the ancient iron window latches. They rattled, unwilling to give, until I moved aside and Knight kicked the bolts open with the heel of his boot.

For a moment there was perfect silence. Then the sounds of a London night intruded like a discordant orchestra. The murmur of brittle autumn leaves, the huff of a carriage. We stepped out onto the pointed tip of the ledge buttressed by a four-foot knee wall and a battered gutter. The flutter of a piece of linen, bright white against the stained shingles. Where two children slept, tucked into a corner and blanketed with a down comforter.

Moments later, Constance Knight discovered us, back in the crawl space. The father and his children, crouched in the small bay like creatures seeking shelter from a predator. And I the observer, standing apart. The window remained opened, the rusted hinges grinding in a breeze.

Edged in moonlight, Knight buried his head in the curly hair of his sleeping daughter, his other arm clasped around the shoulders of his slumbering son. As though unwilling to disturb them, Constance stood in the narrow doorway, face drained of color, the sharp rise and fall of her chest her only sign of agitation. Clenched fists at her side slowly melting.

She finally came to life, locating the right words, clutching her children, rocking them back and forth with no intention of letting them go. As though an unseen cord connected them, Knight looked away from the children and met the eyes of his wife with a surge of emotion so powerful that it pushed me from the room.

⚜

Afterwards, the salon where Knight and I met briefly was cemetery-quiet, an enervating hush blanketing the household. He filled two crystal-cut tumblers, one whisky, the other sherry.

He thrust a glass in my direction. Although the back of my throat was dry and the row of buttons on my shirtwaist dug into my skin, I left the sherry at my elbow untouched. I couldn't wait to be gone from the house. The address of the Saracen's Head, Blackmouth Street, gnawing at the back of my mind.

Knight muttered into his drink. "Trevyn is proving unstable."

It was a good thing I wasn't expecting thanks. "You mean your wife's cousin."

"What are you implying?"

A defensiveness I should have expected. "I'm pointing out that the governess is a relation to your wife. Nothing else."

We stood in the middle of the room as though sitting in one of the overstuffed divans would be an admission of defeat, weakness, or both. Despite the show of strength, a hand balled into a fist, the jut of his chin, Knight was distraught, his words following no particular logic.

"I don't care if she's a relation. We can send her back," he said as much to himself as to me, as though trying to fight his way out of a cul-de-sac. "Her parents are on the continent, something about her elderly father requiring the air in Italy, or so says my wife. It would be simple enough to do."

Simple enough, then why not do it, I'd wondered, not for the first time that evening. Why not send Trevyn packing with a year's allowance if she'd repeatedly demonstrated her inability to keep track of the children?

"You believe she is responsible for placing them on the rooftop?" I had considered the possibility of a somnambulist accomplishing such a feat. The governess couldn't weigh more than one hundred pounds. But if the children had been doused with laudanum, asleep and unaware as she carried them one at a time.... They had been deliberately placed, out of harm's way, the knee-wall high enough and impossible for them to climb over had they awakened from their drugged sleep and attempted it.

A hesitation at my question while he took a drink, grimacing. "Of course. There's no other explanation. If my wife didn't know about your peculiar expertise from her friendship with Alice James, you would never have become involved in what should remain a private matter."

Something in my expression must have changed.

"You're surprised? Henry James is quite the man in the publishing world these days, as is his brother, William, for entirely different reasons, and all of them were circulating in New York last spring." A deliberate pause that went on longer than it should have. "My wife and their sister, Alice, struck up an instant friendship during our time in the city which happened to coincide with Miss James's convalescence there. They've resumed their association now that Alice is living in London."

I wouldn't have known, having last seen Alice months ago in America. She'd come first to me as a friend and then as a patient, at

William's insistence, after I had begun studying with him at Harvard.

There was something unnerving about Knight knowing anything about our circle. "I can understand you'd like your situation with the governess and the children to remain a private matter." My mind suddenly took off in different directions. "At the same time, I find it strange you believe it fair to exploit another family's tragedy for your own purposes. Particularly when your own is experiencing difficulties."

"Is this your way of referring to the publication of the Rivington scandal? And your role in it?"

"And you want to ensure the continued success of *The Illustrated London News* by exploiting a tragedy. You think that wise?"

He banged the tumbler down as though he'd spotted a fly in its depths. "I do. You find the concept revolting, then? That's rich. Ambition and aggression are the hallmark of your countrymen. I saw it firsthand during my time in New York." He let out a short breath, holding my gaze. His turn to prompt me. "The photographs will be published in tomorrow's papers. The women. The prostitutes or actresses or whatever we're to call them. Mary Holland and Annie Childs."

Some part of me, the foolish part, hoped the Rivington photos wouldn't be next.

"You're relieved, Buchanan." He'd lost the honorific, the *Miss* Buchanan. "Stories of a prostitute or a tawdry actress are one thing, the story of a young American heiress under your care quite another, is that it? Spare me the hypocrisy. You're relieved, for the moment at least, that the Rivington scandal, and your involvement in it, is *not yet* part of the public discourse."

Knight had regained his stride, found his way out of his dead end, for the moment. "I'm not going to ask again." He drew himself up, looked down at me. "Do not involve yourself with Griffith's investigation or in the persecution of Aaron Tarski."

CHAPTER 12

The carriage heaved to a stop. The door opened and the driver at my elbow helped me onto a narrow street off Drury Lane, a section of London that was a foreign land and as far from the Knight's household as I could be. It was late, quarter to midnight.

Earlier in the day I'd consulted the Baedecker map in the Berkley Square library to identify a snarl of angry streets behind Drury Lane, the alleys where Jane Douglas, Mary Holland, and Annie Childs had been murdered, and finally, Blackmouth Street and the Saracen's Head.

The night was clear despite the yellow haze that seemed to have settled permanently in the corners and creases of the surrounding buildings. I began to walk more purposefully with a vague sense of where I was going, skirts trailing in mud and worse.

A mound of rags bumped my arm, awakening me to my surroundings. The narrow street was alive, a pulsing mass of greys and browns, stooped figures melting into the stained air until they were barely distinguishable. The buildings crowded toward each other like rotted teeth. I caught a figure under the flickering, uncertain light of a lamp, a man or a woman, it was difficult to tell, the face bloated by drink.

Behind the sordid glare of Drury Lane music halls and theaters, the alleys of Shoreditch displayed their treasures like bizarre curio cabinets. Stalls lining the roadways with an assortment of offerings it was best not to examine closely; some gaped empty at this time of night, others just coming alive in the unnatural light.

The streaming naphtha glow set up the roar and rattle as tight groups gathered to pull on a pipe or gin bottle. A small mob clustered around a boy with no legs. The bark of quack doctors, selling certain cures for every malady, sent Latin incantations into the air. I slowed my pace, absorbed by the claim of a practitioner's list of medicaments and phrenological and physiological diagrams. A barrow drawn by a man, toppling with chairs and tables, snaked by. His wife walked alongside with a thin, doubled up mattress under one arm, swinging a bundle with the other hand.

I moved toward the mouth of the laneway before ducking into an even narrower street. This time I looked neither left nor right, unwilling to take in the signage for the mysterious creatures on display in enclosed places. Hairy men, hairless dogs, gorillas, Aztecs and giants. The darkness constituted no small part of the area's wretchedness, home to crooked doorways and otherworldly phenomena, away from the main road with its flaunting playhouses and aromatic gin dens.

Everywhere, pervasive, the odor of the human condition.

I rummaged into the pocket of my cloak. The ten cigarettes I had allowed myself were packed in paper, from the tobacconist off Bond Street, so keen to provide a pleasing mixture for my husband. I hadn't corrected him. A nasty vice, particularly for a woman of alleged breeding, but it served its purpose. That first haul of smoke into the lungs would pacify the nerves crackling under my skin. I'd considered the small amount of Dover's powder remaining in the false bottom of my oxblood leather jewel case. Which I hadn't needed, my general anxiety too close to the surface as it was. The powder, the magic, was reserved for other days when I required the jolt of heady recklessness in my blood and the crystalline clarity in my head.

I released my hold on the cigarettes. The note. The *summonses*, with the bold black lettering at the bottom of my wardrobe. First the call to Bethlem and now to the Saracen's which I took to be a public house. That these streets and these recent murders were somehow connected to Sophie Rivington seemed an impossibility. But an impossibility that, nonetheless, wouldn't let me go.

The stink of the street pushed one thought aside as another one rose. A walk with my father, years ago. It could have been in Boston's Back Bay, soaked in the stench of fish, fishermen carrying their catch on rods, hefted across drooping shoulders, carcasses with glassy red eyes staring heavenwards. Children half my age, wizened by hunger, gaping from stoops as we passed like a royal procession. My father gripping my hand tightly, his footsteps angry, pulling me along until we were once again smothered by the velvet security of his carriage.

Astonishing how simple it was to disappear—my father had taught me well—particularly in this quarter of London with its odor of rot and desperation. Men and women, heads stooped, hands in their pockets, braced themselves against the dark. There was safety in numbers. It was preferable to passing the night in dingy quarters on gin-soaked mattresses with volatile lodgers quick with the fists.

Another knot of people a few yards away numbered well over three dozen. Two women in front of me, their faces cotton-white tipped with angry spots of red on their cheeks. They watched a waxworks show, standing on their toes in discolored slippers, straining to hear.

"What d'ya see?" A voice pitched high enough to etch glass.

"'Orrible fakeries of the murders." Orange curls bobbed up and down, the edges of a shawl sparkling with black jet and fake silver.

A barker blared details into the night. Those fortunate to be at the front of the crowd pushed their way in with their pennies to see for themselves the ghastly objects strewn on the ground.

"Never 'eard nobody go on like 'im in my days. I declare there ain't no chance for none of us."

"Thank God I needn' be out after dark, but the others come 'ome late-ish and I'm all of a fidget till they comes."

"Soo' it won't be safe for nobody to put their 'eads out."

The audience crackled like kindling, ready to be lit. Some people dropped away but their places were taken by fresh sightseers. Every time new arrivals joined the crowd and the barker and the ghostly bloodstains, the flames shot to life again. The onlookers never faltered but stared at the pavement and the brick work of the adjacent house, imagining the scratches and marks in the wall as if these traces helped them realize the horror of it all.

Casting around the periphery, my gaze stopped at a figure standing slightly back from the crowd. There was nothing outwardly unusual about the man except for his cane, tipped in metal with a curious design that I couldn't determine from a distance. He held it loosely, casually, almost an afterthought. He was not looking at the barker but at the assembly, studying it as though it were a giant experiment under glass. His face obscured by the brim of his hat, features blotted out by the dark.

"Jess think," the orange curls again. She glanced a little way past the roaring barker and the hideous waxwork, and around the corner. "That ways there, past the public 'ouse, there blazin' in the corner, leads down to those blasted lanes where anyone can be murdered."

"I'll be mindin' my ways, that to be sure. 'Alf beast, 'alf man, they calls 'im."

"Not that they be doin' enuf about it. Effie done tell me she saw a bill in the public 'ouse window, offerin' 'undred pounds for the conviction of the animal."

A derisive snort. "We worth that much?"

"If we don't be'ave, we are."

As if on cue, the crowd roared at something the barker offered. I tried to keep the man with the walking stick in my sights, my eyes riveted to the glint of his cane, its handle a carved metal skull that momentarily came closer into view. I watched as he shouldered his way through the throng and disappeared.

A public house glowed in the corner as the faint sounds of a piano-organ ground out a delirious tune. The area was cobbled and gloomy except for the knot of women and children, their attention held by the place where Mary Holland had been slaughtered. There was nothing there, no blood stains, no stench of brimstone, only what the agitated imagination summoned. The organ man played with the fierceness of a wind-up toy, the tune hallucinatory.

The light from a streetlamp struggled in the broth of the fog. It took little to imagine the murdered woman lying on her back, lengthways along the footway and outside the entrance to the stables, her head toward the east, her left hand touching the gate.

A feeble breeze kissed a sliver of exposed skin above my cloak's collar. My scalp crawled with the sensation that I was being watched. The shadows were disorienting, looming behind me like a physical presence. Then a heavy hand on my shoulder. I stiffened, conjuring the man with the cane, face flattened like a one-dimensional icon. Then I slowly turned around.

CHAPTER 13

A woman with jet eyes stood so close I was assaulted by her boggy breath. And a sharp sense of relief. Her voice a rumble, her hand falling from my shoulder. "Fine welcome for monsters fresh from hell." An incantation I was supposed to understand. "'Twas raining terrible that night, and thunder and lightning."

I moved away from the small knot of people cordoned around us. The woman tailed close behind, shaking her head as though ordering her thoughts. It was not clear whether she was muttering to herself or to me. She hunched beneath the weight of her patched coat and into the story she seemed eager to tell, each word coming out in heavy breaths.

Three blackbirds, feathers oily in the night, pecked at the seeping mound of garbage, momentarily stopping my progress. The woman made windmills with her arms to drive them away, her tongue clicking against her teeth. "I'd seen her late that evening or maybe 'twas early that morning." She pointed a shoulder toward the alleyway. "Say a few minutes after midnight, leaving the Frying Pan, the public house in Brick Lane. She been sharing a common lodging house on Thrawl

Street with an old woman. She'd been telling me that a week before, she'd moved to another lodging house in Flower and Dean Street but then was back at Thrawl Street, worse for drink and wearing a new black straw bonnet trimmed with black velvet."

I found myself listening, drawn in by the story. Was this a witness, telling the truth, or at least her version of it? The last hours of Mary Holland or Annie Childs? Or more hysteric mania?

While I wondered, she stamped a foot at one of the birds who ignored her, then she paused, taking in the fine wool of my cloak, her innate prejudice honed over the years, saving her time. "There's no use lying about it to the likes of you, rich with no worry in the world," she said, a woman with nothing to lose, "whilst *she* didn't have two farthings to rub together or a pot to throw them out of, whether she was in the playhouse or plying her trade on the streets."

The organ man changed tempo, the tune swinging drunkenly from frenetic to melancholy, the wind-up toy seemingly out of control. His audience seemed no longer appreciative of the change in repertoire and the crowd, several yards away from us now, began to break into pieces, falling away along with the dolorous music. But the woman held fast.

"You know that the lodging house turned her down, it did, cause she didn't have the 4d for a bed?"

"I didn't know." I turned fully toward her. The shadows and light cut harsh lines into her face.

She nodded wisely, a street sage. "But that was our Annie, swearing she would go out and get the money for her bed. Ellen Smythe met her mayhap an hour later at the corner of Ludgate and Osborne Street. Ellen was on her way home after going to see that lightning fire broken out that morning on the docks."

I remembered the irritated sky as I made my way to Bedlam, the night after I'd received my first summons.

"Annie was alone, well into her cups. Again, won't be lying to you. People are quick to judge. Too quick. The woman was hell-bent on earning her doss money, she was. 'I have had my lodging money three times today,' she says to Ellen, 'and I have spent it… it won't be long before I'll be back.'"

She stopped there with an image of Annie alive, a small, middle-aged woman swaying eastwards along Drury Lane to the spot where we now stood.

I asked, "Your name?"

"Don't matter. Shouldn't matter to the likes of you."

Sliding a hand into the fold of my cloak, I extracted a few coins. Her eyes almost disappeared into her face as she followed the movement before her palm snapped up the offering. It wasn't easy to believe that she was getting something without having to give anything in return.

I looked around before asking, taking in what looked like shadows, men and women moving like wraiths among the buildings and alleys. "Have you ever seen a gentleman in this area carrying a cane, with an ornate—unusual—handle?"

A wound opened on the woman's face revealing blackened gums. I knew what she was thinking. Everything came with a price. And as the daughter of an infinitely wealthy man, experience led me to agree.

"Why for the asking? Your fella in the wrong parts of London? Up to no good with the likes of actresses like Mary? Though youse a beauty, I'd say, though no 'counting for tastes."

"Not exactly."

Bony shoulders beneath the patches of her coat lifted carelessly. "Why you asking?" she repeated. Then glanced around, in the event someone might be eavesdropping.

I fished for another coin. "In which direction can I find Blackmouth and the public house the Saracen's Head?"

The woman stared straight ahead, a curtain of limp black hair obscuring her face. "You almost there." The money vanished into her palm. "You be watching yourself. Lots of the ladies pitch outside the Saracen. So don't be trying to poach on nobody's territory." A cackle at the absurdity that quickly turned into a rolling wet cough. "You don't want yer bright hair pulled out in fistfuls." She tilted her head to spit before lifting her arm to point in the direction behind her. "Just follow the alley alls the way till you get to Bletcher Street, no more than five minutes' walk."

I felt her eyes on my back after I thanked her and set out to find if she'd told the truth. How long she stood there or if she decided to follow me, who knew? With little time to lose, I hurried along, first through a darkened alley, littered with glowing braziers illuminating sunken faces, and then into the ruddy light of Bletcher swaying with public houses and women in search of custom. Brightly clothed like exotic birds in a dense fog, they moved to a strange rhythm, a complex dance, from one doorway to the next.

Coffee houses and hotel restaurants were within my experience but the entry to the Saracen's Head was nothing I'd encountered before. Raging like the first ring of hell. A battered sign, letters burned into rotten wood, heralded the entranceway. Whoever or whatever I was to meet waited beyond the smoke belching from the cramped entrance. I hesitated, ducking into a shadowed doorway to the left of the public house, an unclaimed space for the time being at least, reeking of spoiled fruit and lye soap.

A draught of tobacco was needed to focus my resolve. I reached for the tissue-wrapped packet of cigarettes and matches under my cloak and extracted one with steady hands. The burst of a tiny light momentarily illuminated the corner. Just long enough that a face flared to life.

I should have run but my movements were slow. But then, I'd never run from anything in my life, or had I? There was nothing to do except look at Aaron Tarski blocking the doorway. The cigarette remained unlit, the flared match having fallen from my suddenly clumsy fingers, the singe of phosphorous tracing the air.

"Mr. Tarski."

He responded by staring into the darkness over my head.

He appeared the way he had at Millbank, his features slack, eyes unfocused, thin tufts of hair sticking into the air. Few feet separated us, and I wondered if I was strong enough to push him aside and make for Blackmouth Street.

His head lolled from one side to another, like a broken puppet's, the effect of a muscular tick or something else, I couldn't tell. His hands stuffed in his pockets, perhaps clasping a knife. Or worse. I clamped down on the last image I had of him in prison.

Two days. They had released him. Shortly after I'd left the prison. Without money, without work, with nowhere to go. And with my indirect consent. Tamping down the specter of the photographs, I imagined Griffith in a suffocating rage in the corridor of Millbank Prison.

My hand, still holding the unlit cigarette, approached Tarski's shoulder, hovering there. A ripple crossed his face. "Have you lost your way, Mr. Tarski? If you could say what you are looking for, I can help."

Tarski didn't acknowledge the question. "Are you looking for lodgings?" I improvised, withdrawing my arm, palm snapping the cigarette in two.

He cleared his throat, a death rattle, and just as startling. "You try to help me." The Slavic accent was strong.

I nodded. "We could go to one of the public houses for a meal. You must be hungry or thirsty." He shook his head, shifting his weight from one hip to another, clenching his fists in his pockets. I gathered my cloak, a signal that we were leaving, trying to lead us both away from the deserted doorway and into the street.

The stench of old sweat closed in as Tarski took another step closer while his face contorted so that it was difficult to tell if he was angry or afraid. He was possibly stronger than he looked and it would have been simple for him to overpower me, hold me down and—do what? Strangle me? Slice me into neat segments? If my assumptions were wrong about Tarski, what else might I have missed? He was not capable of carrying out an intricate murder, but he might be capable of following his primitive instincts.

"I will find you a place to eat and a place to stay. I promise you."

"I can't go back." His eyes were wet. To prison? In the unfocused gaze there was confusion but no hint of violence. The man was desperate but with an aimlessness about him.

"You don't need to go back to prison, but you must let me pass now." I edged alongside him until he caught my arm, locking his fingers around my wrist. A spike of panic followed by a quick reassessment. I may have been wrong after all. Screaming wouldn't work.

He was determined and surprisingly strong despite his meager weight. I twisted my wrists, but his hands were bone-hard manacles. I brought up a knee that was lost in layers of fabric then wrenched against him until there was a hot burst of pain, my skull hitting the doorframe behind me. An odd taste in my mouth, silver spots appearing and disappearing in front of my eyes. Then silence swallowed by darkness.

CHAPTER 14

The sound of birds. Robins in the elms outside my bedroom in Boston, rousing me at an absurd hour after an evening of too much champagne. My eyes slit open, then my mind cleared. I felt the hard ground and saw a smear of blood when I moved my hand, a broken cigarette. A strange whistling which did not come from birds but from the woman with the jet eyes, now on her knees beside me, breathing hard.

"Didn't I warn you to be careful, missus?" she asked.

Ripples of nausea. My hand went to the back of my head, to a lump the size of a coin. I closed my eyes again and then began to sit up, leaning against the side of the door frame. "What happened?" The question entirely inadequate.

The woman straightened to sit on her haunches, her cloak bunching around her. "Wouldn't know. Just saw the fighting."

With eyes half opened, I asked, "The fighting?"

"Two of 'em." Her eyes glinted, reminding me of a gnome I'd once seen in an overgrown garden. "And one a gentleman. With that cane you were looking for. Sure he ain't your husband and you got yourself caught up in something no good?"

The world tilted, one thought lurching against the other. "Where are they now?"

The woman released a moist cough, looking at me as though I'd asked her to reconnoiter Buckingham Palace. "Could be anywhere 'round here. At least weren't the Shoreditch Savage or you'd be laid out in lavender."

The side of my face burned. There was a vertical frown line between the woman's eyebrows and she winced when I looked up at her.

"You be needing some doctering. A split lip and bruises but ain't serious."

Arms straightening against the ground, pressing my spine along the door frame, I eased into a sitting position. Muttering to myself, ignoring the splinters jutting from the wood against my back.

The woman looked confused or at least pretended confusion at my words, wiping her hands down her muddied skirts. I murmured thanks, pulling myself up the wall until I was standing. The world tilted again before I closed my eyes to steady myself, resting on the wall behind me. I felt the woman take hold of my arm, offering support, adjusting my cloak with several subtle tucks. I dragged air into my lungs, counted ten seconds before opening my eyes again.

Blackmouth Street swam before my eyes. The rutted cobblestones, the warped doorways finally coming into focus. It took a moment before I realized the woman was gone.

I closed my eyes. Opened them again. Then I stepped from the doorway. I surveyed the street, to the left and right, through the fog, empty now. Wanting to call her back. I'd intended to give her the contents of my purse, but I patted my cloak, discovering instantly that my silver and the reticule had vanished. Gone with the woman, I thought, remembering the subtle adjustments to my person, the sleight-of-hand no doubt relieving me of my goods. I smiled as crookedly as a swollen lip allowed, the oily film of blood against my tongue. All was right with the world.

Listing onto Blackmouth, I walked alone, feeling the swell across my cheekbone and the pulse of a bruise on my mouth. It was dark and late and the environs had seen far worse than what I presented.

I skimmed the surface of my brain. I'd learned nothing, was left with nothing save for the outline of the man with the cane, a bruised face, and the memory of my encounter with Tarski. A free man.

Adrenaline straightened my spine. *The photographs.* Knight and the *Illustrated News.* Two days pared down to a few hours until daybreak.

I passed a man with pan-pipes, cymbals, a triangle, and a drum on his back. Beside him an acrobat wore striped trousers and walked on stilts while behind him an old woman played the hurdy-gurdy with a parakeet on her shoulder. Under crooked eaves, a deformed wretch hunched over a chamber pot. I shivered, the first shock of perspiration evaporating into the air. Along with the realization that I had to return to the Saracen Head.

I hadn't gone far, it turned out. Smoke curled from the low stone entranceway, the sign hanging as crooked as a dog's hind leg. I ducked my head under the lintel, the rumble of voices mingling with the sound of ash smoldering in the giant hearth. My eyes burned. Under my feet something wet, ale or worse. Sliding into a bench at the back of the cramped room, I surveyed the half-dozen tables through a shifting cloud of smoke.

Four men slumped over their tankards. A publican with thin lips and a widow's hump slapped a damp rag over the surface of the bar. Behind him shelves were littered with broken glassware and tankards and if I'd wished to pry under the counter, I was sure to fine gallons of cheap gin.

But no woman with the jet eyes, no Tarski, and no man with the cane.

What was I doing here? Had I missed my summoner, thrown off course by the woman with the jet eyes and Tarski? I wasn't the type to wait.

Maneuvering myself from the bench, I took the few steps toward the bar, to the publican who was now drinking deeply from a mug. He wiped his mouth with the back of his hand. "Don't think I seen you here before." His eyes lingered on my swollen lip, but he was smart enough not to ask about its origin.

Then I remembered I hadn't a penny on my person. A strange sensation. "I'm looking not so much for a drink," which I couldn't pay for even if I'd wanted to, "than for a person."

He barked a laugh, thick and rheumy. "You think we is giving it away? Besides, it's closing time, if the lady hasn't noticed." Jerking his head to the four men. Two were snoring. The other two, glass-eyed, swayed on the bench.

I put an elbow on the counter, ignoring the stickiness under my arm. "A quick question."

His gaze narrowed. "We don't answer no questions here. Want no trouble."

Pretending to reach into my cloak, I patted down the exterior pockets as though looking for coin. A glint of anticipation appeared in the man's eyes. "Anybody unusual drop by tonight?"

"You mean other than yourself?" He scratched behind an ear as though giving the question consideration.

Keeping up the pretense, leaning back from the bar, I dove into the inside of my cloak where there was a discreetly hidden pocket. Smiling confidently, I palmed the fabric as though searching for a purse and, instead, felt a small, unfamiliar bulk. Strange. My fingers reached beneath the silk-lined wool to a thatch of vellum.

The back of my head throbbed. The publican was saying something, lips moving, but his words drifted off into the smoke-filled space. Eyes suddenly razor sharp, he folded his meaty forearms onto the bar.

The blood in my arteries hummed. I don't remember what I said, backing away, table legs knocking against my knees as I made my way out of the Saracen Head. Outside, the thick air should have been a relief but wasn't. Grey raindrops settled on my head, my shoulders, as I huddled in the stoop where I'd last seen Tarski.

I realized I hadn't let go of the thatch of vellum. With a dense breath, I extracted a sheaf of papers.

There were five pages splayed in my hands, the handwriting as familiar as my own even in the anemic light of the night. But I knew there were many more.

The great tenderness I feel toward you increases with each day...

Reading beyond these first words was unnecessary because I had committed them to heart, to remember and then to forget. Intimate, private letters that should never have been written. That should only have been known to the two of us.

Our last meeting has left me in a state of wretchedness.... Sweat formed on my forehead despite the chill settling into my bones. The letters should have been destroyed, not returned. A vain, willful gesture on my part.

And I am as possessed of a fever such as I have never known...

Letters I'd returned to William James upon their receipt in Boston, well before my arrival in London.

Bile rose in my throat, my thoughts coming in tighter and tighter circles. Someone had intercepted the correspondence, read each page and sent some, though not all of it, back to me. As warning, threat, punishment. I looked quickly right and left again, along the nightmare of Blackmouth Street, head throbbing. The world constricted—the photographs, Sophie, Tarski, all coalescing. I followed the street until I came to the darkest corner I could find, retching the contents of my stomach and my soul into the ditch.

CHAPTER 15

The radiance of the morning was an assault. Knight and I stood beneath the portico of *The Illustrated London News* building where moments earlier he had refused to meet me in his offices above Fleet Street. His secretary, a dour man, face screwed with suspicion, had called for a carriage instead. Now we waited for the clatter of hooves and the jitter of reins to signal the end of a mutually enforced silence.

"You've seen the photographs in the paper, then." A statement rather than a question when we were finally out of earshot.

I had. With daybreak only a few hours away after my return from Shoreditch, I'd applied a compress to my lip and cheek, sleep elusive. Then just as the maids began to stir the grates, I'd clutched at the morning papers, ironed and ominous alongside my breakfast tray. As promised by Knight, Mary Holland and Annie Childs had risen from the ground, their images screaming from the front page of *The Illustrated London News*.

No photographs of the dead Sophie Rivington. It felt less like a reprieve and more like a gun at my head. I sent a scribbled note to the offices of the newspaper, requesting an early meeting with Knight.

Then I tossed William's letters, wrapped in black ribbon, to the back of my wardrobe. They represented an affair that should never have taken place, casually undertaken, by me at least. William James had been a sheltered man, living a careful and abstemious emotional life even within his marriage before I'd come along. I'd been a thunderclap in the aridity of his existence, an infatuation, not love. The irony was not lost on me that one of the preeminent psychologists of our age could not tell the difference.

I'd returned the letters to William when I should have destroyed them. Reckless, I realized. And now they'd found their way back to me. I remembered the woman in the alley, her small careful eyes, the deftness of her hands. Tarski and the man with the walking stick. But how could any of them have come upon letters written to me by William? Letters that should still be in Boston?

The back of my throat was cool with the dripping remnants of Dover's powder, a heady wildness bolting through my blood.

Knight, every inch the publisher that morning, was dressed in a cutaway coat in charcoal, one hand hooked in a vest pocket. "Griffith is apoplectic with the resurgence of unrest in the East End," he said with a twisted joy.

And with Tarski back on the streets. "Your photographs and the accompanying lurid piece had the desired effect." A carriage cut across Fleet Street nearly knocking down a runner, cap flying off his head, before jangling to a halt, the door swinging open.

"Also brought you to my doorstep this morning, although I welcomed the intrusion. We have matters to discuss, you and I." The boy stooped to collect his cap, then spit in the direction of the driver who raised a fist in reply. "It's in your best interests to hear what I have to say if Griffith doesn't come to *fetch* you first."

I stepped into the maw of the carriage catching a glance of my face in the small mirror above the cushioned squabs. Grey shadows puddled under my eyes and lines etched my mouth, bruises covered with powder. I settled onto the bench with its horsehair scratch, Knight opposite me as fear perforated my awareness.

Knight's fear, not mine.

I returned Knight's stare as the carriage lurched forward, the silk tassels on the door shimmying in time, the interior redolent of sandalwood and lime, the cologne of a gentleman. "I'm not readily fetched, Knight. Where are we going?"

"Where we're going depends on the conversation we need to have first." His jaw was stubbled blue in the light. He glanced out the window at the remaining curtain of fog over the river, wrapping the murky brown current in gold tissue. "Griffith is looking for you, and he has ordered a small battalion of his men to search for Tarski. You should be concerned. The Jew was released, thanks to your efforts or lack thereof, a free man for a time." He turned from the window leaning forward, his face close to mine. "That is before he was seen attacking you off Blackmouth Street last night. And by the way, your attempt at maquillage doesn't fool me."

Tilting away from him, I pressed my head against the cushioned backrest. "The man isn't capable of the crimes of which he stands accused. The article that accompanies the horrific photographs of Miss Childs and Miss Holland doesn't describe Mr. Tarski in the least. *"Hideous malice, deadly cunning, insatiable thirst for blood… beings who look like men, but are rather demons, vampires."* You've done a superb job plunging the East End into panic and hysteria."

"Tarski attacked you."

"He did not." How did Knight know? Seen by whom?

Knight shook his head in amazement. "You're lying—to yourself and to me."

"I'm alive because the true murderer is still at large. That's the truth of it. If Tarski is a killer, why didn't he finish me off like the others?" A tang of tobacco hovered over the scent of cologne in the close quarters, adding to my irritation. Now it was my turn to glance out the window, at the barges moored in their usual cluster around the river like an oily slick. My breath left a mark on the glass when I said, "We had a conversation and I hit my head against a doorway. Tarski was in no way directly responsible." I recalled the man in the cape with the walking stick, an indecipherable shadow in the picture I was trying to construct.

"What were you doing in Shoreditch?"

"None of your concern."

"I thought we'd agreed otherwise." He paused. "This *investigation* you seem to have undertaken will not serve you well. I warned you the day we met, standing over the body of that dead actress."

I coiled my hands in my lap. "A murderer is at large, preying upon women." In case Knight needed a reminder. "And while I'm convinced Tarski is not the perpetrator of these crimes, I will do what I can to help identify the killer."

"Your arrogance is astounding."

Framed in the carriage window, London's factories and steeples washed over me like a dark benediction, for a moment blocking out Charles Knight.

"We're a few moments from the police station on Commercial Street." Knight stared straight ahead. "Griffith has the Jew right where he wants him. You're to identify him as your attacker, an attempted strike by the Shoreditch Savage, and Griffith will get his murderer."

If I had not been ready enough to slip off the bench and out the door, I would have laughed.

"I'm about to become the killer's latest victim, attempted victim. Is that it? More fodder for your papers? It makes me wonder if you or Griffith didn't set up the entire fiasco on Blackmouth Street."

Knight smiled as though he'd tasted something bitter. I was locked in a carriage with a man who, as I first suspected, had much more to hide than even I did. *We had an arrangement, Knight.*

I took a chance, the Dover's powder vitalizing. "You haven't published Sophie's photographs."

"Don't test me."

"You're the one being tested, Knight. But by whom and by what I'm not yet sure."

"Are you threatening me?"

"How can I possibly threaten you?"

He stiffened as though I'd touched an open sore.

I didn't bother to tread carefully. "Because of what I know of your family?"

"My wife has the situation with the governess well in hand."

"A capable woman—I'm sure she does."

For a moment he looked as though he was about to argue but then the carriage began to slow, the rumble of cobblestones replaced by a growling crescendo of voices. The wheels sawed back and forth like a cradle. I looked out the window. Both sides of the street framed a patchwork of faces followed by hundreds more mottling the road.

Knight followed my gaze, parting the curtains to peer out the window on his side of the bench. "This is what you should be paying attention to."

"The rioting in the streets." Someone or something hit the side of the carriage.

"And what it means."

"I know what it means."

"I don't think you do." A fuselage of rocks punctuated his statement, ricocheting off the side of the carriage door. Knight jerked his head in the direction of the street. "Anger and indignation are the ruling passions of these crowds and they turn a blind fury upon anyone they fancy to blame for these murders. The newspapers have recorded half dozen such riots, aimless and potentially explosive, parading through the East End. Politicians have no choice but to notice. And for once, the poor have a hand at their betters' throats."

More than his words, the excess of the mob outside was like a seismic charge, shocking me into a primitive understanding. The realization had been too slow in coming, leaving me queasy as though a curtain had just been yanked aside to reveal a black and twisted painting. From outside the carriage, a swell of voices, a drumbeat, coming closer. My world was full of lunatics. I knew from experience what violence looked like, the clawed hands, the errant fists. The carriage shook, slamming me toward the window. From the street, wild eyes stared back. Open palms beat against the door. Then a drop of spittle, running down the thin glass barely separating me from the crowd.

Anger and unreason. A potent and deadly combination. "None of this can end, can it?" The unrest, the articles in the papers, the questioning of political order. The *murders*. The photographs of Sophie Rivington were the least of it. I righted myself on the seat pointing a finger at the window and the roiling mob. "Because if it does, what are the consequences for you?"

He didn't have the chance to answer. The carriage heaved forward, cratering unsteadily. I couldn't take my eyes from the little wedge, a flimsy lock, that could and would be ripped away, throwing us onto the street. Hard knocking against the carriage wheels, drumming on the doors. Horses shrieked, exhaling fear and panic. The cries mingled with glass first shattering then raining shards on the empty seat beside Knight.

The carriage rocked again, once, twice and the third time I collapsed to my knees. Knight's breath came in harsh waves moments before the weight of an army leaned onto the carriage door, splitting it from the feeble lock and frame with a shudder.

CHAPTER 16

It seemed that the whole of London rushed in, a surge of red-rimmed eyes and hoarse voices. The odor of dung and spent coal. Only Knight's shoulder held the remnants of the door in place. Refusing to cower in the corner, I rose from my knees just as Knight's hand on my arm fastened me in place like a bolt.

The pressure on my arm increased. "You're mad if you think you can just walk out into that mob. If the rabble doesn't pull you apart first, you'll be taken to Griffith and Commercial Station."

I heard the shouts of the driver and the clean snap of his whip. The carriage rocked viciously in response, Knight jammed against the disintegrating door. The discussion itself was mad—even, controlled, measured. The insanity of what waited outside pulled my mind back into focus with the precision of a punch.

"You have an alternative?"

"I know where we can safely wait until the crowd disperses." A brusque nod before he slid off his seat then moved his shoulder from the door. I tumbled from the carriage behind him. The crowd windmilled around us, shouting obscenities, fists raised, blood roaring.

The odor of wet wool pressed against my face. I threw my weight into the anonymous chest, shoving hard with my palms, a man almost taking me down, skirts tangling around my legs. My pulse surged with the dregs of Dover's powder.

Knight lunged in front, pulling me behind him.

A phalanx of police officers advanced on horseback, several of their numbers on foot swinging clubs, the silver buttons of their uniforms glinting sharp metal, harsh voices shouting orders. The mob appeared to take a collective breath, their attention now focused on the horses and men with their weapons beating the air.

Knight looped around, grabbing my arm, this time with no hint of civility. His shoulders hunched, crouched low, he suddenly appeared as though he was part of the crowd, cut from the same coarse cloth. I bundled my skirts in one hand and snaked close behind.

The warren of roads was transformed from a week before into a hallucination that looked both alien and familiar, a terrain under water. Road signs hung haphazardly, Wentworth Street, Hanbury Street, Cross Road. Facades stained in the morning light, leering down from what appeared to be a great height. Tenements, warehouses, a tangle of street vendors setting up their wares. The mob faded away replaced by girls selling tissue-paper flowers, clothes-pegs, watercress and lavender. We passed a cane-chair mender and the closed shop of a glazier.

No longer knowing where we were, with the thrum of the mob still in my ears, I was out of breath when we stopped at a small shop, blinds drawn, giving off the yeasty aroma of bread. Knight pulled open the door and offered a nod to the man behind the counter iced in flour, the shelves behind him heavy with loaves and buns. He didn't startle but continued kneading his dough with quiet ferocity while we left footprints in the snow of dust and grain on the sloping floor.

At the back of the storefront was a low doorway and Knight ducked inside. I followed, staring into the darkness of a windowless room. A single lamp sketched a rectangle of light on the floor.

"Your timing has always been enviable." Knight fixed on the man sitting in the shadows. He moved to turn the wick higher on the single lamp and the room sprang into sharp relief. I had the sense that the man—the man with the cane—had been sitting there for a long time.

CHAPTER 17

"Georgia Buchanan," I said, "but you already know that."

"Victor Cails," came Knight's voice from the doorway behind me.

Cails unfolded from a chair to acknowledge the introduction. His cane, topped by an empty, silver skull, tilted against a line of barrels dusted in flour. "Join me in having some of this fine ale." He gestured, the magnanimous host, to the cracked pitcher next to him.

The small space felt like a trap, fetid and warm, scarcely big enough to hold the three of us. Knight motioned to the low bench opposite Cails. I sat with the stiffness of a corpse in the first throes of rigor mortis.

Cails poured two mugs that he placed on the ground between us. Adjusting the chair so it was closer to the bench, he sat down with movements that were assured, his face intelligent and lupine, an unsettling combination. It was difficult to tell his age, somewhere between late thirties and early fifties, hair thick with threads of silver visible. A pocket square poked out of a jacket unbuttoned to display a somber navy waistcoat.

"London's East End is in fine form today." Cails' tone was conversational, voice low and graveled, persuasive in its baritone. "One can just feel the *excitement* in the district and elsewhere."

Knight undid the first two hooks of his overcoat with a hand freshly raw at the knuckles. The lines of his face seemed to have solidified, his jaw more pronounced, the brow heavier. "And the police have little to show for their efforts." His pronunciation seemed broader, having lost some of the careful consonants along the way from Fleet Street to the East End.

I'd faced lunatics in the confines of a cell before but never this.

We could have been in a sitting room, a salon, a private club instead of a storage space heavy with the stink of yeast. The two men had picked up the residue of a conversation as though they had left off only moments earlier. The violence just a few streets away still shuddered in the air. It appeared Knight and Cails were immune.

Cails's smile was benign. "The police are simply hoodlums of another type in the service of the state rather than in service to the people." He cocked his head and his brow shot up hopefully. "I shouldn't think you'd agree, Miss Buchanan."

"I've never given it much thought."

"Perhaps you should."

I turned toward the publisher, a heavy shadow in the corner. "Why did you bring me here, Knight?"

Cails decided to answer the question for him. "Knight knows the location of many such safe harbors in London. You'd be amazed at the publisher's range of interests."

"And you just happened to be here as well." The first time I'd spied Cails he'd been at the scene of another mad scrum near the Saracen after which he'd vanished into the crowd. Who had followed whom that night?

"A fortunate coincidence." A lie that he expected no one in the room to believe.

"As was the night you came upon me and Mr. Tarski outside the

Saracen."

Cails's eyes were flat and cold but a small sign of irritation played on his lips. "You might be grateful."

I remembered the woman and what she'd told me about the man with the curious cane. As for the letters from William, I ignored a cold tap down my spine, and the possibility that they might have been placed there by Cails.

"Won't you have a drink of ale, Miss Buchanan," Cails asked. "It will calm you after an incredible fright." The pitcher and mugs sat ignored. "Unless, of course, a woman of your rarified tastes expects finer."

"You have an association with both Knight and Griffith." An understatement. I sensed this man's interests transcended the mere greed of a publisher and ambition of an Assistant Commissioner.

Cails regarded me for a long moment, apparently pleased by my display of forcefulness which he knew would do me no good.

Knight broke his silence. "You'll regret asking."

"What possible difference will it make," Cails lifted a shoulder, "if she knows? You've come this far, after all."

How far had I come? And how much closer was I getting? The room seemed to shrink, as though that were possible. I rose from the bench. "We've come as far as Knight demanding that I don't help Griffith in his prosecution—*persecution*—of Mr. Tarski." My attention focused on Cails. "Nor is he predisposed to my undertaking an investigation of my own."

"And what else do you know, Miss Buchanan?" The persuasive baritone. "Allow me to identify some of the circumstances in which we find ourselves." The bench pressed against the back of my knees as I slowly sank back down. Suddenly, Knight and Griffith were only thunderclouds on the horizon. While Cails presented a far greater and immediate threat.

"Griffith and his retinue seem to have decided that they are dealing with a madman, one that strikes at night and in out-of-the-way places and so that his victims are unable to scream or cry out." Cails voice was unsettlingly calm. "In no case does he leave at the scene of his crime a weapon or any other object that might be traced back to him. And although he is not a random killer, he exclusively targets prostitutes and actresses when there is nothing to suggest a previous relationship with any of them. Thus, no accomplice that might betray him, no witness or clue that can identify him, and no clear motive."

A furtive mouse scampered behind one of the barrels, a scratching sound. I forced myself to be still, taking in the narrative that Knight and Cails had created out of thin air. My mind wavered, at first refusing to see the truth taking shape. A truth that was as cold as it was monstrous. They'd conjured someone to act on their command. To kill. Not that I had any proof. Not that they wouldn't deny every accusation. Not that they might decide to silence me.

The room came back into focus along with the sense that Cails and Knight were waiting for a kind of perverse acknowledgment from me.

I swallowed my outrage. "This caricature you've drawn with the help of Knight and his newspaper is a deliberate distortion. It intentionally impedes police efforts. They are looking for a type of murderer that doesn't and couldn't possibly exist."

Cails nodded approvingly, crossing one leg over the other. "You are an intelligent woman, Miss Buchanan, the more remarkable given that most women of great wealth typically remain in their gilded cages, safely anaesthetized from the world. It makes one wonder what has made you so different from the rest."

I heard the mouse, the scratching sound, like a rusty hook.

"You spend your time studying the mind, so I hear, which also makes one wonder why you spend so little time examining your own."

The room was becoming warmer, the air thinner.

"Yours would be infinitely interesting, I'd venture." A speculative glint in his eyes.

I hesitated, picking my way through a response. Cails would not be easily played. "It doesn't take much to determine that you and Knight have common interests, of a political type."

Knight shifted on the bench, arms crossing his chest, reminding us that he was still in the room.

Cails maintained his speculative pose. "You've answered your own question. Very astute." He drew out the last two words.

"Of a political type," I repeated, ignoring the pulse at my left temple, "that embraces a revolutionary fervor, wherein the exploitation of the poor becomes a tool, a means to an end." I nodded in the direction of the low doorway. "As in the mob outside."

Cails gave an approximation of a smile. He shifted in his chair, the leather of his boots gleaming dully in the half light. "You should understand exploitation is a harsh term that must be used carefully. If the means delivers a greater end, then the definition is a morally flexible one."

Beside me Knight dipped his head in silent response, studying the floor.

"*Whoever lays his hand on me to govern me is a usurper and tyrant, and I declare him my enemy,*" Cails quoted. "Pierre-Joseph Proudhon, the man credited as being the first anarchist and one of anarchism's most influential ideologues."

The name meant nothing to me. "I'm vaguely familiar with the ideology. I've an acquaintance with Marx."

Cails's eyes sharpened. "Proudhon warned against Marx's authoritarian aspirations. Anarchy is a vehement distrust of the state, Miss Buchanan."

I was aware of how well we learned, in the course of a lifetime, to rationalize variations of the truth, whether personal or ideological, some better and some more vile than others. I'd lived with distrust, doubt, suspicion, a porous foundation upon which, some might argue, my vocation was based. At times it was necessary that we contradicted the truth, or constructed it, for our own purposes because without some sort of a lie, we would have nothing.

What lie was Knight living, I wondered, and Cails, both men foundering on the faith of misdirected ideologies? "You may offer your political beliefs dressed in philosophical posturing, but what we're left with is the prospect of further murders. More women will die if you have your way."

Cails turned slightly, his clean jawline and steep nose limned in the half-light. "Bravo, Miss Buchanan, I do value directness, that uniquely American trait."

"My directness only reiterates the ugly reality that you have so carefully and brutally conceived. All in the service of your anarchist's cause." The wick on the oil lamp shivered, the tight space, the yeasty odor, suddenly overwhelming. "You would sacrifice the lives of how many women to achieve your goals?"

Cails was relaxed, his eyes fixed with an almost listless consideration as though I mattered not at all, whether I came or went. "You might be surprised. Progress could help raise these women out of the hell in which they've been trapped by forces not of their own making. Are their lives even worth living, toiling as they do, selling their bodies to keep them in bread and drink?"

"And you set yourself up as judge as to who is worthy or not, and worth the sacrifice."

Cails's hand brushed the air with unconcern. "You believe these women, existing as they do in the stink and roil of the East End, are worth your consideration?"

Part of me knew there was a trap in his questioning, an expectation of a haphazard, contradictory reply. "They're worthy of consideration." I thought of Annie Childs and Mary Holland lying in the Montague Street mortuary. "As much consideration as you or I."

"You speak in banalities, Miss Buchanan. I expect better coming from you." A lethal quality infected Cails's voice. "Although your pastimes do speak to an interest both in the rich and benighted, if not in the poor, precisely—unless the poor are useful specimens, like another species of laboratory rats, forced to participate in whatever hopeless experiments you decide to pursue in a clinic or public asylum. You study and conduct experiments on them, do you not? You would argue that their participation is for the greater good, sacrificed at the altar of science and inquiry." He settled back in the chair. "Follow the logic. Why is my argument so offensive to you? The greater good is the anarchist cause. Change will not happen without it."

"Whose definition of the greater good?"

"You answer questions with questions."

"And you find facile ideologies an excuse for immorality."

"Immorality? Really? Finally, your temper is up. I was wondering how long it would take to get a visceral response from you." Cails shifted his body so that he faced me directly, tense and still at the same time. "Such misplaced confidence when you should be petrified." His gaze skirted my face as though committing to memory the color of my eyes, the set of my mouth, the geography of my shifting expressions. The small pulse pounded in my left temple while he studied me beyond the point of comfort. "You're not, by any chance, afraid, Miss Buchanan?" Cails looked to Knight, who was now standing, for agreement. "Why Knight—I believe this otherwise very sensible woman suddenly fears for her safety. Perhaps for her life. And not from the mob I might add."

Cails rose to his feet. My nerves crackled. He didn't need to step any closer, his message telegraphed with the clarity of a precisely aimed shot. I calculated how many more steps to the door and whether it might be locked from the outside.

Knight appeared to do a quick calculation of another kind. "Think, Miss Buchanan. Consider for a moment the consequences of your actions, this investigation you've decided to pursue."

The consequences of my inaction, I *knew*, would result in more women hacked to death with surgical accuracy in the streets of East London.

"The least of her worries at the moment." Cails turned to the cane behind him, brushing off the handle before gripping it firmly with strong elegant fingers. His hand cupped the skull, a silver-plated cranium with translucent gems in the hollowed-out caverns where eyes might have been. "Georgia Buchanan believes that we are behind the Shoreditch murders." He tapped the floor with his stick sending up a drift of flour. "She fears she is going to be the next woman to die."

I eyed several of the stout barrels lining the wall, the right size to conceal a body. Knight and Cails were silhouettes in the gloom, soaking up what was left of the light and air in the room, the oil lamp stuttering like an imbecile.

"You fear the worst." Cails leaned into the words. "*Fear*. An emotion that brings all one's failings and weaknesses to light."

There was a bizarre logic to his planning if I could only have made sense of it. Cails's plan. The realization offered little comfort. I threw down the bargaining chip. "The photographs in Knight's possession are only of use to you if I'm alive."

Cails stared at me, the beginning of a disbelieving smile creasing his narrow face.

"My murder would serve no purpose."

"Murder?" Cails's tone mocked, his face sharp angles and lines from cheekbones to chin. Then a flash of ice. "True power rests in the exercise of restraint and Knight can tell you that I despise excess of any kind."

I considered how far my bravado might go.

Knight looked up from the floor, flicking his eyes at Cails.

"You've much to consider, given your current predicament." Cails pressed on. "Shall I enumerate? There is your father to think of— because who knows what he is trying to hide with his relationship to Archibald Rivington. There are those who would contend that he purchased the ambassadorship for his friend in exchange for influence, a potential political embarrassment for your country at the very least and an unwelcome situation for your father if exposed. Some matters are better left unexcavated after all."

A low, reasoned voice, so convincing. "Then the unsavory details of a suicide sliced open for public viewing. Is there a strain of madness running through the Rivington family? Or something more sinister perhaps? And your unfortunate role in the matter, as an alienist with associations at Harvard and the Salpêtrière." A wide smile split his face. "Have I left anything out?"

Certainly, he had, quite deliberately. The unspoken always had a way of leaving its mark. Victor Cails, the anarchist, I thought, would like nothing more than to have the daughter of an absurdly wealthy American industrialist to pit against his ideological fantasies.

I played my part in the foul catechism. For the moment. "You're asking me to do nothing to help the police make a case against Tarski or anyone else. Do nothing that would direct attention away from the slaughter in the East End. And do nothing to help bring a close to this murderous rampage."

Cails offered a warm smile. "Don't look affronted. There's no need to flinch from the crude realities, Miss Buchanan. You are your father's daughter, one who knows how to strike a bargain."

Which would lead to more dead women.

"Never a difficult day in your life. Until recently."

Knight sat on the bench, adding nothing to the exchange. I suspected his behavior admitted to a long and familiar relationship with Cails and he intuited the meeting was at an end.

Both hands on the edge of the bench, he looked up to catch Cails's eye just as the older man said,

"I'll let the two of you resolve the details." As though he had already lost interest. "I know you now understand the overarching terms of our agreement, Miss Buchanan. And while you needn't fear for your life, we will ensure if not your *death* then your *disappearance*."

Death. Disappearance. I struggled to ignore my pulse, light and quick. Then tried to swallow, my mind scattering, words drying on my tongue. I understood power, my father's power. But Cails. Who was this man? I snapped my eyes to him. He stared back.

My reputation. My father's. The Rivington family. And if having me disappear was not enough?

The room was airless, my breath short. I dropped my gaze first.

Knight was already at the door, pulling it open. Then with his back to me, Cails bowed his head to clear the low lintel. His footsteps seemed to leave no trail on the powdered floor.

CHAPTER 18

Outside on the street, I pulled in breaths of coal-thick air. *Disappear for a time.* A glance at the watch pinned beneath my cloak told me it was close to noon although my body and mind were working like it was the middle of the night. When I looked up again, Cails had vanished. Along with what he knew about me.

Knight gripped my arm. He led me with uneasy familiarity through the maze of alleyways, a hedgerow of dead ends. Wagons crawled in the rutted path and the occasional pinched face peered out from an unscoured corner.

Victor Cails gave his own kind of assurances that the killings would continue, in number and vicious degree, and now I was part of the grisly mechanism. I had no evidence to use against him and he had the Rivington photographs that he would use against me. I wondered what he would do to Knight should his greater scheme come undone. And Knight—if only I knew what he was afraid of.

My mind volleyed back to that first meeting at Bedlam—Griffiths, Knight, and I crammed into the asylum library. There were the four of us, somehow connected, like points on a grid. I knew Knight and

Cails's motivations but what about Griffith's?

I reeled back with sudden clarity, as if I'd been struck. "You're using Griffith. Keeping him spinning." The revelation glaring. "His entire police brigade looking like fools."

Knight glanced over his shoulder but didn't let go of my arm. "It's not difficult to do. Griffith approached me and the newspaper, demanding we stop stoking the killings with our coverage of the murders. Your name arose, the mind doctor that he was threatening to involve in the case. To shut it down. Then I told him we had the photographs of the dead Rivington girl. That certainly got his attention. Should come as no surprise—I'd learned of the scandal during my time in New York."

Their twisted agreement. Another layer I'd missed. So much more than simply greed on Knight's part and ambition on Griffith's. "Why Griffith's interest in me, specifically?"

Knight kept walking, dragging me alongside. "You should ask your father. George Buchanan has made enough enemies in his life. His kind always does."

A tangle of people congested the street, a woman cackling, sprawled up against a wall, a dog thin with mange, cocking a leg. My mind pitched from one fragment of thought to the next, none reassuring. "What complaint does Griffith have against my father?"

From somewhere came the overwhelming stench of sharp chemical and rot. We stopped abruptly in front of a tanner's shop, the sting momentarily clearing my head, Knight's gaze nailing me in place.

"*Complaint?*" He spat a laugh, releasing his grip now that I hung on his every word. "Shouldn't come as too much of a shock. How do you think George Buchanan made his fortune? Though you probably don't know, do you? Having never bothered to ask." He looked at me almost with pity. "Your father simply foreclosed Griffith's family's estate, generations' worth, or at least his solicitors did. Because that's what he does. What his people do. Mop up the random assets of good but impoverished families. After all, not all members of the peerage can marry American heiresses. I'm certain your father doesn't even know the details of the transaction and the Griffith name would never come to mind if he were asked."

Knight's words, clear and sharp. "Griffith's humiliation is of epic proportion and if you understood the English peerage better, you wouldn't look so shocked." Knight was suddenly confident, almost lounging now, arms crossed. "Griffith is a fool, believing he can orchestrate a stop to the murders in the East End. As you put it—we don't wish it to end."

For the first time I considered letting Cails and Knight make good on their threats. Publish the photographs of Sophie Rivington. Spread news of the scandal far and wide. Destroy Sophie's family, my reputation and what little was left of my father's. But that would do nothing to stop the murders in the East End in which I was now dangerously complicit.

I would be made to *disappear*, a part of Cails's grisly strategy that I was just beginning to understand. I needed evidence, I thought, my mind running. I needed to get closer to Knight, closer to Cails—and away from Griffith.

I didn't resist when Knight summoned a hansom. And I didn't resist when he crowded me into the vehicle before clambering inside next to me. Directions barked to the driver before Knight heaved the door shut. We crawled down Huxton street and through the mob not so much dispersed as reassembled, a wretched and volatile procession that lacked any precise form or destination, their fear and hatred disbanded for a time.

The unseeing eyes of Mary Holland and Annie Childs stared up at me accusingly. *I am guilty of the good I did not do.* No one else was as close to the Shoreditch murderer as I was.

Silence carried us the next few miles, the crunch of the cobblestones and the discolored squab above Knight's head helping to keep my focus, that I had no choice but to follow the road to the end. The commotion of the streets subsided to a murmur until we pulled to a stop.

What a difference a few miles made, the unstated boundary between the wealthy and the poor. The gutters with their stalls and assemblages of fish and ribbons, door keys and cabbages, tapers and nails giving way to the calm and order of white limestone and shadowed porticoes.

The square in Mayfair where Knight's townhouse sat was empty, its serenity marred only by the ramrod-straight shrubs disturbed by a faint breeze. Tall gates assured the peace. Knight's gaze was now cool, aloof, yet I could see disquiet flashing at the edges, something that I had come to associate with Charles Knight. The publisher who wasn't what he seemed.

"Griffith won't think to look for you here."

I swallowed, breathed. "What of your wife. Mrs. Knight."

"You're staying with us to help with Trevyn. Supervising her convalescence." And to have Knight supervise me. My every instinct told me to push open the carriage door and bolt, but I forced ice water into my veins instead. Where better to find what I needed than under Charles Knight's roof.

More women would die—because of what I would or wouldn't do.

"Your mistakes are compounding." As though I needed reminding. "Think of what would happen if Griffith finds you. Don't you just fancy yourself the Shoreditch Savage's lone survivor? Testifying against Tarski. The *charlatan* from Boston whose good works have only led to more death. The public scrutiny would be endless."

The carriage steps hit the ground, the driver waiting for our exit. The house was as I remembered. The shuttered windows, the graveled walk, elegant lines that soared to a tower room.

I trailed Knight through the colonnaded side entrance of the townhouse with its pillars and checkered floors to a salon whose candied assortment of chintzes and plaids set my teeth on edge. My prison.

And where I found Alice James seated across from Constance Knight.

CHAPTER 19

A lice's hands pleated the fine cashmere shawl over her knees. A plate of heaped pastries at her elbow sat untouched.

"I will close the windows," Constance Knight rose from her chair, moving across the salon before bringing down the casement with the finality of a guillotine. She shook and then arranged the heavy brocade drapery before suddenly recognizing our presence on the threshold. "Miss Buchanan?"

Knight sank his hands into his pockets, possibly considering a variety of versions of the truth fit for his wife. I thought of his freshly raw knuckles. He had reassembled himself, having straightened his cravat, shot his cuffs and brushed any evidence of the humble bakery from his sleeves.

"Georgia," Alice's quavering voice, "how entirely unexpected."

I sensed that Constance was not a woman easily flustered, her gaze moving from her guest to me and then back again, quickly coming to some decision, recovering brilliantly from my surprising appearance in her drawing room alongside her husband. There was something sculptural about her bearing, elegant with inquiring eyes and sharp cheek bones. I'd forgotten, somehow, that hers was a stealthy beauty that lacked the delicate, forgettable features deemed so desirable in our age.

A slight smile. "What a pleasant surprise. Of course, you and Alice are fast friends."

"Mrs. Knight, please accept my apologies for the intrusion. Alice, it's wonderful seeing you looking so well." I examined Alice's face, the flushed cheeks and the pinched lips, amazed at how adept we were at performing a distorted version of normalcy.

Knight nodded in Alice's direction murmuring the appropriate greetings before addressing his wife, eyes shorn of expression, his tone taking on the wise neutrality of the head of the household. "Miss Buchanan came by my offices today and while securing her a carriage, we were assailed by the mobs in the East End."

His wife's smile faded. "I can't begin to imagine…" She stopped herself. "At least you were accompanying Miss Buchanan. To think of a woman alone in such circumstances." She didn't presume to ask what I was doing at the offices of her husband and the nature of our business. Moving to her side with brisk efficiency, Knight took her hand in his, a small theatrical gesture, laying the groundwork for my stay in Mayfair. A tall woman, Constance almost looked her husband in the eye but for an inch. After a few moments, she removed her hand from her husband's, motioning me toward the divan.

Alice played at polite obliviousness, composing herself with useless motions, first squaring the plate of sweets at her elbow, then arranging the bolster at her back and finally returning to pleating the softness of the cashmere on her lap. "These pastries look wonderful, Constance, but as you know I have so little appetite these days. Georgia, strange coming upon you here of all places. I've been waiting for your visit now that you're in London."

Knight gave Alice a tight, absent smile while examining a print of cherubs in a verdant gold field positioned above the divan. "You may visit with Miss Buchanan *here* whenever you choose, Miss James. I shouldn't wish otherwise." His gaze left the cherubs to shoot his wife a look. "Constance—Miss Buchanan will be staying with us for the foreseeable future, to help with Trevyn. I think it would be best."

Later, behind closed doors, perhaps there would be questions but at the moment there was only cool acceptance in Constance Knight's regard. She gave her husband a chance to add something else but when he didn't, she clasped her hands at her waist, head tilting. "Of course." Then turning towards me with a practiced smile. "We are in your debt, Miss Buchanan, for upending your life to come to our assistance. I can't thank you enough... for the other night. And now for this... it's much too generous."

I murmured the right response smoothing over the awkwardness, the strange circumstances that had brought us together, unwillingly, in this room. It seemed absurd, suddenly, that in this placid household, amid the chintz and paisley, the quotidian domestic, I would find evidence to put an end to the murders in the East End.

Then there was a minor fluster of taking my cloak, informing the housekeeper, and questions about dinner before Constance left the drawing room, Knight with a proprietary arm at her elbow. I lowered my head to exhale and Alice James and I were alone.

⚜

Alice attempted to sit up straighter, then, clearly exhausted by the effort, deflated into the divan. "I hadn't expected to see you here of all places, Georgia," she repeated, the shawl now a pool around her waist.

"A situation with their governess that I may help address." I remained standing, taut as a bow. "You referred me after all, Alice, to Mrs. Knight, I believe."

"Quite right, I did. Somnambulism is it?" She raised her rounded chin above a swathe of lace without waiting for a confirmation from me. "Constance mentioned something to that effect. Distant relation or not, Trevyn can't be roaming the halls much less the streets at all hours. Constance has tried to help her, you understand, gave her several warnings, as a matter of fact, even suggested that she take a tincture to help her sleep, not too soundly, naturally, given that she needs to listen for Charles and Violet."

"Miss Trevyn may be ill."

"If so, she can seek medical attention—by the look of it, *yours*." The words floated over my head, trapped like an unexpectedly bad smell between the ceiling and the floral and paisley flecked walls. "I have come to know Constance very well over the course of several years." Alice sat up straighter. "You should understand that Constance is not given to flights of fancy, to moodiness nor to a consumption of sentimental novels, her disposition as sound as the grandfather clock ticking in the entranceway of this home."

"By that you mean her assessment of Miss Trevyn's ailments is to be trusted."

"Precisely. Constance's wisdom and fortitude are astounding. I simply could not endure it." Her hands fluttered before falling back to her lap. "Only imagine if the children were to come to some disastrous end. It also speaks to Constance's loyalty that she does not wish to dismiss Trevyn if she is under distress, to send her back to her parents who can scarcely afford...." The sentence trailed off then began again with more details about Trevyn's family having experienced difficulties, the father's consumption and his requiring the air in the Italian alps.

She pattered on while I allowed myself to sit opposite her, wondering if I should let down my guard while my head was still full with what I'd learned about Cails and Griffith. I was also aware Alice and I were repeating a familiar pattern, only this time not in my rooms on Mount Vernon Street in Beacon Hill.

What was wrong with Alice James? Difficult to determine. Over and over, I had thumbed through the worst of Professor Charcot's photographs looking for clues, the images detailing the particulars of nervous and degenerative conditions—the choreas, ataxias, tics and fits, the *tabes dorsalis*. Charcot had, through his investigations in his native France, used patient photographs to demonstrate a physiognomic map of passions, those ghostly traces of unbalanced emotions that might reveal insanity. All in the hope of a cure. Or so we mind doctors told ourselves.

All of which made me reconsider Constance Knight and her unlikely friendship with Alice James. Two women of an age but of entirely different circumstances and constitutions. Constance, wife and mother, whose courage and strength I'd witnessed in the face of a potentially staggering tragedy. Alice, child-like and frail, an exposed nerve who would fall into a fugue state if confronted by an edged word.

I settled a bolster at my back. "How are you feeling, Alice? How is your health?"

First surprise at the change of subject then a familiar shrewdness in her gaze which, for a change, she didn't bother to hide. "Always the questions, Georgia. You are relentless." She leaned her head against the cushions and looked at the ceiling where the chandelier cast strange shapes, competing with the overwrought patterns on the walls.

"Very well then." A girlish sigh. "As usual, the doctors have entirely too much to say about my health but with little result. The last physician, recommended to me before I left New York to stay here in London with Henry, was that silly Russian who charged an exorbitant fee for application of electrical currents. Another milestone on the long pilgrimage toward wellness." A hint of impatience before she relented. "I'm not about to dismiss the whole thing out of hand. After all it was William who offered an alternative, Dr. Mitchell."

"I recall."

"I'm sure you do. All I recall are acres of time in bed, food, vapor baths, massage and galvanic currents applied to nerves and muscles."

"How is Henry doing now that you've joined him here?"

"Henry? Henry have time for me? Why, I've hardly set eyes upon him since coming to London, since *The Aspern Papers* published.

If he's not in Florence then he's in Venice with that smart set he's taken to. I'm staying with Katharine Loring for the time being at her apartments in Clerkenwell Green."

Her companion, Katharine Loring, who had taken on Alice and her intractable illness and labile moods when the rest of us had tired of them. The whispers about a Boston marriage I ignored. "I'm sure Katharine has suggested fresh air, getting out more." I gestured to the window and the low glow of the sun. "The autumn weather has been uncharacteristically pleasant so, no doubt, a carriage ride or visit with friends such as Mrs. Knight is not out of the question."

"I could not live without Katharine." The tremor in Alice's voice was exaggerated. "Katharine is occupied, always occupied because I can be of so little help to her. There are the few servants she's retained here in London who need direction, a char woman and such, household accounts totaled, letters to be answered, calling cards collected, social engagements politely declined. It is a world from which I've been spared: the inflammation from stimulation, isn't that what someone called it, like a rash that can quickly spread? She doesn't deserve to be shut up here in London with me." She plucked at the shawl over her knees, glancing sideways. "And my humors. What did Willi always say? My flights into illness, my willed malaise? Have you heard from him, by the way?"

Willi. The diminutive startled me. "William is a busy man."

Alice's breathing quickened, a faint but familiar sequence that demonstrated her changeable emotions. She picked up a pastry then put it down again on her plate. "I suppose that's true, now that he can no longer rely upon you to assist him. You were of such benefit and service, I'm sure, to his research and studies." Her fingers stilled by her plate when she asked abruptly. "And to me, of course. Treating me as your patient all those months, through the worst of it."

I examined her flushed face. "I hope it was of some help. Through the worst of it."

A small smile broke through. "Wish I could say, Georgia, wish I knew. Exhausting, all of it. Poking into my mind, my emotions, and for what?" A pause. "It must feel to you a bit like playing God."

"I'm not quite sure what you mean."

"Well, you are the chosen one, the one who is all seeing and all knowing. Telling your patients what it all means when perhaps it means nothing at all."

"Is that how you see it, Alice?"

Her smile faded. "What made you decide to travel to London?"

"You know I've spent time in Europe."

"Paris was it not? With that Frenchman, Professor Charcot, that time? My, your interests are peripatetic, flitting from one thing to the other." I made note of the criticism. "Although London doesn't seem like such a good idea any longer, wouldn't you agree?" Alice continued. "Katharine is reluctant to even allow me the papers. Why I'm always watching out for her with a cyclopean eye, as she's ready to chastise me for reading my collection of newspapers which I've secreted away like a pilfering servant over the past several weeks."

"Are you certain that's wise?" I couldn't imagine how Alice would absorb the horrors of the Shoreditch murders. Daily life was enough of a challenge.

Alice let out her breath in small puffs, cashmere bunching under her palm. "I will admit reading about such terrors is like a fist squeezing my heart. Katharine brims with exhortations, warning me against opening my mind and nerves to such nightmares, reminding me of what I can expect as a result—my wild deliriums."

The faint chime of the clock. I pictured Katharine returning for tea and Alice rattling the papers on her lap before folding and then shoving them back beneath her chaise at the apartments in Clerkenwell. "Most likely a good plan. No wonder that nerves come undone with what's happening in the East End. You shouldn't read about such horrors."

"While you live them—the horrors—caught in a riot this morning? I would be distraught for days, trapped in such a maelstrom. Of course, your nerves are impervious to the symptoms that prey on mere mortal women, particularly those who subject themselves to overstimulation." Alice's posture was once again that of a collapsed doll without enough stuffing to brace her. "You and Constance, I admire your fortitude."

"You're stronger than you know, Alice."

A tight smile. "Of course, but then Constance has her husband by her side. A strange match, although a durable one, it seems."

The observation was peculiar, coming from Alice. "Why strange?"

She smoothed the shawl on her lap, looking away, almost coy. "Some might say Mr. Knight's done rather well for himself, come up in the world since his marriage. The son of a vicar, although from an old family. And she the daughter of a baron. How else do you think he came into the ownership of *The Illustrated London News* and who knows how much property and other business interests?" A pause. "Rather fortunate for him."

"A vicar's son." I wouldn't have guessed it. "It appears you and Mrs. Knight have formed a close friendship, shared confidences."

The room had darkened, the late afternoon a surprise, rendering Alice in shadowed profile, her pale hands finally stilled on her lap. "We have."

CHAPTER 20

Three days later and I was the one pacing like a madwoman. I'd learned nothing more about Cails's and Knight's plans, gathered not a shard of evidence.

I recounted what little I knew. Cails was an anarchist, Knight inveigled in his plans to keep the unrest in East London flourishing. Tarski in prison; Tarski out of prison. The more murders, the more mystery, the more newspaper stories, the more mayhem the police and the government could not control. Griffith and his pursuit against me that would rain ruin both on my father and the Rivingtons. William's letters—somehow connected or an aberrant detail?

All of it an indiscernible monologue that went round and round in my head, murmurings just out of the range of coherence, scarcely formulating the question much less the answer. Then back to the question of the summonses. First to Bedlam and now to Blackmouth Street in Shoreditch. Who was sending me those cryptic notes and why?

Plans had gone smoothly here in the house in Mayfair, none of my making. No signs of Knight. Trunks of my clothes appeared in my rooms, sent from Berkeley Square. An invitation to lunch in Clerkenwell from Alice James and Katharine Loring that I declined.

My meals were taken alone and I had seen only servants and Constance Knight, my host who was also my unwitting jailer, once over tea and once over lunch where the topic of the governess was unrelenting.

An afternoon ago, in the conservatory, the febrile autumn turned grey, drops of rain heavy on the glass roof overhead. Wind roared outside whipping up gravel stone from the side garden walk, beheading what was left of the trellised roses. The governess paced, flinching at my questions:

"How do you feel when you wake up from one of these unusual slumbers, Miss Trevyn?" I tried not to pace along with her.

She tipped her head, perplexed. "I don't remember anything. I don't dream. And then my body and limbs are heavy, my mouth dry as cinders."

"Have you ever taken laudanum or any other type of tincture for sleep?"

"Never. Perhaps when I was a child and sickening from a fever. But," she stopped, looked at me directly, "I don't indulge in any such medications if that is your line of inquiry."

"I'm not trying to find fault."

"But you find it curious, don't you?"

I did. Miss Trevyn was calm, levelheaded, sane. More than I felt these days. For the first time in my life, I was in hiding, avoiding Griffith and those infernal summonses.

As for my putative charge in the Knight household, I observed Trevyn's relations with the children that were nothing but composed and ordered, as regular as the lull of the metronome on the piano in the salon. Her measured tones proved persuasive, Charles and Violet compliant and complacent in following her requests, playing in the ivy-choked garden by the portico or doing their ledgers in the school room. They had little to do with me or any other adults, their solemn little faces most often seen in profile as they were swept upstairs to the nursery or bundled outside for their walks in the park.

The governess, far from wishing to forget her recent struggles, insisted on finding the reasons for her irregular behavior. And I had no answers. The young woman who first appeared like a wounded bird was as sound as a young oak. It was Constance Knight who didn't like to think so.

Each morning, in my handsomely appointed rooms, I glanced at the newspapers on my breakfast tray, dreading the headlines that would tell of another killing in the East End. But it seemed Cails continued to play God, electing to take his time before calling another woman to his unholy kingdom.

Or was I too quick to judgment? I had no proof that would support any of these assumptions about Cails. I knew nothing about the man other than the persona he chose to present. Of what was he capable? He appeared to give little thought to right and wrong. He was clearly a master manipulator. He exhibited scant empathy or remorse. Was it possible that he had found a coldly rational madman to do his bidding, someone who not simply killed but also savaged and mutilated his victims to greatest effect? Not Tarski, I was certain. He lacked the predatory impulse, the need for control, the mission-oriented focus that I sensed were key to the psyche of the murderer. I tried to bring the killer's profile into focus, but the outline remained elusive, a hastily rendered sketch that offered neither broad strokes nor fine details.

Whenever I had the chance, I returned to my prime concern, finding evidence to connect Cails and Knight to the murders in the East End. I rifled through private drawers, scanned bookshelves in the study on the second floor, glanced through a partially opened door to the Knight's bedroom.

What was I expecting to find? A written confession? A sheaf of papers expounding the details of Cails's anarchist plottings? The Shoreditch killer's weapon?

Although it was midafternoon, a dim light glowed from the depths of the Knight's bedroom, a four-poster bed flanked by a striped chaise, an escritoire in the far corner. A window sashed tightly against sodden clouds, and beyond a dressing room, the door slightly ajar to reveal the edge of a bed, a low bookcase, and the angle of an imposing armoire.

I glanced over my shoulder and down the length of the hallway, empty except for my shadow stretching along the parquet floor. A door closing downstairs, the reverberation coming from behind the kitchen, every noise in this house already too familiar to me.

Edging into the room, I caught the scent of bergamot and lemon. I slid to the window, eyes cast down at the escritoire, polished surface clear save for an ink stand, a small vase with violets, shimmering purple. There were two slender drawers which opened with a sigh, revealing nothing more than ribbons, calling cards, a childish drawing, the bright yellow chalk smeared.

I swallowed a combination of shame and guilt, nudged the drawers closed, retreating from the window. Then looked up. The dressing room. Where Charles Knight most likely slept, a not uncommon arrangement for married couples. And where he might empty his pockets, carelessly tossing aside notes, papers on which were written names, addresses. *Something.*

Only reminding me that I'd found nothing of use these past days under Knight's roof. Not a scrap of evidence linking him to Cails or to the murders. And nothing to indicate why Knight, an esteemed publisher, might find himself connected to an anarchist.

A few steps and I was on the threshold, the shelves with the tumble of books, the armoire with its dark recesses and sly, hidden corners. A small mirror, upright on the top shelf.

Where I locked eyes with Constance Knight. Her face framed in gilt, spearing me with a stare.

CHAPTER 21

Blood hummed in my ears. I turned around, the room coming into focus with Constance Knight at the center, eyes dark against the pale oval of her face.

"Mrs. Knight, I should apologize. There's absolutely no excuse for my being here."

A slight lift of her brows. She stood serene and inscrutable in a maroon morning dress as though she expected to find a house guest lingering in her private quarters.

"I was looking for Miss Trevyn." I shook my head at my own foolishness. "I'd last seen her racing after the children. I thought I might find them here." The lie hung in the air between us.

There should be a confrontation, at the very least, a volley of questions or a cold dismissal, but any momentum had stalled in the silence. From the corner of my eye, I could still see the armoire, the bookshelf; whatever was hidden there would have to wait. If I wasn't found out first.

Constance finally broke the silence, her voice low and clear "No need to apologize." Smile widening. "After all, my husband and I are the ones who are in your debt with regards to Miss Trevyn's peculiar affliction. And it makes perfect sense you would be keen to keep an eye on her comings and goings. In any case, what does it matter? It's fortunate that I find you here. I'm eager to learn about any progress you may have made with her."

The composed expression, hands folded at her waist. I wondered what she was really thinking, what she suspected, beneath that controlled demeanor. For a moment we remained a frozen tableau until, without another word and a turn of her heel, she swung from the room, the situation firmly in her control.

Down the two flights of stairs, across the atrium, past several servants, their capped heads bowed, and then we were in a sitting room off the conservatory. Wood paneling, two horse-hair stuffed wing chairs draped in worn green velvet, and a mahogany writing table under a broad window. I eased into the chair opposite Constance while she rang for the maid. Such a normal gesture, as though she hadn't caught me in her bedroom, by her husband's dressing room, ready to ransack their personal belongings like a hostile intruder. Which I was.

I forced a smile and the tension in my shoulders to ease. "I'm hardly a miracle worker, Mrs. Knight. But I believe Miss Trevyn to be of sound health." An inane comment but I owed her one at least.

"Perhaps you are!" Constance stroked the arm of the chair with one hand. "I'm mortified to say that, for the moment at least, the immediate drama has passed. It's been a week since I found my cousin wandering in the gardens at midnight, appearing to be asleep."

Somnambulism. Constance Knight's calm and measured tones were laudable given the situation with her children. I tried to picture Trevyn, night rail billowing and buttons askew, escaping out a back door with unseeing eyes.

Sleep disturbances. Or a double consciousness, as some would have it. Activity that took place within sleep, in dreams, in the emergence of different personalities, visitations, the hallucinatory and the non-rational. I recalled Charcot at the Salpêtrière who would, with one wave of his hand, one look of his eye, and one command—*dors*—deliver his subject, usually a pretty young woman, into a hypnotic sleep. "*You might have run a red-hot needle into her and she would not have felt it...*"

"She might have left the property and wandered out into the streets had I not intervened." Constance Knight looked up to nod at a maid in the doorway. The woman entered quietly before placing a tray with glasses and decanters on the low table between us.

The maid slid from the room. "Whisky or sherry?" Constance Knight's question was almost conspiratorial, delivered with a smile. "Never mind that tea nonsense. I find the former quite restorative in the late afternoon."

"As do I."

A quirk of a brow. "I thought as much."

I watched as she reached for the decanter to splash a generous portion into my glass, a carafe of water alongside. A moment later the liquid was hot and smooth against my throat where my lies still lodged.

"And it's Constance, please." She raised her drink to her lips. "I think we can dispense with the formalities given the situation we find ourselves in."

I tipped my glass towards her in agreement.

"I'm not one to worry but realistically we can't continue with the threat of these disturbances that put the children at risk. Truth be told, I've spent far too many nights looking for my cousin on the streets of Mayfair and beyond when I can't find her in the garden or elsewhere."

I murmured my concern, attention wandering, my gaze skimming the mahogany desk in the far corner sitting like an undiscovered continent, its surface cleared of personal effects that might give away history or hint of character. Or proof of guilt.

"I feel somewhat responsible as this illness seems to have overtaken my cousin here in London. And I'm loath to turn her out. She is a relation, her parents of reduced means, and if there is a possible cure..."

I had no answer, the matter of Trevyn's illness perplexing, a distraction somehow that was taking me away from the tragedy of Annie Childs and Mary Holland. I continued to listen, concentrating on Constance Knight's voice and a small yellow stain of sunshine blotting the herringbone floor.

"You are a mind doctor, Georgia." As though the title conferred magical powers. "There must be a cure. I wish only to help my cousin."

There was no cure if there was no illness in the first place. "It's not as simple as applying a poultice to a wound, unfortunately. The mind is a mystery that we're only beginning to unravel. I can offer help, but I can make no promises, Constance. And I shouldn't want you to think that I'm a physician when I've merely studied the neurological sciences."

"Studied them in depth, I'm sure." Curiosity lit her dark eyes. "Alienism, isn't that what your discipline is called? A strange term and yet I suppose it makes sense. What else is insanity, really, than the quality of being alien to oneself?"

"From the French, *aliene*, or insane. But I think I prefer your definition to the more traditional one."

She dipped her head at the acknowledgment. "You are a woman of many talents and wide experience. Unusual, some might say." She paused. "I hope I'm not being indiscreet, but Alice has told me, admiringly I might add, a little about your life. About how your father encouraged your studies, even at an early age." She raised her glass, looking at me over the rim. "He permitted you to follow your interests and attend classes at Harvard and in Paris. With Alice's esteemed brother, yet." She leaned forward in her chair. "Frankly, both Alice and I are envious, Georgia. You are fortunate, blessed with an unusual father."

"I concede my father is an unusual man." I hoped to push any discussion of my father to the sidelines. "And yours?"

She pressed the rim of the glass to her lips for a moment, as though considering. "Somewhat indifferent, I'd have to say, but that's another story for another time." Looking away and then back at me with a sudden intensity. "You are the beneficiary of a unique upbringing which undoubtedly contributed to your considerable accomplishments. And for those reasons alone, I have every confidence in your skills concerning my cousin and her illness."

I allowed several moments to pass before saying, "She may not be ill."

Confusion flickered across Constance's face followed by a questioning frown. "I don't understand because you are—what's the right word—*treating* her nonetheless. A hopeful prospect, although I've not the faintest idea what that process entails."

"I've taken the opportunity of speaking with Miss Trevyn on several occasions, for several sessions, but I'm afraid I can't divulge the nature of our discussions."

"Of course. I wouldn't expect you to, although," and her voice notched lower, "I've heard of various therapeutics, galvanic baths, gynecological interventions and such that are considered helpful in many situations involving female matters. Oftentimes the womb is the source of the contagion or so we're told. My mother was beset for years with female troubles and with the help of doctors availed herself of any number of remedies."

I was suddenly aware that our voices were too loud for the setting, the refined proportions of the room at odds with the jarringly intimate echo of our discussion. There was a restlessness about Constance Knight, a kind of inverse acuity behind the apologetic smile. It occurred to me suddenly that I liked her, her curiosity, strength and intelligence.

I considered my answer. "What you are asking, Constance, is what does your cousin's treatment consist of?"

"If my concern for my cousin seems inappropriate..."

Constance's concern for her cousin was admirable so much so it threw into relief her calm acceptance of the children's wellbeing under the governess's care. Then again, many children of the upper classes were sent away to school at a far earlier age and into far more careless hands. I recognized that it was not unusual for months to pass by without parents clapping eyes on their offspring. From Constance Knight's standpoint, at least Miss Trevyn was not a stranger under her roof.

Taking another swallow from my glass, I returned to Constance's question. "Your concern is far from inappropriate. The best explanation I can give is that essentially Miss Trevyn and I talk, or more specifically, I simply listen to what she has to say."

"You talk."

"Yes, it's a type of exchange, a way for the mind to order itself." I could have but didn't wish to explain more, about my belief in the malleability of personality, the ability of thoughts and words to reshape reality. The process was impossible to translate into words.

As if to remind me of my failings, the image of Sophie Rivington shimmered before me. The piano, ever silent, hulking in the corner of my sitting room in Boston. Sophie perched on the bench, her legs moving compulsively beneath her skirts. Sophie had been on the mend, better at ignoring the tremor in her hands that would ordinarily send the sheet music on her lap drifting to the floor. Or so I'd believed.

A delicate clearing of her throat. Constance watched me with an uneasy half-smile, as if she too had known about Sophie Rivington and the many ways I'd failed her. Would I fail her cousin as well? My head felt full and there was a pain behind my eyes that intensified not only with the unwelcome thoughts but also with Charles Knight's near silent entry into the room. Commanding the threshold, he wore an overcoat and a scowl. Behind him hovered the housekeeper.

Small footsteps in the hall and then Violet's sudden appearance, clutching a rag doll, a rainbow of faded colors, missing buttons down her dress. Her brother, an eye pressed to a kaleidoscope, wasn't far behind.

Knight was an exclamation mark on the threshold, his children scattered around him. "I'd left paperwork here somewhere." His gaze left mine for a moment, pretending to survey the sitting room.

"Good afternoon, mama, good afternoon, papa. Good afternoon, Miss Buchanan."

"You're behaving today for your mother?" Knight ruffled the boy's hair. Violet nodded while doing up a button on her doll's dress with small, clumsy fingers. Branksome stood behind them, hands clasped at her waist.

Constance rose from her chair, a full smile tightening the edges of her wide mouth. She opened her arms as the children ran to her and then placed a hand on each tousled head, pulling both tightly toward her. "Certainly, you're behaving for your Mama. Don't you always? Now I want you to go to the nursery and listen to Miss Victoria. She's feeling rather poorly so I expect the best conduct from you both. And if you're very, very good, then maybe your Papa and I will allow you to have your tea with us early evening. Before our supper."

"May we play hide-and-seek before our tea?" Violet asked, crumpled face beseeching.

Charlie added, "Like last time?"

Constance shook her head, soft amazement in her voice. "Silly children. We'll speak of such things later."

"Tea with your mother and father." I said the words with an exuberance I didn't feel, watching Constance's relaxed manner with her son and daughter, arms still wreathed around them. "I believe that's even better than a game of hide-and-seek."

Knight didn't move from the doorway, power in his pose, one hand thrust into his trouser pocket. Violet looked up inquiringly at her father who stooped suddenly, protectively, between his daughter and me, appearing ready to scoop her into his arms. Charlie began hopping from one foot to another with the energy of a puppy, stopping when his mother put a finger to her lips.

"Your mother is quite right. We can have your tea together later today." Knight took the kaleidoscope from his son's clutching fingers.

"Now off with you to the nursery. Run along with Branksome." Constance clapped her hands lightly ushering them out the door.

CHAPTER 22

"I'm not to blame." Victoria Trevyn sat off the nursery, surrounded by tiny boots and felt jackets, tiring of my unending questioning.

My earlier conversation with Constance Knight had made me wary, challenged my confidence, forced me once again to probe my own capabilities. Nor was I any further ahead with Trevyn or Cails or Knight. Despite having spent a week at the house on Mayfair.

"Why should I trust you—you're a friend of my cousin's." Trevyn's pale eyes were wary. She sat across from me at the small children's table.

I shook my head, the aroma of chalk and damp in the air, my knees tucked close under the cramped table top. "Even if I were Mrs. Knight's closest friend, what goes on here during our conversations will never leave this room."

"My cousin wishes to blame me, to assign me a disorder that I do not have—and I don't know why. These incidents, I barely recall any of them in the way she does." She looked at me, lips open in a small exclamation. "These events are absolutely confounding and without explanation. Never before have I experienced anything like this."

I imagined Constance Knight's fear and helplessness at the thought of losing her children, warring with her sense of responsibility toward her younger cousin. Blame could reasonably be her first reaction. "What reason does she have to accuse you?"

"Perhaps she would like to turn me into an invalid."

"And why would that be?"

Victoria turned away and peered down at a pair of galoshes abandoned against the wainscoting, stained with mud. "Although I'm ten years younger, I do remember her mother, always sickening, always ailing, and my cousin looking after her. Lord Ralston was never about, so it was said in the village, and the responsibility fell to his only daughter." She shrugged. "Perhaps Constance grew accustomed to the role of nursemaid."

"Your cousin had no siblings."

Her eyes still on the boots, the governess relaxed her shoulders, picking one up and rubbing at the encrusted mud. "She had no brothers or sisters. No surviving siblings, that is. My cousin is an only child. That was the reason for her mother's illnesses, her state of collapse, losing her infants… in such a fashion. One after the other they would die during her confinement or shortly thereafter."

No small wonder at Constance Knight's composure and strength. Still births and infant mortality were a constant in our lives. However, I could imagine the special horror of an adolescent girl witnessing her mother's seemingly unending suffering. The experience would also go some length to explaining Constance's nurturing instincts. I considered, not for the first time, that there was much to admire about the woman.

"What about Mr. Knight. Has he spoken directly with you about these recent events?"

"Other than that night, when I first sought your help," she said, then shaking her head. "Mr. Knight leaves all of the domestic decisions to his wife."

And why wouldn't he. The running of the household fell under the purview of women, including the servants, and even more so in this instance given that the governess was a relation.

"Do you ever administer laudanum or other soporifics, tinctures, medicaments to either Charlie or Violet?"

She dropped the boot, aware that I'd asked the question before. "I do not."

"To calm them down when they become too rambunctious? Or to get them to sleep? I understand that Charlie has a high temperament— it's a common and accepted practice in many households."

We continued for another few moments but Trevyn was telling the truth, demonstrating neither anger nor outrage at my further questions. She ate well, took exercise, her focus on the children unwavering. She experienced no vagaries of mood, neither high nor low.

For whatever reason, I thought of John Everett Millais's work, *The Somnambulist*: the pale wide-eyed girl walking on the verge of a cliff in her nightdress, her peril and the mysterious glimmer of an unseen moon captured on canvas. But in this instance, Victoria Trevyn didn't fit the picture.

⁂

The following day after several hours spent uselessly thumbing through books in the library, I returned to my rooms, flinging myself onto the chaise by the window. Limbs twitching, I longed for a cigarette. A series of cigarettes. I should leave this house, I thought, be done with it. Nothing to be found here. Instead I was simply waiting for Cails's next move like one of Griffith's especially incompetent police.

Unwilling to sit any longer, I rose from the chaise and moved to the side-table. Although I hadn't found much of use from the private reserves of Charles Knight, I had taken a bottle of whisky from the dining room sideboard earlier in the week. Now the liquid burned down my throat, leached into my chest; it seemed Constance and I shared the same taste in drink. It was not precisely the pall of tobacco but good enough for the moment, bolstering my resolve. I would wait until the house settled for the night. No one would notice my leaving from the servants' entrance. A day might go by before Knight would learn that I was no longer under his roof.

But what of the photographs? There was no possibility I could find evidence to use against Cails and Knight in under a day. Let alone identify or find the Shoreditch Savage and set Griffith back on his heels.

My thoughts spun while I waited for the alcohol to deliver a reprieve. I listened to the staccato of a branch hitting the windowpane. The hiss from the fireplace grate. Then a soft knock, apologetic, hesitant. Setting down my glass, I moved from the side table and across the carpet to pull open the door.

The purring of the gas light from the hallway haloed two small figures in the doorway. Charlie and Violet rocking on their heels holding hands, their identical wide-set eyes, dark, like their mother's, looking up at me.

Violet spoke first. "Miss Buchanan." Voice warbling. "Miss Trevyn's asleep again."

"In her wardrobe this time," Charlie said.

⁂

Instinct was a primitive force that, for once, I chose not to ignore. I pushed past the children and into the hallway only half aware of their stumbling behind me.

"Stay here," I shot over my shoulder, then thought the better of it, tamping down my racing pulse. "There's nothing the matter, nothing to concern yourselves with. Go find Branksome or Cook. In the kitchens where they'll have a treat waiting."

The hallway seemed airless. I ran up the stairs to the nursery, my heel catching on a loose thread in a rug before I righted myself and burst through the doors. I faltered on the threshold, surveying the room. A low fire in the grate, a few books strewn on the floor and no wardrobe. A cold breeze from the window, the leaded casements swinging open. Taking a heavy breath, I recalled the last time I'd stood there with Knight, the empty beds, the scent of crushed almonds. Looking up, I remembered the governess's room. The low door, with its crooked lintel, now partially open.

I threw it wide. And then nothing that I'd ever wanted to see again. My blood stopped and I was conscious of my arms outstretched, leaning against the door, nails digging into the lacquered wood.

Victoria Trevyn, in the caverns of the open wardrobe, a flame of a scarf around her neck, a white stool kicked from beneath her stockinged legs. Stockings darned with neat little stitches. Eyes closed, as though she were sleeping.

I surged across the room, crouching to scoop up her body, lift her under her arms and onto my lap, relieving some of the pressure from around her neck. But not nearly enough. Hands scrabbling, frantic, I clawed at the knot. It was gordian-tight, the more I pulled, the less it gave. Tipping her chin forward until it rested on my shoulder, I grabbed the scarlet silk, trying to wrench it from the back, over her head.

It didn't give. My eyes cast around frantically, a glint of metal, in a small sewing basket in the recesses of the wardrobe. Without letting her go, I snatched the scissors and sliced through the silk around her neck.

Moisture on my cheeks, perspiration I thought, until I realized my tears. Her body was warm, light. Gently pulling her face away from my shoulder, I noticed again the thin lids closed over her eyes. Then I felt for a pulse with shaking fingers.

The rhythm of life, surprisingly strong, in the bruised curve of her neck, just above the clavicle. An odd memory stirred. A doctor in a gore-streaked apron, his eyeglasses flecked with blood, looking down at a patient under a stained sheet. *Death can take its time.* He'd shaken his head, a weary amazement in his eyes.

I swiped at my cheeks with a free arm. Felt the faint rise and fall of Trevyn's chest, looked for movement behind the closed lids. Tried to bar the past and the image of Sophie Rivington's protruding, open eyes—*dead eyes*—from my mind.

I slid Trevyn from my arms and onto the floor by the wardrobe, flicked my forefinger lightly on a cheek. Repeated her name several times until her lips moved. A small groan and then the faint scent of crushed almonds.

"Victoria, you're awake. Look at me." I heard the catch in my throat, the break in my voice. Kneeling beside her. Her eyes slit open then sagged closed again.

"You're fine. Here in your room off the nursery. I'm with you now. You know me. Georgia Buchanan."

She swallowed, coughed, moved her head side-to-side. Then suddenly opened her eyes with such force that I reared back on my heels. What had I expected to see in their depths, the pupils dilated with laudanum? Horror, fear, despair? *Anger.* So pure that it could have reached out and seized me by the throat.

The room swam for a moment and then righted itself. I forced myself to admit that Victoria Trevyn already sensed what I'd suspected. The flame of a scarf lay discarded by the wardrobe, a make-shift noose that had been slipped around her neck while she lay asleep, lay *narcotized*, to make her death appear a suicide. She'd been drugged again. But this time as a prelude to her murder.

CHAPTER 23

My head was clear, my body tight with shock, as though I'd been doused with cold water.

A mug of milk and the sharp air from the open window in the nursery cut through the remaining opiate in the governess's system. I bundled her in a cloak, latched closed the window in the nursery and sped her down the stairs to my rooms.

An hour later, she slipped out the garden door from the conservatory with a valise packed with fifty pounds, a farewell from me. Despite her protests, I promised to forward more to the address in Turin where her parents would be waiting. A short note was left in the schoolroom, explaining the reason for her abrupt departure— her father's worsening illness.

I sped back to my rooms, reconsidering my earlier decision to leave the Knight household. There was no benefit in my remaining. Or was there? I thought of the open window through which someone had entered the nursery to drug and kill the governess. This time the children had not been taken and had not been hidden in a secure place. Instead, Charlie and Violet had come to find me. The pattern was changing, becoming deadlier.

I thought of Constance Knight, her concern for her cousin, the danger to the children. But with Trevyn gone, perhaps the danger had passed. Or so I told myself. Perhaps Cails would find another way to come after me, a way that didn't involve the children or the governess. If he was behind this attempt at all. I needed time to think, sort this out with a ruthless logic.

The walls of the hallway crawled with calla lilies and their stems seemed to reach for me. I tried not to think of what would have happened to Trevyn had the children not come to get me. What had they seen? Worse still, whom had they seen?

I slid past the library, only a few steps more to the stairwell, before jolting to a halt.

"Shoreditch Savage."

I took a few steps back, turned to see Constance Knight in the library. The hallway felt cold, flames shivering in the fireplace behind her. Sitting in a high, wingback chair, she idled behind a sheaf of newspaper in her hands, reading aloud. Then she lowered the top half and looked me resolutely in the eye.

I forced myself to be still. "I didn't see you there, Constance."

A small frown. "You appear in a hurry, Georgia. I hope there's nothing amiss?"

"Nothing at all."

Constance nodded, forehead smoothing. "Shoreditch Savage," she repeated, returning to the newspaper in her hands. "The name linked with the murders off Drury Lane." She rattled the paper, repeating word-for-word. "*A noiseless midnight terror. The strange character who prowls about the East End after midnight. Universal fear among the women. Slippered feet and a sharp knife.*" She looked up for a moment, tranquil in her grey dress with its lavender trim, despite what she was reading. "What is your opinion, Georgia, as a mind doctor?"

I was thinking I needed to be gone from this house. Forget that I'd just witnessed the attempted murder of a young woman in Constance

Knight's home. Forget that I was horrified for her children, Charlie and Violet. Instead, I smoothed my skirts with cold palms, keeping my voice calm. "I haven't given it much thought other than to lament the passing of those lives."

"Really?"

My mind rocked from one unconnected thought to the next. I should tell her about Trevyn. She would know what to do, equipped with that composure and steely intelligence, so carefully underplayed.

Settling back in the chair. "The prostitutes you mean?"

Annie Childs and Mary Holland. I willed myself not to move from the hallway. "The women."

"Yes, of course. Poor creatures." She returned to the paper. "*The Daily Telegraph* and the *Times* offer a description of the murderer as aged thirty-seven, five-foot-eight inches in height, rather dark, beard and moustache. Dress—shirt, dark jacket, dark vest and trousers. And some type of cloak. Speaks with a foreign accent."

I didn't have time for this. "It doesn't appear as though the description refers to anyone."

"I couldn't agree more." A look of concern. "Are you sure you're alright, Georgia? You appear out of sorts."

"Absolutely fine. I'm fine, Constance."

She decided to believe me. Folding the newspaper under her arm, she paused to glance at a long blue vase of late autumn gladiolas set on a marble-topped table. The arrangement overflowed the bowl, the rush-like stems unseemly in their voluptuousness. Making a small noise under her breath, she rose from her chair and, with her back to me, began adjusting the flowers. "I understand that you follow the papers, at least that's what my husband tells me. So, none of this should come as a surprise to you, Georgia."

I dredged my mind for something to say.

"You know, along with everyone else in London and beyond, that the editorials continue with pointless ferocity, searching for an adequate explanation for the murders."

I was afraid she would invite me into the library and to sit down. I thought of Victoria Trevyn stealing from the house. And of a murderer who had somehow slunk into the nursery, tampered with her drink and then slipped the noose around her neck. All the more reason I had to leave without a word. To draw the danger away from Constance and her children.

Constance pulled an errant leaf from one of the stems. "We have any number of interpretations from the broadsheets. The killer is a religious maniac bent upon the expiation of sin in the slaying of..." she hesitated, "whores. His crimes are revenge for some real or imagined injury suffered at their hands. He is a member of some heathen sect, most likely a Jew, that practices barbaric rites. He craves notoriety and seeks to horrify the nation with acts of savagery. And let's not forget an editorial in The Times claiming that the Shoreditch knife has done more to publicize the plight of the poor than all the actions of anarchists and radicals combined." She turned to face me, eyebrows raised. "Then the lunatic theory. Of which you must be aware."

Lunacy, heathen acts, religious mania. Whatever the theory, it resulted in death, for which Cails and Constance Knight's husband were responsible. If it could be proven.

I found myself nodding at whatever she was saying. "There are days I don't believe we've come much further than leeches, purges and bleeding when it comes to my vocation."

"I understand your frustration. I've read recently that homicidal mania is incurable, difficult to detect, and often lays dormant. The asylums are full of such beasts and might one of thousands have slipped out unobserved?" The faint bustle of servants in the hallway behind me and Constance Knight's unwavering gaze.

I had to leave. "Disturbing to be sure."

"And the situation is worsening by the day." Constance retrieved the paper from under her arm, opening it to the front page. "I hope you don't think it forward of me, but I've come to think of you as a friend, Georgia, someone I might confide in. Please tell me if I'm overreaching in any way."

Her eyes never leaving mine. "Not at all, Constance."

"I suppose, given our conversations recently and what Alice has told me, you're accustomed to people opening up to you, divulging their thoughts and feelings. You have that quality about you, Georgia, that invites confidences." She seemed to waver. "I usually don't feel the need to share what goes on between my husband and me."

The fire spit and crackled. Every nerve on the alert, I stepped into the library. "If there's anything troubling you, Constance, and I can help…"

"You're all too generous, my dear. It's strange, isn't it? When I think of it, our circumstances aren't really that dissimilar."

My fingers curled around the doorframe.

"An absent mother, a powerful father." She stepped back from the bouquet, examining the arrangement. "It's not a wonder we've established a friendship so quickly. If I dare call it such." She paused, her words uncharacteristically muddled. "I don't believe my husband would object to my confiding in you, as a friend. Although he and I typically don't speak of such things. But in this instance, Mr. Knight was clearly disturbed."

Speak of such things. I let my hands drop from the door frame. Not for the first time, I wondered how their relationship worked, whether Constance Knight hid her native intelligence from her husband as so many married women did. He was the vicar's son and yet after their marriage, he had taken over the running of her estate and her family's paper. Did she question him about his politics, about his view of these sensationalized murders?

She turned from the flowers and picked up the paper. "My husband told me the Metropolitan Police were sent a letter which they've taken seriously enough to launch a determined attempt to find the author. They prepared facsimiles of the letter and sent copies to the presses, my husband's paper included." Her lips compressed into a line. "It is from the purported killer, what the editors took as a confession."

Her gaze on me, searching for reassurance?

"They believed this one to be from the Shoreditch Savage himself. A horrific goad, really, a threat," she said with a pall of desperation. "One that Mr. Knight obviously felt he could not afford to ignore. Would you like to read it yourself… I can barely bring myself…" she passed the paper to me, the headline shimmering obscenely.

I am the Shoreditch Savage

In the 'morrow two women will be ravaged.

Block letters. Simple black strokes. Another childish rhyme, like the first one I'd received, sending me to Bedlam. And then to the Saracen Head.

I recognized the handwriting.

Something in my head yawned open. My summoner and the Shoreditch Savage. I couldn't complete the thought. I said without thinking, "Why would they print something like this?"

"They are eager to have someone recognize the handwriting. To help find this fiend before he makes good on his promise." Constance turned back to the vase of flowers, making a bouquet with her hands. "Two more women. *Tonight*, it would seem."

CHAPTER 24

I asked the carriage to stop at Blackfriar's Bridge, rain glittering on the road. My intentions solidified despite the vaulting of my stomach, the grit of sleeplessness in my eyes and the false courage of a cocaine lozenge, my last one found in the pockets of a morning gown, scaling down the back of my throat.

I'd escaped the Knights just in time, an hour behind Victoria Trevyn, and as though I was meant to find my way back to the alleys behind Drury Lane. Which, of course, I was. My summoner and the Shoreditch Savage. The connection seared my consciousness like a brand.

The carriage clattered away behind me, eaten by the night, while I stopped to take in the view where the river widened and narrowed like a beating heart. I tasted the salty bite of low tide. Gas lights flickered in bay windows lording over the city's wharves and spires behind which the warren of streets tapered like occluded arteries.

Looking up into a fine rain, I pretended to ignore several men approaching. As they closed in, caps pulled low over their faces, they gave the same smile, as though they had all been caught doing something wrong. I quickened my steps.

The men receded into the dark.

Fulstone Street ahead. I resisted the urge to break into a run. In the shadow of Christ Church and opposite Spitalfields Market, the Saracen sat at most a mile away, the public house where Annie Childs had been seen drinking on the morning of her murder, the papers had reported. Where Mary Holland had lingered to attract her customers.

Too much death. Listening to the pulse of the streets, I struck the image of Victoria Trevyn, the streak of scarlet around her neck, from behind my eyes. I felt permanently awake, far too alert, my jaw tightening and shoulders contracting. I wasn't sure whether to curse or bless the agency of that last lozenge.

The streets narrowed, twisted and turned, before I stopped at a safe distance from Drury Lane. I fought the sensation of disquiet twining around my muscles and bones and heart. The air had thickened, fog and smoke braiding together, water and fire, shrouding the few bent figures hustling about their business.

I continued for what must have been another quarter hour until I saw the Saracen, thick curls of smoke emerging from the entranceway. This time I didn't hesitate.

Inside the soot-caked walls of the pub snarls of men hunched over tankards giving off fumes of hopelessness and desperation. Broken glass and sawdust crunched underfoot, the low ceiling smothering grunts of conversation. I wondered how I could have forgotten the mirror, hanging behind the bar, its surface blackened to a pitch.

My entrance caused few stares when I chose an empty table in the far corner, away from the door, where I could survey the room. I sensed that my summoner knew my movements well, knew why I'd missed his first summons. Although I could only wonder whether he was the player and I the audience. Whatever the answer, we were expecting each other.

A man with a tangled beard and sloped shoulders brought a carafe of hard cider. I slid a few coins over the splintered wood of the table. Then over the rim of my mug, I looked toward the entrance where four men entered, hurrying, walking with purpose and pushing past an older fellow slumped over his ale. Elbows jostling, they sat down and shouted orders in the direction of the publican.

One of a few women sat opposite them, her head cast low, features finely drawn. Her mouth was swollen, most likely from a punch delivered earlier in the day. Little wonder she took deep draughts of her gin. Who would be so desperate to be seeking their doss on a night when most women had probably shuttered their doors in tenements and rooming houses in the East End?

Dressed in a serge cloak the color of dust, I wouldn't be mistaken for a harlot or an actress and I was hardly desperate. Great wealth inured not only from want but also from fear—for myself at least. I'd encountered madmen before, but I sensed this Shoreditch killer was of another genus entirely, hardly the minion that Cails and Knight would prefer him to be.

I thought of a time at the Salpêtrière, in a patient's room, a mute who had caused consternation for months among the attending physicians. He'd been old, paper thin, seemingly asleep on his cot, marinating in hallucinations and old sweat. Lazarus refusing to wake from the dead while I observed him with the dispassion I'd been taught. It had only been instinct that had made me glance downward for a moment at the sudden flick of his wrist.

He'd held a blade, finely carved with an opalescent edge, pointing upwards at me. Four inches of metal. The knife had lashed at my waist and I'd moved in time. The attendants had subdued the patient and I was left with a strange sense of exhilaration, of having subdued fate.

I borrowed from that feeling now, my eyes skittering across the room. The Saracen was full, the air clotting with pipe smoke and ash from a careless fire in the grate. A loud roar, an upset of some kind, spread like a stain at the far table while at the same time, a knot of men and one woman entered. I recognized the woman immediately, the jet eyes punched into her face, the straight, heavy hair. She'd led me to Tarski, or Tarski to me, the first time, then relieved me of my purse. Perhaps the Saracen was simply her haunt and she was not waiting for someone. But I doubted it. I put down my mug of cider and slowly rose from the table.

The woman startled when I placed a hand on her shoulder. I slid onto the bench next to her. In a smile or a grimace, hard to tell which, the woman bared black teeth stumps, feigning surprise. Then fiddling with the mismatched buttons of her coat, she sat up straight, and made a decision that pulled the uncertainty from her face.

"Don't you be calling the coppers. You got nothing you can prove." She twisted her frayed collar as if it was too tight.

"How do you know the coppers aren't waiting outside?"

"Maggie," barked the man opposite us. Block jawed, he picked nervously at a wart on his chin. "Watcha been doin' bringin' the coppers here? Now I know I can say to this fine lady that you have nuffin to do with the wrong side of the law."

Maggie's eyes brimmed with a wary calculation. "Coppers are crawling around the place as it is. Meantime, the bugger gets away with killing like we is sheep in a pen."

"We doan need no extras then. You hear?" said the man, in case the point needed clarification.

"My purse, Maggie. Gone. And my sterling, too."

She snuffled then pulled a soiled handkerchief from her coat pocket. She blew her nose elaborately.

"Who sent you here, Maggie?"

"Nobody. Can't a soul have a drink from time to time?" Jet black hair jutted from her skull in dogged tufts and everything about her face was awry. Heavy brows lowered above eyes that had descended so deep into their sockets that their color was not jet but indeterminable.

Her shoulders hunched around her ears. "You can't prove nothing." She didn't turn away, her expression a mixture of submission and resentment, like a dog preparing for its next beating. "I saved you, didn't I?"

"You did," I nodded. "Did anyone send you to follow me? Here today? Or any other day? The man with the cane, the unusual walking stick? If you're truthful, I can help you. First, by not summoning the police and secondly by rewarding you for your help."

The man opposite us coiled away, his attention directed to a contest involving sailors and spitting tobacco. "Two flies crawling up a wall," Maggie muttered over her shoulder stealing time to consider her answer.

I paused, my attention hooked by a shadow in a side entrance, a few steps away from the bar. It was not so much the quality of the cloak, a rich dark wool, but the movement that fixed my attention. The sway of the fabric, an outline of boots polished to a hilt, and the gait, that was familiar in a way that I couldn't define. And there was a side entrance to the Saracen that had escaped my notice.

"There's nothing I can do ter help you. I was just coming here for my cuppa." Maggie's defiance caught my inattention along with a steady stare that liars always favored.

"I will give you money, Maggie, if you reconsider."

"Help you with what?" Maggie's gaze dropped.

"You tell me."

Maggie hauled a deep breath and slowly levered herself to her feet, both hands anchored to the table, shoulders squared. I adjusted the hood of my cloak to glance back to the corner of the bar. Several men reeled on a bench to an unheard melody and I rose, keeping a focus on Maggie while thinking about the side entrance.

Maggie traced my gaze.

"I'm willing to pay handsomely." I didn't take my eyes from the corner of the bar. The man in the cloak shifted behind a tower of empty bottles but I could still see the wool hem and the glint of leather.

Maggie squinted, her palms now flat on the table. "How much and fer what?"

"Why don't we start by your showing me the environs." I looked at Maggie levelly. "You frequent this establishment, from what you've told me."

"Hardly a crime."

"Stealing is a crime, Maggie. Showing me the side entrance to the Saracen is not. And it might even net you a few pounds." I motioned her to follow me to the front entrance and out onto the street.

In a few moments, we stood on the south side of Aldgate on Berner Street. It was a burrow of small, two-story slums, a crush of tailors, furniture makers and tobacco purveyors, but at this hour of night there was only the regular staccato of the rain. The promise of this Shoreditch Savage had wiped the slate clean, robbing the East End of its usual clamor. A dark miracle.

Maggie made no move to run, but her nose turned up like an animal sniffing for danger. She kept to my side when we entered the narrow alley behind the Saracen to arrive at a low scarred door bolted with an iron rod from the outside.

"You ain't going to find nothing here but trouble."

I waited for a moment, willing the low door to open and the stranger in the cloak to emerge. Beside me Maggie stamped her feet against the damp, sending up an impatient spray of brown water. I ran a gloved palm over the rusted bar guarding the side entrance, giving a slight push. The door remained tightly sealed.

"You looking for him, right?"

"For whom? You tell me."

"The man that did that ter you." Maggie gestured to my face, tracing a fading bruise with a finger in the air.

"The man with the cane, you mean?"

"The other one. The simple one." Maggie looked at me slyly, sideways. "The foreigner. The Jew."

Suddenly she seemed eager to please, no longer the thief caught with a crowbar in hand.

"You know the foreigner."

"I can take you to him."

She rubbed her nose with the back of a hand, face slack with the hope that, like most of my ilk, I would mistake poverty for lack of intelligence. "Where is he—far from here?"

"Close enough."

"Three shillings for you then." I crunched the silver into her fist.

Heads bent against the drizzle, we walked in silence crossing to the west side of Berner Street. Maggie kept a few steps ahead, leaving me to wonder who was leading whom. We came to a narrow court flanked on the right by a building marked the 'International Working Men's Education Club,' and behind, a row of cottages.

It was peculiar, a choir, strong male voices raised in song floating on the night air. A socialist club, I recalled, having read about it recently in the newspapers, patronized mostly by Russian and Polish Jews, more than one of whom had been implicated in the recent murders.

The side door of the club was half open and the kitchen's gas light streamed into the alley. We walked from the light into the encroaching darkness where a snaggle-toothed row of cottages began. They appeared uninhabited, derelict, the cobblestones under our feet turning to mud as we pressed on.

Maggie turned to her left and then stopped abruptly in front of what appeared to be an old stables. She inserted a shoulder into a narrow breach of a low door, pushing it open.

⁂

A brazier burned defiantly, drinking up the oxygen in a corner where a man lay on a narrow bunk, propped on a mattress of mildewed straw. The air was only slightly warmer than outdoors, beads of condensation forming on the edges of a narrow window, any view obscured by a heap of rags. The aroma of horse lingered, a combination of leather and flesh, although a trough running along the middle of the stables looked as though it hadn't been used in years. Overhead beams sagged where hay bales may once have been stored. A blacksmith's oil cloth coat hung from a rusted hook.

I ignored Maggie's mutterings and advanced toward the cot.

When I touched Tarski's arm, he startled awake. His hand lashed out, but his movements were so uncontrolled that he grasped nothing more than a fistful of straw, then held it tightly to his chest.

"*Odchodzic.*" His words slurred as if he was talking in his sleep, his accent thick porridge. Although I had no Polish, I sensed what he was saying. *Go away.*

"Mr. Tarski. Are you ill?" Heat radiated from him like a furnace. He shifted on the bunk, his back to me.

I turned to Maggie. "When is the last time he's had something to eat or drink?"

A half-hearted shrug of the shoulders. She pointed to a metal bowl in the corner and a jug of water.

I reached for my pocket extracting a one-pound note, thinking of the man in the cloak at the Saracen and wishing I could be two places at once. "Why is Mr. Tarski here? From whom is he hiding?"

Maggie snatched the money, shrugged. "Jes found the bugger here."

I smothered the urge to grab the woman by the arms and shake her, my fists clenched so tightly that my nails dug into my palms through the leather of my gloves. "Is he hiding here or is he being kept prisoner?'

"You daft?"

Maggie was cleverer than she let on. Swallowing my impatience, I sank next to Tarski. His hair was matted back from his forehead, eyes open but without focus, an opiate at work, making it impossible for him to stay awake. Beneath the smell of hay there was a layer of muddy silt reeking of sewage and brine, of what London's East End had disgorged.

I looked up at Maggie, making my accusation clear. "It's obvious that Mr. Tarski is not here on his own volition. He's being kept prisoner and I would like to know by whom."

Maggie raised both hands, like she was calming a dangerous animal. "He's slow is all. Nowheres else to go."

I played along for the moment. "How did you know he was here? And why are you bringing him food?"

Maggie frowned deliberately, to demonstrate her confusion, a network of deep lines creasing her face. "I just finds him here."

"I'm certain it's not that simple." I kept my voice level, rising gradually from my knees. "If someone is paying you to keep Mr. Tarski here, tell me. I will pay you *more*."

Maggie's eyes bored into mine and I returned her stare. A careful calculus shone behind those small dark eyes. Outside, a light wind rattled the eaves in counterpoint to the rain, adding to the tension. "I will give you a moment to think about my proposition."

I walked back to the low door that Maggie had left open a splinter, prying it open a bit further, then surveyed the alley. From the first-floor windows of the club, the strains of a melancholy baritone sang in what I took was Russian amid rays of sodden light. The rain was coming down in sheets, now turning the alley into a muddy channel. I loosened the top button of my cloak to glance at the watch pinned to my blouse. It was close to one in the morning.

Despite the sodden earth, there was a sudden crunch of gravel. My head snapped up to see a pony harnessed to a two-wheeled barrow. The driver, cap pulled low over his face, proceeded as though there was nothing unusual in the fact that he was traversing the area well past midnight, as though someone was expecting him and his delivery.

Maggie hovered behind me suddenly and I searched my cloak for more silver.

"Maggie—stay here with Mr. Tarski." I shoved the notes into her outstretched palm. "Stay with him. Do *not* leave."

The woman sucked in her lower lip, the sudden windfall too rich to digest or refuse. The hostility in her voice ignited for a moment then dampened. "My name is Fisher."

"Thank you, Maggie Fisher. Please bolt the door," I looked around the stables and noticed a rake leaning against the far wall, "with that." I pointed. As I made the gesture, something else caught my eye, glinting against the straw at the foot of Tarski's cot.

His breathing was shallow, his eyes half closed. I palmed the area beneath his makeshift bed until I felt something cold and compact resting under my hand. A six-inch blade next to a leather sheaf. I stared down at the knife as though I'd never before seen such an object. Then, my mind blank, I placed it carefully in its sheath before slipping it into my cloak. Tarski shifted in his sleep.

Behind me, Maggie watched carefully. Our conversation so far had been short on explanations.

"We are in agreement," I said. We pretended neither of us had seen the knife. "I will pay you double whatever it is you're getting."

Maggie looked at me as if I were the simpleton when there was more money than she had ever seen hanging in the balance. "You have me word. I won't leave this place and I'll bolt the door with the rake till you comes back." Then she grinned with her good fortune. She'd been an actress in an earlier life, I was convinced.

I pulled back the low door, urgency undermining better judgment. The six-inch blade in my cloak was evidence that I didn't need to think about at the moment. Nor was leaving Maggie behind with Tarski. I pulled up my hood, heard the door close behind me and the rattle of the rake wedged into place.

CHAPTER 25

A low gate at the end of the alley gaped open, my boots making sucking noises in the mud as I followed the ruts tilled by the barrow. I heard the jangle of reins, then the shrill cry of a horse. Moving from darkness back to light, I saw the small wagon, the bent head of the pony and the shape of a figure on the ground beneath a spill of skirts and cloak.

A man rushed from the side of the club, a torch in his hand, and behind him a cluster of followers. In a slant of light, I saw the driver of the barrow, cap pulled from his head, rain pouring down his cheeks. A roll of screams began. Then one man separated himself from the cluster and backed out of the alley, shouting for the police.

I made my way toward the pony, unwilling to look directly at the figure on the ground, sidling up to the animal and running a hand over her flank, feeling the nerves jump under my palm like sparks of electricity. The animal's eyes bulged at some unseen horror. When I looked down, then bent closer to the body, I saw a narrow river of blood that shimmered under a sudden sulphurous flare of a torch.

I knew if I lifted the woman's chin that the blood would still be bath-warm and flowing from her throat, filling the narrow canal and down the yard to the side door of the club.

"Jesu'," someone said, a man holding the torch behind me. "Her neck is fearfully cut."

Her hand lay by my boot, as though appealing for help. There was no need to press two fingers against the warm skin because there would be no pulse. There was no sign of struggle and the woman's clothes didn't appear to have been disturbed, the soles of her boots visible from beneath her skirts. I took this in with a disturbing calmness.

And then I swore under my breath, filthy, desperate words. I was too late.

The cold of the ground travelled up through my riding boots and for a moment I felt that I would be sucked down into the mud. The crowd was growing, people flapping their arms as though ridding themselves of an unwelcome contagion. My hand closed over the knife under my cloak as I looked back down at the body.

The woman lay on her left side across the passageway, her face tilted toward the right wall. Her legs were drawn up, her feet close against a metal grate. Her head rested beyond a wheel rut in the mud with her dress unfastened at the neck. Her hand, the same hand that I had first noticed, rested on her chest, smeared with blood. Her other hand was partially closed, as though clutching something, bearing no rings.

Again, her clothes had not been disturbed by the killer, I thought, forcing my mind to work, shutting out the horror by focusing on particulars. Eyes rolled heavenward as though to ward off the evil being done to her, the victim appeared as if she had been laid out by an undertaker save for the work of a knife's blade. The incision at the woman's neck began on the left side, below the angle of the jaw, severing vessels and cutting the windpipe completely in two. Blood mixed with rain ran down the gutter into the drain the opposite direction from her feet.

I was transported back into autopsy theatres, in Boston, at the Salpêtrière, on Mortuary Street. When had the woman died? The fact that the clothes were not wet despite the rain indicated that she had not been lying in the yard long. Perhaps ten minutes earlier while I'd been in the stables with Maggie and Tarski? Why had no one heard her cries?

I tried to visualize the murder, the picture coalescing with the body of Annie Childs on the mortuary slab and with Dr. Llewellyn's autopsy notes. The deep wounds, the savage cuts that tonight hadn't gone far enough. A surge of revulsion, sour in my throat. The attack had been coldly obsessive, yet incomplete, abruptly halted by the approach of the barrow.

Holding torches over their heads like truncheons, two police constables rounded the corner. The small crowd loosened around the corpse.

Gas jets streamed into the alley leading the way to a cul-de-sac, I suddenly realized. Which meant the murderer had only two means of escape, passing through the International Working Men's Club or through the main gateway. Thoughts unspooled more quickly now, delivering jolts of information, none of which made any sense, except one.

He's not finished for the night.

I tried to think logically. The murderer would not seek refuge in the club, gathering notice, as he had further work to do, his lacerating attack cut off mid-stream. He was killing serially, one woman after another, with an intention that was specific, believing his homicides were justifiable, that his acts were purposeful. *Two* women tonight.

Thanks to puppeteering from Cails and Knight?

He was most probably unassuming in manner and appearance, daring and calm in the face of unimaginable violence. Prostitutes and actresses would have no reason to fear him at first. He wore a long coat to cover up blood from his crimes as he killed in public spaces.

And his name was not Aaron Tarski—as I'd long suspected. But so far had failed to prove.

⁂

I fled past the low gate, past the cottages and stables where Maggie and Tarski waited. Brushing up against a stone wall, stumbling over a loosened brick, I made determination my compass. The killer was close by, a few steps ahead of me, his first priority to put distance between himself and his crime. He would not feel safe until he reached a broad thoroughfare in which to lose himself.

I turned northwards following a small seam of light along Berner Street then toward Aldgate Street where the vein broadened. Clutching Tarski's knife in the folds of my cloak, I watched for any movement, the stillness unnatural.

Aldgate was only partially covered in flagstones, the mud seeping from the ground, devouring the hem of my cloak. I glanced over my shoulder, the gas lamps' glow accusing somehow, outlining the deserted doorways and shuttered stalls.

If I didn't find him, intervene in the next moments, he would finish with his next victim, taking his time to slice her from neck to nether regions. Two women would be dead. But motive seemed elusive. There seemed to be no visible relationship between the offender and the victims. There was anger, displays of rage. My mind raced. And the quasi-sexual component, the harvesting of the viscera and reproductive organs. A coincidence? My thoughts were cut off by the faint clatter of a carriage rounding the corner, a furious pace, the jangling of reins, mud splattering before horses solidified from the fog and rain. I flattened myself against a wall, fingers digging into crumbling brick. The carriage careened to the side, speed slowing until the wheels moved at a braking churn.

"Madam, this is no time to be out on the streets." The voice floated from the carriage window, the face featureless and flat. I didn't have time to decide whether to stay or run. I tried to grasp the reality of what was happening, but my intentions kept sliding away from me, stumbling toward panic.

"Miss Buchanan." The voice nightmarishly familiar, I wanted to turn away from what might lie behind the carriage window. "Whatever on earth are you doing here?" The carriage door swung open to reveal Dr. Phillips, the mortuary physician, banging on the roof, yelling for the driver to come to a full stop.

Peeling away from the wall, I let out a deep breath. There was a look on Phillips's face like he'd tasted something foul. "Whatever on earth…" he repeated, hatless, his bald pate shining in the dimness.

He must have seen my agitation, but I tried for calm, sensible, like I had every reason to be in East London on such a night. "You've no doubt been called to the murder by the workers' club." My most normal voice possible, as though we were back on Montague Street, leaning over a dead woman on a slab of metal, one sane individual speaking to another.

"I happened to be at Leman Station when I received word." His breath misting the air. "What do you know of it?"

"Nothing." I shook my head, unable to produce an explanation.

"Dear Lord." He looked at me as though I'd just crossed a continent on foot. "Come with me at the very least. You can explain in the carriage. You can't remain here. It's not safe."

I looked pointedly to my right and then left, indicating toward Drury Lane aware that my arm shook. "I'm waiting for my driver. He should arrive shortly." The explanation was hardly convincing.

"You haven't told me what you are doing here, Miss Buchanan. Or what's gone on this night—you must be petrified. Or at least you should be. I simply can't allow for you to continue on your own."

I began walking, counting my steps to remain calm, my boots sliding along the wet pave stones. "We are wasting valuable time, doctor," I shouted over my shoulder putting distance between us. "You should be at the murder site seeing to the victim, collecting evidence. The constables are waiting."

"I insist." He held out his hand, one foot hovering, ready to disembark. It was a strong hand, sheathed in leather. I remembered the scalpel in his palm, the blood-spattered apron. The carriage looked suddenly like a coffin.

"You're too kind. I believe I see my driver at the next corner." Craning my neck, I peered deliberately straight ahead, picking up the pace until I was almost running along Aldgate Street. The carriage would have to turn around, giving me valuable moments to disappear into one of the side streets. Despite the shock coursing through my bloodstream, I was exhausted, spent. But I kept on moving, my cloak damp, entangling my legs. I slipped to my knees before hauling myself upright again.

My lungs burned as though I had the ague. Church Lane. And no crunch of carriage wheels. Phillips had decided to accept my lie.

I turned into a choked alley, feeling as though I'd been dragging a corpse instead of skirts heavy with the waste of the East End. Only after several moments did I allow my pace to slow, to regain my breath, to allow myself to think, the rhythm of the driving rain furious in the background.

The killer would not remain in or around Aldgate, let alone hazard Drury Lane with stained hands. Church Lane, dimly lit and out of the way, offered deserted door stoops and heaps of rubbish to hide behind.

I checked my watch, water trickling down the front of my blouse. Half past one. I turned in a circle, eyes scanning tumble-down buildings with broken windows and crooked doorways. Warehouses, the entrances wreathed with thick chains, proclaimed Taylor Perry, a garbage hauler, and Kearley & Tongue general merchants.

From the Saracen to the stables and then the alley behind the socialist club—I was no longer certain who was following whom. But I knew that the killer was now out of sorts, thrown off his plan, his ritual slaughter interrupted by the cart and pony.

My vision blurred as I wiped moisture from my face. When it cleared, I saw him from behind recognizing the now familiar sway of a cloak. A top hat hunched down on his shoulders while he leaned onto an alcove like a patient suitor waiting for an assignation.

Then he began to walk. I followed, keeping an even distance, as though we were connected by a length of cord. Fenchurch Street, Leadenhall and then Russel. With each step I felt more and more elated, the albatross of dread taking flight.

It would come to an end and I would have my answers. The evidence I needed to stop the murders. The killer dodged onto a small, stone-cobbled square, White Square, ill-lit and deserted. A lamppost stood at the entrance of Church Passage, in the eastern side. The man stopped in the shadow of a crouching warehouse for an instant and then slowly rounded the corner to disappear.

I moved carefully across the square until I stood directly under the lamppost anticipating that he waited for me, as though we'd silently agreed somehow to this macabre tryst. There was a cold logic to this madness that could be reckoned with, a strange mixture of the delusional and the violent, devised for a twisted purpose. A random lunatic was what I least expected.

The invisible cord that bound us pulled at me. There were three approaches to White Square, one carriageway and two narrow foot passages. I walked toward the southern corner, drawn by the need to keep on moving and convinced that the man in the cloak would seek refuge in the darkest spaces. Behind rose two tenements lit by a single lamp. I stopped, feeling sweat and accumulated rain inch down my spine. I twisted my neck to gaze at the gray of the buildings and the black of the sky.

The moisture spread like a blossoming bruise on my bare skin followed by a searing heat that settled at the base of my skull. Heat turned to scorching fire. The lamplight shuddered, the post swayed, until every bit of light leached from the square. A smothering noise like a pillow descending, breath stopped in my throat. I slid to the ground. And then I knew nothing but silence.

CHAPTER 26

In the corner sat a woman, naked except for a chemise. She poured a bucket of water over her straw bed, lay down in it and then covered herself with a sheet. Despite the room's stench, she smiled at someone in the distance and in a low voice repeated unintelligible phrases. A jumble of words spewed from her mouth.

I observed, unable to do more than watch as the woman rose from the bed to lunge at the mud floor. She walked on all fours and then stretched like a lizard on the ground. Her eyes fixed, she surveyed the dirt as though searching for gems.

The room dissolved and now I sat with Alice James. Alice lay on a daybed, snail-like, ready to pull back in her shell. She pouted, an awkward shaping of thin lips, Alice unnatural as an ingénue.

He hasn't been by to see me in weeks.

Your brother is a busy man.

He once wrote me mock sonnets.

You are his sister—he loves you.

Alice's face began to crumple, her features puckering into an embroidery of cuts, blood congealing on cheeks and forehead.

Nausea clogged the back of my throat, cutting off my breath, catapulting me awake, gasping. I must still have been dreaming because even with my eyes open, I saw nothing. Panic flowed through every vein and muscle, awareness dawning.

I was on my knees, arms tied behind my back, wrists and waist burning against rope. My eyes opened wide and strained against the darkness, a thickness blocking my breaths, cutting off my voice, my screams. The silence was impenetrable, and I sensed that even the rain had stopped.

My eyelids scratched against a surface. It took several moments to realize that a thin scarf was wrapped around my head. If I labored, I could make out a figure leaning against a wall, a woman collapsed onto his chest, like a spurned lover, begging for mercy, another chance. He still wore the top hat, the cloak motionless now, more shadow than man.

I was meant to see these slow and deliberate actions through a scrim.

My wrists and fingers were numb, a prickling of nerves deadening my lips as I struggled to breathe. On my knees as though in prayer, tethered to the ground, I tried to keep my mind intact. Through the fine mesh covering my eyes, I saw and yet I didn't see, like attempting to find my way in a pitch-black room. I watched the man in the cloak pushing the woman away from him almost gently before inserting a knife under her left eye and then drawing it under her nose, cutting it from her face. The knife continued with a gash down the right cheek to the angle of the jawbone, the nose laid over the cheek.

A mouthful of rags deadened my screams. I drummed my wrists, one against the other, pushed against the rope around my waist, convinced I would choke on the vomit rising from my throat.

The woman slumped to the ground in a grotesque choreography. Her clothes were pushed up to her breast, the stomach laid bare, a gash from abdomen to throat, the flash of white rapidly covered in red. The night had warmed, the aroma of blood and feces carried on a damp breeze. The cloak swayed as the man bent over to draw out glistening intestines, placing them between the body and the left arm.

Then he turned toward me. Nothing but the power of the mind. An unsound mind, I repeated to myself uselessly. The top hat obscured his face, but I heard labored breathing, louder even than my heart vaulting in my chest. I thought of all his women, jagged wounds, eyes gazing up from the cobblestones, as I focused on the knife in his hand. And in his other, carefully nestled as a robin egg in a leather-sheathed palm, was an ovary, its unmistakable shape almost lost in the lip-pink shell of a womb.

I didn't know where to look, at the circle of blood growing ever wider underneath the dead woman or at the flash of steel that dominated even the darkness. The decision was made for me. He drew himself up like a giant black crow, black against the blacker sky, lunging. I expected what—a canvas gone blank, searing pain, choir of angels? Instead my wrists were suddenly freed, blood pulsing hotly through my veins reminding me that I lived even though I didn't deserve to. Like a deadweight, I collapsed to the ground, sobbing dryly, the cloth in my throat blossoming like a sponge. I didn't know how much time passed but when I gathered the courage to look up, he was gone.

CHAPTER 27

A childhood memory flickered, Narragansett Bay, my head caught by the sea, hair streaming behind me. A nanny pacing just beyond the surf. I was submerged in water, the only sound the pounding of my heart, a signal that I still lived.

But I was in London, not in Massachusetts on some distant shore. I raised my head, afraid to tear away the curtain shielding my eyes, unwilling to let in an even worse darkness. Instead I clawed at the ropes around my waist with the hysteria of a mad woman. They refused to come undone but at least my fingers moved again, the blood flowing more easily.

A deep breath and then I raised fists to my eyes, surfacing. Pushing aside the stiff fabric, I saw clearly now, a dead rat by my knees and the remainder of a chamber pot, the contents a stew in a puddle of rain. A woman lay unmoving just paces away but I turned my back. The fabric in my hand that had covered my eyes was rough even through my leather gloves, landscape burlap or coarse linen, which I shoved into the pocket of my cloak next to the outlines of the knife. Tarski's.

The killer was gone. And he let me live. Air stuck in my throat as I remembered the assured arc of his blade and remembered the glistening ovary in its womb, cupped in his palm like an outrageous offering. Rising from the ground, I realized that I was still tethered like a dog or horse to a hitching post. I pulled out the knife to cut through the nub of rope at my waist until it fell loose and frayed.

The square was deserted, four corners filled with shadows, abandoned warehouses, no one in sight. Thoughts were taking too long to coalesce, but my body assumed control of my mind, legs moving stiffly at first, then one foot forward, then another as I retraced my steps. *Our steps.*

Horror turned inward now having no place else to go, moral escape impossible. I started running. Away from White Square, away from the body, the second one that I had seen that night.

I was abandoning her, I thought, propelled along by some profane current. To leave the unknown woman alone was an abomination but finding the killer was the one impulse that held me together, drove me forward, kept my lungs from exploding.

The streets blurred, squat buildings, slanting tenements, the whole of it a feverish jumble. My eyes aimed at the ground, looking for what? Fresh gouts of blood? An abandoned knife? I lurched ahead, going nowhere, the bricks in the road taking on the form of a face in shadow, an oval blackness, featureless.

Shoulders hunched, hands buried in my pockets, I grappled with too many contradictions, the whole world slowing to a slurry of vague images. The brain was the most mysterious of organs, so unlike the mechanical workings of the heart with its identifiable chambers and regulated rhythm pulsing blood through our systems like the steam of an engine. The mad presented with normal outside casings, no boils, no weeping wounds, the disease hidden inside folds of gray matter.

If I could only open his brain, peer into his mind, unspool the coils of blood and gore first to understand and then to stop this butchery which was anything but senseless. There was a pattern here, of circumstance and motivation that defied the behaviors of a lunatic.

Cails and Knight had found or made an extraordinary specimen to be their black hand.

I stumbled, my ankle wrenching. The pain in the back of my skull roared to life. I straightened, walking, darting, then walking again. I realized I wouldn't find him because he wasn't looking for me. He was done with me this night. Fresh beads of rain slapped my face and I walked some more until I found myself back in the alley by the Socialist Club. Where the night had begun.

The low gates were now sealed shut to salvage the remnants of the earlier murder, to preserve the vestiges of the noise and confusion and whatever evidence remained. Only one torchlight burned, splitting through the darkness.

A mouthful of air, rank and foul. My mind veered to where Maggie would be waiting with Tarski, the rake against the door locking out the world. Staying in the shadows, I wanted to be done with it all, to go back to the start of the night by following the sinister glow from the Socialist Club to the alley behind with its row of hovels fallen over like tipped dominoes.

The alley pinched to nothingness. It was too quiet. The voices of the choir long dispersed, and the splintered door of the old barn giving way under the pressure of my shoulder too easily, no rake or lock to impede an intruder. My heart slumped as my vision adjusted, directed to the only point of light, the brazier in the corner, smoldering. Empty. No Tarski. No Maggie.

The night was a scorched field, everything laid to waste. Exhaustion had replaced the blood in my veins. I collapsed onto the stinking cot, allowing my mind to go blank. For an instant. Then I heard the bite of footsteps on gravel. The door was barricaded. Or was it? I heard the rattle of the stable door scraping open.

CHAPTER 28

My fingers throbbed. I was instantly awake, my eyes singed open. Dust mottled the air forming a halo around the man profiled in the morning light. Bracing a shoulder against the door, he pulled it shut behind him. In his hand a simple crowbar that had made short work of the flimsy latch that I thought could keep me in and him out. I struggled to sit upright, my mouth rough as sandpaper.

I hoped there was no terror lighting my eyes, like an animal on its back, its belly exposed, a weak thing. Easy work for Victor Cails. The battle for self-control warred with last night's memories. Best I could manage was to greet Cails's observation with silence, willing him to disappear and knowing that he wouldn't.

Knees pressed to the side of the cot, I slowly levered myself to a standing position. I felt petrified under the fabric of my cloak, embalmed with mud. A dullness throbbed in my chest, any courage I had left dissolved with last evening's lozenges at the back of my throat

Cails leaned against the window then crooked a smile. Like a magician's prop, his cane was set on the window's ledge, the silver cranium leering with its empty gape and hollow eyes.

The room tipped for a moment. Then righted itself, the window squared with the wall, Cails in between. An impulse shot through my body, pure as white heat. *I want to kill him.*

He was soberly dressed, hatless, in a grey jacket of costly merino wool most likely from Italy. Hypocrisy came in all forms, my father liked to say. *Give me a true laborer with dirt under his fingernails spouting socialist rant any day than a gentleman with reform on his mind.*

I needed to know how Cails had found his way to this place, stinking of mildewed straw and horse flesh, the small brazier in the corner still chugging out heat.

"You keep Tarski here." A non sequitur that fit into the chaos of my thoughts and helped smother my fury. Barely.

"Do I?" The words so quiet as to be almost inaudible. My hands coiled in the stiffness of my ruined gloves. "I believe you saw far more revelatory incidents than coming upon Mr. Tarski here in this unfriendly place."

Images blurred in my mind's eye. *The Illustrated London News*'s anonymous threats made real. Two new victims to feed the proletarian frenzy. The double event with the killer passing through Shoreditch like a phantom. In under an hour the press would report that he had inveigled his victims, killed the first before moving on to mutilate and kill the second. As an added flourish—leaving the police humiliated and ridiculous in their defeat.

And leaving me, quite deliberately, as his only living witness. Why?

Cails's smile was cold and unsettling, his narrowed gaze swimming over me, and I considered that I had Tarski's knife in the pocket of my cloak.

I'd seen too much. That's what Cails was thinking, the man who was creating and directing this scourge in East London. He kept Tarski drugged, a decoy for an incompetent police force and a scapegoat for the rabble while the real monster did his work unfettered and undetected.

Cails looked down at me from what felt like a great height. Rather than letting my knees give out, I slumped back down on the cot. "You have a fascinating quality about you, Miss Buchanan. Here you are in the most impossible of situations and most of it of your own making. To protect the family of a young heiress and prove the innocence of a worthless immigrant, you endeavor to hunt down a killer of worthless women. Why do you do it? Risk it?" His face lit with curiosity. "The pampered, protected and only daughter of one of America's wealthiest men. Spending your time with the mad, the diseased, in filthy, pestilent asylums. Whatever has driven you to such an extreme?"

I moved my legs experimentally, feet shuffling lightly over the floor.

"You prefer not to speak about yourself. I've noticed that unusual predilection, peculiar in a woman. You dislike attention and prefer that the emphasis be redirected, placed in any other possible path." He took a step away from the window and one toward me.

I now knew too much, or so he believed. *He was here to kill me.* I was finally alert, painfully so, the last of the numbness draining from my body, clearing my mind. But doing nothing to tamp the rage coming to life again, low in my chest.

"Ah, Miss Buchanan, at last a bit of color returning to your face." Cails's expression gave little away but his voice dropped a tone, as though offering confidentiality. "The public exposure is never good for people of your type with so much to hide. Your father is a powerful man but even he prefers not to have his pedestal shaken." A flicker of light at the back of those dark eyes.

A threat wrapped in a promise. What made an ideologue, I wondered, a zealot like Cails, willing to unleash a virulent disease on the very people he claimed to be fighting for? So much political turmoil, the liberals and social reformers and even Irish Home rule partisans claiming these killings for their own ends. And the newspapers with their editorials attacking the government for the entire world to read.

An echo of William's voice reminded me—*We are all ready to be savage in some cause. The difference between a good man and a bad one is the choice of the cause.*

Cails had made his choice. Even if I could have escaped the miserable stables, what did I have to lever against him? That he was a radical fomenting revolutionary discord through the creation of a killer that stalked a serial number of victims?

There was no knife I could produce with his handprint on it.

"Your mind is working feverishly."

"My head aches."

"And worse, I imagine, with what you've recently witnessed."

He thought I knew the identity of the killer. "I have questions."

"You always do." His eyes left mine briefly to survey the stables as though he might have considered lingering for a time. "You have questions concerning my motivations, how I came to be here at this juncture, in this place, with you."

How interesting, I thought coldly, despite the slow churn in my chest, that even a man like Cails felt the need to explain—justify—himself. "Perhaps I do."

I'd never get anything close to a confession but, then again, truth was often closeted in lies. Most of the political classes in London would tell about the sinister plots hatching in the city's environs by anarchists, socialists and Fabians, many of whom were Europeans in exile, foreigners with no homelands. While I had one posed here in the dirt and the straw right in front of me.

Cails's watched me as carefully as I watched him. "Wherever you would like to start." I used a shop-worn phrase that had proven useful in my practice.

"While you say nothing, watching and judging." Mocking. He was so close that if I'd even wanted to rise, I'd be unable to maneuver around him.

"Interesting your choice of words, Cails. Are you concerned about being judged?"

"I'm not looking to justify my actions but to right wrongs. We see the world differently, Miss Buchanan, you through a false lens that does nothing to ameliorate the conditions you wish to address be they inside or outside some poor devil's head."

"You address the material concerns and I the psychological—is that it?"

"If we were to eliminate poverty, inequity and the corrupt governments in the sway of the ruling classes, we would have little need for this interest in the frontal lobes of cadavers."

I managed to say evenly. "If I understand correctly, you see madness, if you see it at all, as a mere consequence of material conditions."

"Not at all. More a consequence of exclusion." A flicker of light again in the dark of his eyes. "We cannot tolerate those who live outside the margins of a productive society. If they are *mad*, they must be institutionalized." A sly smile, as though he could catch me in the argument. "Think of the women you hope to cure—you hope to cure them of the behaviors that place them outside the realm of the domestic. Why? Because we require an angel in the house, not a devil at the hearth."

I sidestepped the obviousness of Cails's trap. "So hallucinations, hysteria, deviancy?"

"Outside the realm of true knowledge and science. Not so long ago we believed deviants to have been conduits of God or Satan."

"You believe in unreason then."

"Just the opposite. I believe in the five senses, death, reason and nothing else." He paced to the window and then back toward the cot where I still hunched, my head now craning to look up at him.

"We are both battling a form of unreason, albeit from different vantage points." I refused to lean away from him while wondering whom I was trying to convince. There was a delirious quality to our discussion in the confines of a former stable, the waft of barnyard and desperation in the air.

The discussion was veering off course. Offering me nothing of any substance that I could use. Except to delay the decision—the murderous act—Cails was about to undertake.

The pain in my neck pulsed but it was weaker than before, competing with slivers of memory from the previous night. The hand at my foot, appealing for help, frozen eyes rolled heavenward. The arc of a knife in a leather palm. The lip-pink shell of a womb.

I raised my eyes to the ceiling, borrowing time, tracing the wide beams burrowed by insects. I squinted into the rotting wood. Would he use a pistol, a knife, a blunt instrument to bludgeon me? The brazier in the corner cooked away, choking the air, curls of dying smoke wreathing the stables. Other than a door, the cot and three rusted hooks, one of which held the sooty oilskin, there was nothing I could use to escape. I pictured Tarski's knife, then blinked the image away.

"The most difficult decisions are oftentimes the easiest to make," Cails said.

A justification? Or did he require my compliance, that I lay myself down like a lamb to the slaughter?

My fingers clenched. The knife in the pocket of my cloak—I could never use it. Could I? Against a man who was behind the murders of at least three women in East London, his guilt as certain as if he'd wielded the weapon himself. A manipulator, a zealot who would kill *hundreds* of women only to have London on its knees for his own political ends.

He read my mind. "Hasty conclusions have a way of being unhelpful, Miss Buchanan."

Heat spread one vertebra at a time along the length of my spine. He needed for me to say the words, to mouth helplessness, like Griffith, I thought in a moment of clarity, in order to take his revenge. How far the mighty have fallen, he would think, his gaze taking in my mud-encrusted cloak now emptied of coins. Then my face which must have been as drawn as a tarnished penny.

It was warm, the brazier huffing out heat, sweat inching down my back. The knife in the pocket of my cloak. I quickened my right hand, ready to reach for it.

Cails exhaled and started to speak. At that moment, the door of the stables burst open.

CHAPTER 29

Cails listed backward, daylight spilling into the stables. Charles Knight, eyes lit with fury, face slicked with sweat, wrenched Cails from behind, snaking an arm around his throat.

A momentary view of the alleyway. Puddles drying and the sagging outlines of the roof of the Socialist Club in the distance. Then voices shouting from what sounded like a half-a-dozen men, Griffith's men, I thought with rising panic. The alleyways would be full of them this morning.

Ignoring stiffness in my limbs, I surged to my feet, but not before Knight tightened his grip on Cails, lips widening in a grimace. Although Knight was the broader of the two men, Cails's body was a relaxed, sinuous line as though he wasn't several truncated breaths close to death.

"Charles." A slight rasp to his voice. "*Charles*. This performance—is it really necessary?" Knight tightened his hold but Cails's voice continued steadily. "You are alarming Miss Buchanan with your display."

"Where are my children?" Knight seemed to stagger with the words. "Violet. Charlie."

A faint draft from the open door swept up errant bits of straw. The two men stood like towers in the dirty morning sunlight.

"What are you talking about? Why should I know what goes on in your household?"

"I won't ask again." A ferocity in Knight's tone that neither Cails nor I could miss.

Dread carved a hole in my stomach, dried the perspiration on my back leaving my hands chilled, my mind cold and clear and riddled with guilt. I should never have left Mayfair. I should have warned Constance.

I sensed that Knight knew how to kill Cails with a slow squeeze of his larynx, cutting off his air until he was clawing at his throat, choking, eyes rolling into the back of his head. Cails didn't struggle, as though expecting the divine intervention in which he didn't believe.

Escape was possible. Looking out toward the alley, I heard the distant voices of Griffith's men. They would be investigating, searching, this morning. But if I left, I left with nothing but savaged women on my conscience and no evidence either to exonerate Tarski or indict Cails and Knight.

And the children. Gone. The loss of a child was an atrocity of nature, a perversion of how the world should work. I shoved the thought of Sophie Rivington away.

"Knight," I said in a voice reserved for the most volatile of patients, willing him to look at me. His head jerked away from Cails and in my direction as though noticing my presence for the first time, eyes darting. "We need to remain calm, to go over details, anything you can give me."

At first Knight didn't answer, just drew his arm back more tightly, slowly but inexorably narrowing his hold on Cails. I made my expression as blank as I could, hoping not to lose him.

He shot a glance at the barren alleyway behind him then back at me. "You can't help. This man—you don't know what he's capable of."

His voice strangled, grasping Cails to him like he couldn't bear to part with the man.

"What is Cails capable of? Tell me." My tone was meant to be reassuring, when all civility, any slick of civilization, had been stripped away like skin from flesh. Knight was radiating a primal terror that poured from him in waves.

I pictured how he and Constance had taken to the streets, prowled every mews and park, dug under every porch and scoured every court to find Charlie and Violet. London was a sprawling city, its undercurrents as vile as the sewage that ran in its gutters. I sensed that the dark corners where Knight's mind had taken him might not allow for a way back. He was imagining the worst and suddenly I along with him.

"It's too late for you, for anybody... I know who's responsible. I shouldn't have waited so long... gone along with it all." His words were hollow, nonsensical. The pressure on Cails's neck remained steady. Then Knight jerked back in one fluid motion lifting Cails to the tips of his toes.

I forced myself to dull a spark of dread. Did I really want him to release Victor Cails? The man who would have killed me if Knight had not broken down the stable doors? Then again, the larynx was a reasonably fragile air passage to the lungs. Easily broken.

Cails said nothing but his eyes found mine and for a moment I thought I was the one rambling and feverish. He knew what I was doing, what I was after. In my mind's eye, I saw the scarlet scarf wrapped around Victoria Trevyn's neck.

"I've helped you before and I can help you again." I took a careful step toward the two men. Knight's free hand clenched spasmodically, his eyes wet, darting without direction. "When did you last see your children? How did you discover they were missing? Where is your wife?" I thought of Constance Knight, her calm and intelligence and command seeping away.

Knight flinched at the mention of his wife and then his face became cold. He'd done this before, I sensed, held someone at the point of a gun or a knife or his bare hands. The arm around Cails's neck was surprisingly muscled for a gentleman. Knight didn't shake, didn't waver, this moment the most important in his life. He waited to answer, nostrils flaring, his mind no doubt considering all the possibilities, whether Cails lived or died, whether he would take notice of me, believe in my efficacy, and whether he would ever visit his children in the nursery again, see them sleep, hear their laughter, return them to their mother.

"I'm not asking you to release Cails," I said. "Simply tell me why you believe he may be involved in your children's disappearance."

Cails, his head at an awkward, deathly angle still managed a coldly wicked grin. "Yes, Charles. Why don't you tell us!"

Knight answered with a sharp twist of his arm. "You tell me, Cails. Where did you take them?"

"You are wasting time."

"Why would Cails be interested in stealing Charlie and Violet?"

"Answer her, Charles."

Carefully, as if handling a rabid animal, Knight placed a black boot between himself and me, cutting me off from what he was about to do. "It wasn't Trevyn this time, if it ever was." Barely audible now, as though he couldn't believe it himself. "She couldn't be responsible. She was seen leaving the house last night by Branksome who was with the children at the time."

I swallowed nausea. Thought of the open window in the nursery. Cursed myself again for not warning Constance Knight.

Cails stared straight ahead, over Knight's head. "If anything happens to me, Charles, you will be exposed. You and your family. I will see to it, in life or in death. You should know me that well by now. I leave nothing to chance."

A strange smile was stranded on Cails's lips. "How quickly you've forgotten your humble origins, *Charlie*. And your impressive transformation from radical to esteemed publisher." He parsed each word. "I raised you up. Raised you from a common pickpocket to the man you are today. Introduced you to the power and finality of gunpowder." He paused. "You could have had a hand in bringing down the world."

Knight's grip on Cails turned to stone, his knuckles white.

"You might have remained a petty thief forever but instead you chose to be a revolutionary plotting the overthrow of order."

I considered who was more in shock, Knight or me.

"Remember while much has changed for you in the intervening years," the graveled voice continued, "it's still your choice, whether you choose to finish life in Mayfair, a forsaken colony or at the end of a noose as a traitor to your country."

Knight's free hand tugged frantically at his pocket. The black snout of a pistol emerged. He dragged it across Cails's jawline.

My thoughts fired in different directions. Cails didn't flinch. "You were always a hot head," he said, eyelids lowering, his voice unchanged, "making assumptions, jumping to conclusions. Unreliable."

"If you don't tell me right now where to find them…" Knight ended the sentence by pulling back the hammer of the pistol.

"It was I who saved you, Charles, you'll recall, not so many years ago." His face was so close to Knight's that their foreheads almost touched. "Saved you from your wretched life, saved you from prison, saved you from the noose. He was supposed to enter the history books, Miss Buchanan, blow up the Royal Observatory. Unfortunately, his device failed."

Knight sucked in a lungful of air as though the waiting bullet had found him.

"And it's a good thing I did find you with that pack of passing schoolboys close behind. Schoolboys! They would have discovered you kneeling and bleeding but still able to talk to Scotland Yard."

Cails's eyes flickered and I was aware that he was watching me when he should have been watching Knight. Because *now I knew*. Knight's knuckles were blanched around the pistol, the muzzle obscene.

"Why don't you tell her, Charles? Go ahead." Cails confident in his power over Knight despite the gun held to his head. "Tell her how I gave you your identity, one that allowed you to court Constance Ralston, marry her and subsequently follow in the footsteps of her father to become the publisher of *The Illustrated London News*. In short, tell Miss Buchanan that I gave you *your life*. A life worth living."

Knight was breathing hard as though he had run half of East London.

"After so many years you've learned so little." Cails's eyes narrowed. "But if there's anything that is worth repeating, it is this. I have you in *my grip*. I've always done and I always will. Further, there's no reason for me to spirit away your children. You are desperate and with nowhere to turn, you turn inwards, which we know is a very dark place. Distrust and suspicion fester there, Charles. And then you think to accuse me. A mistake I will forgive only once."

Knight stiffened. Although he was an inch away from Cails, he didn't expect it when the older man leaned into him, suddenly creating enough space to wrench one arm free and drive the heel of his hand into Knight's face. The shock cleared the clouds from his eyes before Cails slammed his opposite forearm hard into his throat. Melting from Knight's grip, he grabbed Knight's head and rammed it into the wall. The pistol slid to the floor, useless.

CHAPTER 30

Knight was on the ground, knees pulled tightly to his chest, his breaths coming deep and unsteadily. Cails shot first one and then the other cuff, before bending down to pick up the pistol. Straightening, he offered a shrug of what passed for an apology. "Let's give him a few moments. I'm sure he'll recover."

Arms now limp, barely grasping his knees, Knight opened his eyes, rolling his head from side to side like a broken marionette. Leaning over him, I did a quick review. His color was returning, his pupils normal. Cails's blow had been delivered with strategic neutrality.

I watched Cails pocket the pistol and then pull a case from his jacket. He offered a cigarette with the casualness of a croupier at a card table.

For a moment I hesitated but then with a steady hand extracted one when Cails struck a match. He observed me taking a deep draught, before returning the case to a pocket. The cigarette tasted like burning paper, the heat of it on my lips. But I held the smoke in, feeling the scald in the back of my throat and deep into my lungs, desperate for the familiar balm that didn't come.

I dropped the unfinished cigarette, turning it beneath my boot.

Cails tilted his head toward me. "You believe what Knight was prattling on about?"

"That you are responsible?" I didn't say for what. My voice harsh.

"I'm responsible for many things, most of which you get wrong." He rubbed at his jaw thoughtfully. "Though what I've said is the truth. Our young Charlie was a pick pocket when I found him. After the Royal Observatory debacle, we primed him for other duties wherein Charlie Cornish took the place of a rector's only son who lost his life in a foolish prank in Italy during his European tour, the details of which are too absurd to recount. His father, the rector, died soon afterwards."

Cails watched for my reaction. "While the true Charles Knight's inheritance was modest, his education and lineage were impeccable, lofty enough to impress Baron Ralston who believed Charles Knight might just be worthy enough as a son-in-law, and to helm his publishing house." Cails paused thoughtfully, for a moment taken off track. "The Baron didn't last long. I haven't seen such a florid case of the pox in years."

Then he smiled as though we were part of the same conspiracy. "Conveniently for us, Ralston died a harrowingly painful death, a suppurating mass of pustules, howling like a dog, just eighteen months after the wedding of his daughter, Constance. And Knight here," Cails pivoted toward the seemingly oblivious man at his feet, "assumes the mantle of the estate and the command of *The Illustrated London News*. The Baron dies never knowing the truth—that he's allowed an unrepentant anarchist from the worst of London's stews to infect his home, his enterprise and, worst of all, his lineage."

He stared down at Knight. "What have you to say, Charles?

I tried to keep control of my thoughts, my mind churning. Knight roused himself, scrubbing a hand down his face, turning a crazed eye toward us. I considered what was left of his sanity had not quite finished staggering and spinning away. Pausing another moment, he then began hauling himself up. He produced a hoarse cough like something was wrong with his voice. Leaning limply against the wall, all the violent energy seemed to have deserted him.

His eyes focused somewhere to the back of the stables and I wondered whether he realized Cails and I were standing a few feet away. "I arrived home," he began finally, searching for words. "Arrived home." He stopped and towed a breath into his lungs as though it was his last. Arms hanging lifeless by his side.

Language was a curious instrument, as revealing as a badly pitched piano or violin. I'd seen firsthand that when the mind came undone, syntax soon followed. Knight coughed then started again. "I arrived home." He might as well have been alone, telling the story to himself. There were no denials, no dismissal of Cails's story, how Charlie Cornish became Charles Knight. His focus, on his children. "To the sound of the housekeeper screaming." He swallowed hard. "A keening so wild, like a sound coming from an animal." Knight shoved a hand through his hair, the details off kilter yet sharp. "I rarely go there, to the nursery. I ripped open the doors. Branksome, the housekeeper, appeared holding Violet's doll, cradling it like an infant."

I must have moved, sucked in my breath because he looked at me, gaze clearing for a moment, fingers twitching at his sides. "The doll's hair is shorn, cut ragged, the body ripped open. And below, on the floor, a pair of shears."

I should have turned away, given him some room but I couldn't move. Not for the first time in my life, I wondered how much torment a human being could absorb, whether our psyches were like ink blotters permeable only to the saturation point.

Charles Knight, a haunted man with a past to outrun. And with a present that he couldn't endure. I'd barely finished the thought when he turned stumbling, head-long toward the door, without a thought about me, about Cails, or about the pistol that could have been used to stop him. He staggered out of the stables, falling like a drunk into the curtain of soot-stained light and into the alleyway beyond.

CHAPTER 31

Footsteps coming from outside, stomping, not worried about being heard. On the lookout for the Shoreditch Savage, for any evidence he may have left behind, checking each one of the outbuildings in the mews. Cails, outlined in the gaping door behind him.

Jerking to my senses, I blocked Knight from my thoughts, wide awake, knowing what I had to do. There was nowhere to go so I backed toward the brazier, my gaze darting around the stables in a final, hapless survey, landing on the soot stained cape hanging on the rusted hook.

"Knight," Cails said with a shake of his head and a careless glance toward the door, "he will come to his senses. He always does."

What if he didn't? Griffith's men in the Yard could detain him for questioning. They might have ignored the derelict stables but not now, Knight stumbling directly across their path. Perhaps they wouldn't question the publisher of *The Illustrated London News*. Perhaps they would.

"Did you abduct the children? Do you know where they are?" Time closing in like the lid of a coffin. I remembered the open window in

Trevyn's room. *Did you try and kill Trevyn, make it look like a suicide?* Too many questions tumbling through my mind.

Cails's eyes swooped over me, gaze hawk-like. "You can't possibly believe that nonsense, that I'm in any way responsible. What would I want with his offspring?"

"Charlie and Violet are gone. And given what you've just told me, what I've learned, the lengths you might go to ensuring Knight comes to heel...." My voice was ragged. How easily Cails had shaken off Knight's hold, a man a decade younger and twenty pounds heavier. Perhaps Knight had balked at his role in the killings. *Knight as the Shoreditch Savage.* I shook my head, trying for logic this time. It would make no sense for Cails to risk the man he'd so cunningly and carefully placed in a position of power.

My choices, if I ever had any, were dwindling. Cails wouldn't give in and I had nothing that I could use to expose the existence of his demented manifesto. Worse still, no knowledge of the whereabouts of the children and—my thoughts coalescing now—it was only a matter of moments before the police came to the end of the alley to search the old stables.

I heard nothing but a drumbeat in my ears. For once I didn't think, I acted.

I leapt toward the back of the stables and knocked over the smoking brazier with my boot, the spilling embers licking straw before Cails had any time to react. A baffled moment, then a look of surprise at what I'd done. He vaulted toward me but not before the fire demanded his attention. Then a noise from his chest, beyond speech now. Jerking off his jacket, repeatedly striking at the flames, until finally throwing it down to try and smother the blaze.

The straw gave way under my boots, denying me traction. Gaining balance, my arms flailed before grabbing Tarski's metal bowl and raising it over Cails like a club. I brought it down on the side of his head, no planning, no deliberation, desperation in its purest form. A crack, a bone splitting, Cails holding his face just as I brought down the bowl a second time. Cails going rigid before he slumped to the ground, knees first, arms dangling at his side.

Fire made a noise, a hungry, vociferous roar. Smoke wreathed its way around the stables, eating at the straw, stealing my breath, stinging my eyes. In my hand the bowl lay heavy, vibrating up my arm from the contact with Cails's head. Splayed on the floor, Cails was still, too still. For a moment I considered moving him, edging him out the door, into the air where he could breathe. Force a confession from him somehow, I thought in an instant of madness.

With air rationed, his breathing came in short gasps. Blood leaked from the crook of his mouth, eyes half open, stunned, and for once helpless. With a moan that sounded like it came from someone else, I raised the bowl above my head to strike a final blow, shut my eyes and then heard it clatter to the ground. I couldn't do it. When I opened my eyes again, I saw it roll a few feet away from Cails.

The fire smoldered. Then shouting, footsteps, a series of coughs, and the sound of spitting. Griffith's men raking the yard for evidence. My pulse beat fast as time thawed and resumed. I opened my eyes to the smothering smoke then decided to lift Cails by the shoulders. He was heavy but that was always the case with dead weight. His torso slumped back to the ground. Even if I could have dragged him into the alley, I thought disjointedly, only for Griffith's men to see us?

The blacksmith's cape on the hook behind me. My hands seemed to act on their own. Pulling the sooty fabric from the wall, I threw it over my body, covering my hair and my face, stepping over the still form of Cails to edge my way out the open door.

First smoke and a kaleidoscope of buildings in the alley encircling me. A quick left, my legs heavier than they should have been. I didn't get far. A man rounded the corner, his uniform a dull blue, instantly blocking my way.

Heat still seared my eyes, my cheeks, my lungs as the man placed a hand on my shoulder. I tore my gaze up the alleyway, expecting to see an army descend.

"You there—where are you going?" The words intended to stop me. I didn't think about what I'd done, leaving Cails behind in the stables, dead or alive. Hair retreating from his forehead, features indistinct, the constable dug his fingers under the flesh of my shoulder. Stooped, no longer young, there was a weariness about him. "Did you hear me?" he asked as though trying to get the question right.

I sensed that he took me for a man, a suspicious one at that, with what could be interpreted as the Shoreditch Savage's murder weapon in his pocket, if he'd only known. A roil of laughter, bitter and deep, threatened to erupt from my throat. I'd been so close, tethered to that coldly, rational monster, that now I could be taken as his doppelgänger.

Yanking myself from the constable's grip, I was hit with enough force to take me off my feet. Arms wrapped around mine as we rolled to the ground and I sucked in air and tried to wrench free. Grappling for my attacker's face, my hand came away with a policeman's cap while a knee struck my ribs. Tarski's knife, I remembered, just before a fist came down ready to collide with my skull.

Pinned down in the blinding glare of rage, I felt my hand claw around the weapon hidden under too many layers of fabric. My vision blurred under the crush of the man's weight, but my head moved just in time, my arm arcing backward and then upwards, the knife clutched in my hand slicing through the blacksmith's cloak.

I hesitated for an instant as the constable straddled me and grabbed his club, hefting it above his head. He was going to crush my skull, I thought. No turning back. My arm shook, my wrist numbed as I brought up the knife into the man's left thigh. A howl of pain, astonishment creasing his face, eyes blown wide open. He shrank back like a coiled spring. I struggled to stand, dropped the knife and then ran.

CHAPTER 32

We'd called it the abattoir, a place of stained porcelain sinks, of air pungent with the renderings of human flesh. The site of my first dissection, the candidate a wiry corpse of indeterminate age and identity. Returning home to Beacon Hill after a morning of bone and gristle, I'd been grateful for the modern plumbing that my father had insisted be installed in the house. The gleaming tub, the pristine copper, the punishingly hot flow of water blasting from the ivory faucets. It hadn't been hard to imagine dried crimson flecks falling from my skin as I'd scrubbed at my face, my arms, my hands.

I thought of that day until the memory blurred and the edges of my vision went soft. Although it was morning, the London air foamed a greyish yellow, forming a boggy path out of the meandering streets surrounding the alley behind Aldgate Street. No longer running, I didn't know where I was but the voices behind me were receding, claimed by the fire threatening to consume the mews I'd left behind. Far enough away, the clang of the fire reels was more in my head than outside the stables where Cails's lifeless body now lay buried in ash.

A line of houses, grim and derelict, advanced from the pall and I pulled the blacksmith's cape from my head and shoulders and tossed it behind a slop pail. At the next corner, a man in a red cap tended a trash fire stirring smoke into the sallow air. The urge to turn around and go back was strong.

But Cails was gone. Dead. Killed by my hand, his lungs seared by fire and smoke. Another man was injured, not fatally—the knife hadn't gone near the femoral artery—he would recover.

Countless women's lives would be saved and Mary Holland and Annie Childs would be avenged along with the two women who had met their savage end tonight.

The images came in surges. My teeth chattered, the wet of my blouse turning cold, plastering my shoulders. Shock, I thought grasping for coherence, common after serious injury, the circulatory system failing to maintain adequate blood flow to the brain. Organs hoarding what they could to stay alive. My mind vibrated. Charlie and Violet, I remembered suddenly, imagining Knight, his eyes scorching, fixing on mine.

A strange pattern, Charlie and Violet lost and then found with the regularity of a nursery rhyme. Constance in the shadows of the nursery, the children's beds empty, a shutter banging against the securely locked casements. Victoria Trevyn, pale and defiant, her hands clinging uselessly to a brutalized doll.

My steps provided a rhythm, unsteady at first and then more even, sliding away from unreality and gradually toward order. Cails was gone—the children no longer in danger and the East End safer for it. *But where were the children?* It was as though a fever had overtaken me, drenching me one moment in sweat and the next in clammy cold.

A hansom lurched around a corner, slowing to a crawl as it approached, the man holding the reins nodding at me before urging the horses forward. Heavy clouds massed overhead turning the sky from yellow to a sheet of grey. The alleys narrowed and then opened again onto the broad river of Drury Lane, faces sliding in and out of my view.

Clerkenwell and St. John's Lane, number forty-one. I didn't know how I remembered either place or address or how I managed to get there.

I watched as Katharine Loring used her hip to wedge a bag of books against the door jamb. She flipped through a massive key ring, trying to find the one that would let her into her flat, a slim two-story brown-brick house. There was obviously no housekeeper and Alice James, I speculated, was too indisposed to come to the door herself. Katharine finally discovered the right one, twisting the handle and trundling half inside before she heard me call from behind.

Around me Clerkenwell seethed with its jewelers, shops, pedestrians and a tangle of cabs. But here in a side mews, daylight was emptying from the sky, bringing with it a strange calm that I desperately needed.

Short-sighted, squinting through spectacles, Katharine first turned, then froze for a moment before recognition dawned, followed by a look of shock. While most of the soot from my face had been wiped away, there must have been a sink to my features, hollows beneath my eyes and cheeks. Katharine had ministered to wayward women much of her life, I knew. Still balancing her bag of books, Katharine had me by the waist in an instant and I was ushered inside a dimly lit and narrow vestibule smelling of liniment and lavender.

She ran off to find tea, crying out for Alice who after a few moments appeared disheveled in the doorway, pen and notebook tumbling to the floor, a half dozen sheets of paper spilling around her.

Then we were in a mean little room, two ancient and balding wing chairs and a concave settee by a window overlooking the expanse of a shrubbery, glowing bottle-fly green against the oncoming dusk. It had taken me most of the day to make my way from the East End to Clerkenwell, though I recalled little of it.

The fine sheen of dust, the buckling wallpaper barely holding on to its original print, all of it spoke to Alice's reduced circumstances, the double price she had paid for running away first from Boston and then from her brother Henry. I dropped into one of the chairs that was as hard as a pair of unpadded hip bones, aware of the staccato beat of my pulse.

"I need your help, Alice." My mind deliberately blank for fear that what had passed in the last twenty-four hours would seep like a poison into the room.

Alice remained standing, bent slightly at the waist. "My help?" She appeared dumbstruck, letting the improbable sink in. She seemed thinner than when I had last seen her, a translucency to her skin as though she was sickening again. My head spun, grasping at what I could possibly say to her. This was not a time for questions nor for answers. Perhaps her illness could work to my advantage, I told myself, desperation making me reckless. Mental illness was a ravenous beast and Alice's attention would turn inward, leaving no thoughts for me or my circumstances, just as I wanted it.

"Are you entirely well? You look devastated, as though you haven't slept in a fortnight." She lowered herself onto the divan.

"I'm fine, really." I tried to keep my voice even but there was a hoarseness to it. "Not for very long… I'm reluctant to put you out at all but I need a place to stay, Alice. Where I might have some privacy. For just a little while. Otherwise I would simply go to a hotel but at the moment, I can't." I smoothed the surface of my cloak, the repeated motion slowing my pulse.

A flutter of hands before she awkwardly shuffled the remaining papers on her lap into a semblance of order. "Of course, Georgia. For as long as you need." She crammed the notes into an open book on the side table before straightening, slightly out of breath, giving me a curious look. "I would never turn you away, you know that. But I don't want to disappoint as we're hardly equipped…. This is a simple household as you can see." A concerned frown. "I don't wish to pry but I can't help asking, Georgia—why ever not return to Berkeley

Square or the Knight's?"

"Not possible at the moment." Too curt a statement but unlike many lies of late, the sentence was at least true.

"This is so unlike you... you've always been so resourceful, independent."

"I won't stay long and I will reimburse you for your trouble."

The frown deepened. "That's not what I meant at all and you very well know it. Don't be ridiculous, after all you've done for the family."

She peered at me, taking in my mud-splattered cloak, my dusty riding boots, then rose slowly, one hand on the side table. "You look a disaster, like you haven't slept in days. This hasn't anything to do with the Knight's domestic situation, has it? What with the latest of these strange incidences involving the governess?"

Shock jolted through me, releasing me from my stupor, and I sat upright on the hard upholstery. "You've heard anything... about the children?"

"You've been up all night, looking for them with Constance, is that it?" Another glance at my cloak and boots.

"Have they been found?" I was holding my breath.

Filtering through the papers on the side table as though searching for a lost invitation, she nodded absently. "Yes, of course, I've just received word from Constance. There's little detail you understand but clearly the governess must be responsible once again, I surmise." She shook her head. "Not sure what Constance is intending to do with that girl and it appears as though you've made no progress with your treatment. Is that why you're here, some type of falling out with the Knights?"

Barely holding myself upright, I searched for some words for Alice who was looking at me strangely. "Please don't tell the Knights I'm here with you. I'll explain later, I give you my word." I began again. "I'm very tired."

Katharine was at the door with a tray of clattering tea cups but one glance at my face and she took me by the arm for the second time in under an hour to a sliver of a room off the kitchen, leaving Alice James behind, pale and perplexed. It was the live-in maid's quarters, if they could have afforded one, clean and bare-boned. But I didn't care, ignoring Katharine's embarrassed apologies, before I collapsed on the hard, narrow bed smelling of mothballs and camphor, desperate once again for oblivion.

CHAPTER 33

Dread, a noxious poison seeping through the circulatory system. Not enough to kill someone but, perversely, torturous enough to keep them acutely alive. I spent my time in the maid's room or in the stingy little parlor, head buried in the newspapers that I surreptitiously went out and bought with the pennies I'd found cached in a hole in the bottom of the rickety wardrobe in my room in Clerkenwell.

The news was not good. Both murder sites had been cordoned off by the police, but thousands of morbid sightseers suffocated the approaches to White Square and outside the Socialist Club. Windows overlooking the locations of the killings were thrown open with seats sold and eagerly sought. There was much to feed on, a theatre of horror along with vendors selling everything from bread and fruit to sweets and nuts. Newsboys kept the murders alive with the latest particulars, reading aloud to many of the East Enders who were illiterate or foreign.

And I learned the names of the two latest victims whose lives I hadn't saved.

Ada Stewart left the mortuary in Golden Lane in an open hearse and rested in a grand coffin bearing a plate inscribed in letters of gold, as befitted a minor Drury Lane actress, followed not only by her family but also a brougham overflowing with the jackals of the national and local press. Elizabeth Wood, about whom little was known, was buried in a pauper's grave in East London Cemetery.

A cryptic message was left in chalk in a doorway in Gouston Street: *The Juwes are the men that will be blamed.*

They had not found and re-arrested Aaron Tarski but then again, perhaps Cails and Knight didn't want him to be found by the police. Then I reminded myself, the metallic taste of guilt in my mouth, *there was no more Cails.*

Without my cigarettes and without my lozenges my every sleep was accompanied by an inward reel of violence, images spooling endlessly, the deaths of Sophie, Mary Holland, Annie Childs, and now Elizabeth Wood and Ada Stewart catapulting me upright in bed night after night.

Ten days after the double murders, ten days of a hermit's life in the maid's quarters, the newspapers recounted that the authorities would comb the worst slums of Whitechapel and Spitalfields, the area of search bounded by Lamb Street, Commercial Street, the Great Road on the south, by the City boundary on the west and Albert Street, Dunk Street, Chicksand Street and Great Garden Street on the east. For the best part of a week, officers went from house to house, looking under beds, searching cupboards, inspecting knives, interviewing landlords and lodgers. The search was completed five days later with no killer to be found.

Griffith reported to the press: "*The greatest good feeling prevails towards the police, and noticeably, in the most squalid dwellings, the police had no difficulty in getting information. There is a perception among the populace that we are doing our utmost to solve these murders.*" No mention anywhere of a fire in a stable near the Socialist Club nor of an unidentified male body.

Finally, on the second week—there it was in the *Guardian*. Constable Daniel Hicks, released from St. Mary's Hospital in Paddington, recovered from injuries suffered at the hands of an unknown assailant the morning of the double murders. Followed by hysteria that Hicks might have let the Shoreditch Savage slip from his hands with nothing more to show for it than a gaping wound in his left thigh that had somehow just missed his femoral artery. And an abandoned knife. More evidence that the killer must have had some medical expertise as a hunter, butcher, student of surgery or qualified surgeon.

Dr. Phillips's report based his case primarily upon the careful extraction of Ada Stewart's uterus: "*It required a great deal of knowledge to have removed the entrails and with such anatomical precision.*"

When the worst of it threatened to overwhelm me, I told myself that the killings would cease. That Constance and Charles Knights' children would be forever safe. But Knight didn't know that yet—he had no idea that Cails, and the sword he held over his head, was gone.

The story he and Cails had written would have its conclusion—*mine*—I decided in the early hours of the morning when I couldn't sleep. Knight knew my secrets and I knew his. It was a fair exchange. I wanted the photographs of Sophie Rivington destroyed. And Aaron Tarski removed from London, far from Griffith's reach. As for William's missing letters, I perhaps would never know.

It felt like an ending. One that left me restless, dissatisfied. I'd killed a man, with justification it could have been argued, but doing all the wrong things for all the right reasons wasn't enough. I was guilty of the good that I had not done.

CHAPTER 34

Alice and Katharine's household was quiet as a boneyard, an uneven hush marred only by the mop-and-pail clatter of the twice-weekly char woman, and the pious voice of Alice's physician whose visit earlier in the week had been short lived. The doctor came and went discreetly and I was reluctant to intrude much less make my presence known. As I'd anticipated, Alice fell into familiar behaviors, consumed more each day by her emotional precariousness, fading into the divan in the parlor where she lay first in the mornings, then returning after her nap in the afternoons.

Keeping to my room, I became accustomed to the arrhythmic beating of my heart, ears straining to the slightest sound outside my door. One morning, I shot awake in my narrow bed, needled by the residue of a dream, gritty and sharp. Scraps floated through the room, that I was falling, flying across hundreds of feet in the air, nothing below me except London's rooftops. Then a woman's voice, low and reassuring. Familiar and in the hall outside my room. I froze under the rough linen sheets, bones and muscles stiff. Constance Knight had come to visit with Alice. I could only hope that Alice would keep her word, allow me the privacy I'd begged her for.

Our compact held. Alice had said nothing to Constance about my staying with her—or had she? I wasn't sure except for the fact that nothing changed in the small household. Alice and Katharine asked no questions of me but meted out the occasional curious looks when I emerged from the maid's room in clothes thieved from a moth-ridden cupboard. Serges and rough woolens were fitting now, a medieval hair shirt of sorts. Katharine was absent some of the day, fetching tinctures from the chemists, books from the library, the rest of her time as far as I could tell, spent at Alice's bedside. There was no time for the formality of a tea or proper dinner, our meals taken separately or not at all. Conversations were of the most superficial kind, as though we'd all come to a tacit agreement that the less said, the better.

Earlier in the day, a restless walk had done me no good other than to deplete my remaining silver, handed over to a runner in an untidy neighborhood some miles away, along with my note for Knight. I'd decided that we would meet at the National Gallery, a public place. Sleep was elusive but my will was made stronger in the dry-eyed early morning hours. The time when I focused on the hollowing out of my conscience. Painful but necessary. Like the digging of one's own grave, a final reckoning with one's own psyche.

Bleak thoughts were constant companions that tobacco or lozenges couldn't hope to dislodge even if they had been at my bedside table. Besides which a visit to the chemist was impossible, most likely arousing interest, then questions.

Another month or so in Clerkenwell with the notoriety of the killings diminishing and the aim of Griffith's eye wavering, and then I would decamp for Paris or Vienna. Go unnoticed. Disappear.

Another morning began with kitchen noises penetrating the thin walls of the maid's room. I'd slept little and, after making myself decent, soon found myself on the threshold of the cramped dining room. Amidst the cracked crockery, the yellowing wallpaper and the faint aroma of soup, Katharine was trying to rouse an appetite in

Alice. Alice slumped at the table, murmuring something about her head spinning. A dark, greasy stain blotted her skirts and her hair was matted, bathing seemingly having taken too much energy from her in recent days.

The deterioration had been rapid—how could I have missed it? The closed doors and hushed whispers that accompanied another visit from yet another physician, then the cloistering away, the emergence of linens and possets by the hollowed divan. Urgent, muted conferences that halted when I'd turned a corner or surfaced from the maid's room like an awkward guest.

"Please take some breakfast." Katharine held a spoon to feed Alice like a child. Glancing up at me, she didn't bother to hide her worry, eyes pouched from fatigue.

"I'd really rather not." Alice still wrapped in her nightdress.

Katharine made an aggrieved face as though I might be a possible savior. She peered at me from the kitchen as though she hadn't seen me in days. Which perhaps was the truth when I thought about it. We moved like wraiths through the small rooms of the apartment, caught somehow in different dimensions.

"My heart is thundering too hard in my chest," Alice said as I took a place across from her at the table scattered with abandoned biscuits and sticky preserves intended to tempt her palate. A brown bottle of cordial remained corked. I knew she'd developed over the years the ability to pretend that she was on the mend, manage her body and mind's rebellion. But over the past fortnight, a more physical truth had clearly emerged, of flesh consuming itself, a wasting away that was beyond her control.

Katharine placed cheddar on a piece of toasted bread. The fork shook—she wished desperately, I sensed, to see Alice eat, cram one chunk of bread after another into her mouth and rebound with good health.

"I feel vile, Georgia. I can't sleep. I can't eat. My heart," Alice waved her hands, "wants out of my chest."

Katharine didn't meet Alice's eyes but spooned a dab of chutney atop the cheese. A drift of unease of an undisclosed incident hovered between them. Alice's breathing deepened and she gave Katharine a bleary smile.

Her companion's face lit up. "This is not the end, you know. We can ask for other physicians to have a look."

"So easy for you to say. You and Georgia with your robust health." Her breaths quickened. "I have a greater sense of intellectual degradation after an interview with a doctor than from any human experience. I've been seen by so many specialists with only the feeling of degradation as the result. Nothing more, just degradation, and certainly no cure."

"I should have sensed something was wrong, that you were doing poorly." A cup of tea was placed in front of me, weak and unwanted, its depths cloudy. "I could have recommended someone from Harley Street had you told me you were ailing. Someone who could help you."

"You have your own troubles, Georgia, and you needn't be burdened with mine. Perhaps I've not been clear enough—no more doctors." Looking down at the tablecloth, at the faint ring of an indecipherable stain.

Katharine fixed on Alice. "Now you know that's not true. We could use Georgia's recommendations as we have seen improvements in the past when we've consulted with varying physicians."

Alice looked up from the table, eyes heavy with tears. "You worry me, Katharine."

"I worry you?"

"This is… I am… totally unfair… to you."

"You're speaking nonsense, Alice." Katharine put down the bread and cheese, wiped her hand on a damp cloth, then wrapped an arm around Alice's shoulders.

"Please tell Georgia. I can't." Her chin trembled.

And then Katharine repeated what she and Alice already knew and I didn't. The physician, hand on Alice's right breast, feeling for the lump over her pounding heart. Informing her that it was tumorous, an invader, destined to suck the lifeblood from her—

She didn't need to finish the sentence. I was suddenly tired, despite the morning light dousing the room, siphoning off the shadows. Alice had the look of a child searching for some explanation, an indication that she might be cured with the right combination of words. How I wished I could give them to her. Love and loss, a cruel equation. There was nothing to say about mortality that anyone wanted to hear. Noted by her many specialists over the years, including me, Alice's symptoms had long been without foundation, a fantasy. *This* diagnosis pulled her firmly to earth.

"We'll see another doctor, get another opinion." Katharine pulled Alice gently toward her.

Alice resisted, strangely resolute. "I know it's true, his diagnosis. I can feel it."

Katharine dropped her arm abruptly from Alice's shoulders, as though physically rebuffed. Eyes downcast, she turned to rearrange the dishes, the uneaten bread and cheese, the tall bottle of cordial that was prescribed for Alice's nerves, the least of her problems now.

"Would you like to return to Boston?" Katharine asked under her breath, staring vacantly while wiping a crumb from the table, waiting for her answer.

Alice's mouth worked nervously. "I can't return home. There is nothing there for me. Willi with his wife and family and teaching at the University—my brother has shut me out of his life," an odd smile, thin and unconvincing. "You won't recall, Georgia, but Katharine will. That note from him, after that Christmas long ago." Her tone mocked. "*I trust your neuralgia, or whatever you may believe this thing was, has gone and that you are back at school instead of languishing and lolling about the house.* That's what he thinks of me still. Languishing. Malingering." She took a shallow breath. "Henry is not much better, in Florence with his worldly friends and his fame, and with no room for an ailing, dying sister."

A sudden memory flickered, from one of our sessions back in Boston. Alice, lips pinched and pale, an oily rage rising to the surface. Thrusting a white envelope onto my lap. I'd looked down at my hands as if they hadn't belonged to me before extracting a sheet of creamy paper from the envelope. I'd smoothed it flat, my fingertips running over a sketch of a young Alice, and in the bottom corner William's signature, a younger version of the spiky familiar script. A portrait of a sister by her brother.

The memory faded—but it hadn't for Alice. I tried to reach for her hand across the table, like I had something helpful to give her. She startled, recoiling. "There is nothing anyone can say or do. Nothing. Particularly not you, Georgia." Her hand scuttled away from mine.

Katharine fussed with the tea pot, then rearranged a cup and saucer, her mouth twisted in suppressed emotion.

"You've had a shock, Alice," I tried again, for her, for both of us, "all the more reason that now is not the time for catastrophic thinking about your health. And no time to doubt the love your brothers have for you." Even to my ear, my words were unraveling, unconvincing. "Things may not be what they seem, simply black or white. You'll see life differently tomorrow, once we have a chance to sort through your situation."

Alice's eyes gleamed with what seemed like the last dregs of her energy. "I'm finished with doctors. I'm finished with sorting out my feelings, settling the war between my body and my will. I am relieved, *do you hear me*, relieved that my life is coming to an end. A liberation of sorts. The two of you allow me that at least."

The tea cup shook in Katharine's hand. She blinked like something had flown at her. "Your life is not coming to an end. I don't believe it for a moment. I still insist that we see another doctor, and Georgia agrees. Don't you, Georgia?" She turned to me, hopeful. "There are so many of the very best specialists here in London that we would be remiss in overlooking."

Alice looked away, the faint spark of rebellion dimmed. Without a word, she took the plate with the bread and cheese and brought a bite to her mouth. We sat in silence and in defeat, pretending that she was eating while Katharine fussed with the dishes and I made a show of folding my napkin, my eyes dry. I would not think of losing Alice now. A display of weakness would do her no good.

Alice shivered, although the fire in the hearth put out heat like a foundry. Katharine made motions to fetch her a shawl, her favorite one, the Scottish plaid, from the front bedroom. I rose to my feet, away from the anger and the exhaustion, Alice's eyes fixing on me as I pushed back my chair, promising to bring the shawl.

It was cooler in the hallway and away from the dining room. Down the end of an oak-grained corridor the scent of camphor floated in the air, leading me to the front bedroom, door ajar. A monastic bed against the wall, starched linen and sharp hospital edges. The window was closed, thick curtains creating a perpetual twilight. It was a sickroom already, save for an elaborately filigreed chest under the window, like part of a bride's trousseau, on top of which the shawl nested.

The plaid was warm as a cat in my hands, cascading to the floor. Then a drift of notepaper slipped from its folds and hooked my attention.

William's precise handwriting looped before my eyes.

My loveliest Georgia.
Without you, the weeks stretch on like a feverish illness.
I won't ask any more of you but what you are willing to give.
My life is drained of color, of vitality when you are
not within my reach.

The quiet grew, filling my head to bursting, and then my ears rang as if there were shouting nearby, the silence splintering. Here in Alice James's bedroom. Notepaper littering the floor. More of the letters that I had sent back from London to Boston, the ones missing from the packet tied with black ribbon at the bottom of my wardrobe on Berkeley Street.

CHAPTER 35

Charles Knight stood under the arrogant gaze of Charles I astride his suitably magisterial horse. The portrait, dominating the cavern of a room in the National Gallery, brooded over the thinning crowds. The elaborate cravat and somber tweed jacket contained Knight as the gentleman he pretended to be, posture ram-rod straight, the light from the dome blanching his features. He seemed as lifeless as the bronze figures lining the adjoining gallery walls.

My alertness was painful, attuned to everything from the shuffle of an old man behind us to the chill of the fog that still clung to my cloak. I slammed the door shut on images of Alice's greedy eyes devouring William's letters in the twilight of her ascetic bedroom. She was unwell, had always been unwell—an *unsound mind*. I imagined her stealthily procuring the letters from William's den in Boston, picturing as she slid open the bottom drawer of his desk. Bringing them with her to London.

And now she was dying. Perhaps the letters gave her a kind of perverse comfort, a connection with her beloved older brother. That was the only explanation I could fathom. A confrontation would provide only anguish for her. I would spare her that. My lip and cheek burned with the memory of discovering William's letters under my cloak at the Saracen. How had they come to be in Maggie Fisher's hands? Questions that would have to wait.

My vision focused on Knight feigning interest in the giant proportions of the painting in front of us.

He presented today as Charles Knight, London Publisher, arms folded across his chest, the thin line of his lips dismissive. His affect was defensive and reminiscent of patients who, after months of therapies, suddenly regressed, crawling back to old behaviors as though nothing had changed even though everything had.

There was no sign of Charlie Cornish, buckled over and defeated in the stables behind the Socialist Club, standing across from me.

He dispensed with a formal greeting. "*Art is always and everywhere the secret confession, and at the same time the immortal movement of its time.*" The words fell from his lips like a spell that at one time might have worked their magic. My expression must have disappointed him. "I thought you said you were familiar with Marx—I'm paraphrasing."

"Clearly not familiar enough."

He gestured to the Van Dyck. "Cails would remind me that the King lost his head."

"And shares your name."

Knight rewarded me with a stingy smile and a slight incline of his head. "Here he is, the King leading his horse through the landscape, the very image of power. But did you know he was only five feet tall?"

"I did not."

"Of course, you didn't. That's the power of the ruling class, of the Divine Right of Kings, to throw star dust into the eyes of lesser men." He adjusted the perfection of his cravat.

A trill of laughter behind us, startling; a young woman and a matron who released a heavy sigh and the scent of vetiver cologne.

"But you're not here for a history lesson," Knight said as we both returned to the stark browns and blues of the Van Dyck, the brush strokes an angry impasto.

Aside from the women and the old man who toured the hall behind us with an aimless shuffle, the gallery was empty, the atmosphere laden with pigment and history and the tension between us. Earlier, the museum entrance on Trafalgar Square had been choked with the usual throng of patrons. Men in bowlers and top hats, the occasional troupe of school children and governesses but no signs of the constabulary. The fact did nothing to ease the tightness in my throat. A few more months was what I needed to prove to myself the murders had ceased and for Griffith's interest in me to wane.

"Your children are well?" I wanted to confirm once again that Cails was no longer in the world. Where Violet and Charlie had been found and by whom on the night of the double murders was still a mystery. Despite her visits with Constance, disconcerting to me as they'd been, Alice had been too wrapped up in her own troubles to ask the question or at least discuss any answers with me.

"You're not here to discuss my domestic travails." Knight's jaw tightened.

"I might be if they involve Cails." I kept going. "You accused him of taking your children just a short while ago."

"I was mistaken."

"Really?" He was glaring at me now. "Or did you think it in your best interests to resolve your differences. Given the knife Cails holds at your throat."

His eyes dropped. "I was surprised to receive your note, Miss Buchanan. Forgive me, but I thought you'd disappeared after that morning."

Disappeared. I should have been inured to the shock of someone wanting me dead, but somehow I wasn't. Knight had anticipated that Cails would kill me rather than see me leave the stables alive. His indifferent glance took in a few jarring details, the rough serge of my cloak, the high neck of my blouse, unadorned by broach or pearls, my gloveless hands. I wasn't the Georgia Buchanan he was familiar with but then neither was he the Charles Knight that I'd met only weeks before.

I saw him again, on his knees, both physically and mentally, his two selves warring one with the other in the abandoned stables. Victor Cails looking on. I wondered about his recollection of events, knowing how trauma could alter the mind.

Knight sounded almost bored, leaned in toward the portrait, as though to examine it more closely. "In case you're in need of a warning, you should be afraid of showing yourself in public."

From the corner of my eye, I observed a clutch of chattering women near the entrance to the gallery. They swayed like a choir until their attention took them elsewhere. The museum attendant in the corner paid no mind, staring into space as though following an imaginary winding road.

I didn't like the threat and wondered whether I'd waited too long to tell Knight the truth. Afraid of what I might learn. "Cails has disappeared," I said finally. Ceased. Vanished. *Murdered* was, once again, the more difficult word.

Knight grinned and then shook his head, marveling, no doubt, at my naivete, the specter of Victor Cails not so easily destroyed. "Cails does that from time to time. Disappears. What of it?"

"This time is different."

"And you would know."

I pressed on. "Have you heard from him? Has he made more demands of you? Made your children disappear?" A pause. "No, I didn't think so."

Knight turned away from the portrait to look directly at me. "Why would I believe you?"

"Believe the evidence in front of you. I am alive." I lowered my voice, although the museum attendant hadn't looked up once. "No more troubles in the East End. The sudden silence. For weeks now. How else can you account for it?"

"If Cails has disappeared, he has his reasons." Those reasons must have given Knight pause. Suddenly his gaze circled the room looking for anything predatory before coming back to rest on me, lips tightening. He slipped a hand around my upper arm. It might have appeared as though he was importuning me to stay. "Your position in the world won't protect you from the likes of him."

"As you would well know. Look what he has done to you." I didn't shake him off, leaning in closer. "Tormenting you and your wife by taking away your children. Simply to remind you of the power he holds over you." I watched him twist with this information, understanding how difficult it was for him to accept. Then let an instant go by, watching his expression, the familiar tightening around the mouth. "You're a free man now, Knight, whether you recognize it or not."

His eyes snapped to mine. "Free? As though such a thing exists. In exchange for what?" Knight was slowly shedding his gentlemanly cast, the lines around his mouth deepening, shoulders hunching like a pugilist. The choice of weapons had changed, and he sensed it. At one point it had been gunpowder and murder and anarchy, according to Cails's script. Now it was photographs, according to mine.

The pressure on my arm eased as Knight pulled me over to the next painting, not caring about attracting attention now. In a gilded frame, Mary Queen of Scots by Clouet pulsed with impending tragedy despite the glaze of youth. Her stare already held too much knowledge, the red of her dress embroidered with pearls set against the dark background, as though anticipating her grisly fate.

Knight jerked me closer and, from a distance, someone could mistake us for lovers.

I spoke first. "I want the photographs." My head almost touched his shoulder, a better angle from which to appraise Scottish Mary. Knight pretended to smile, acknowledging the necessary evolution of our association that had now crusted over like an old wound.

"I'm certain that you do, but I no longer have them."

The red and black of the portrait blurred, the back of my neck tightening, thoughts coming in staccato bursts, none pleasant. "Then who does?"

Knight straightened away from me. "Griffith."

I wrenched my arm free. "Why?"

The gallery was empty and we were alone, and for a moment I wondered if I'd imagined the jam of people on Trafalgar Square, the old man's shuffle in the gallery, the clutch of noisy women. Imagined them like I'd imagined there would be none of Griffith's men waiting for me.

Knight shrugged. "He demanded them. Threatened to raid our offices with several warrants in hand."

"You told Griffith we were meeting here today."

"What you mean to ask is: are the police going to seize you the moment you walk out of this gallery?" He raised his brows. "Who can tell?"

In case he needed the reminder. "I know about your association with Cails and about your past life."

Knight's stare doubled down on me. "You have no proof. Cails's story is worth even less now that the man has disappeared, as you allege. Never forget that Cails gathers information like a wolf tracks scent. I still have access to verifiable facts concerning both the Rivington matter and your father. Even for an infamous gold and railroad speculator, his outsized arrogance is impressive. The *Boston Globe* recently reported that George Buchanan boasted he could hire one-half of the working class to kill the other half. The apple doesn't fall far from the tree."

Pulling himself up to his full height. "There was a time when I'd have been riled by your cool regard, that knowing silence you use like a weapon. But my reality is not threatened by you, Buchanan. I can thank Cails, fate, or my own Faustian nature for having risen from the bowels of this city to become who and what I am today."

"Cails holds you prisoner whether the man is dead or alive."

Knight dipped his head, pretending to consider the portrait more closely. "You really have no idea, despite your pretensions as a mind doctor, an alienist, about anything concerning my life."

I was reminded of the Charles Knight I'd first met in the library at Bedlam, full of false assurance and confidence that somehow presented as a coherent identity. He finished his examination of the painting, pulling back. "You've lost, Miss Buchanan. Forget what you think you know about me. Go back from where you came, to America, before Cails or worse comes back to get you."

CHAPTER 36

Anxiety crawled along the surface of my skin. None of this had turned out the way I'd intended. Knight didn't believe that Cails was gone, and now Griffith had the photographs. For an instant, I considered telling Knight that I'd killed Cails.

Panic was clouding my thinking. It was only a matter of time until Griffith found me. And he would no more believe my tales of Cails and Knight than take me for a pickpocket. It didn't take much to imagine Dr. Phillips, in his bloodied apron, telling Griffith about my presence on the back streets of Drury Lane that night. Then there was Constable Hick's recollection of his knife-wielding assailant. Cails's body recovered and identified in the abandoned stables—

I was the killer now. And Griffith would have more than he ever imagined to take his revenge.

Knight decided the meeting was at an end, striding from the gallery without a backward glance. I wasn't finished. I overtook Knight at the top of a wide case of stairs, leaving the plundered riches of empire behind, the domed atrium where countless stolen treasures rested, Italy's to the left and Spain's to the right. It was my turn to grasp his arm, the muscles hardening under my grip.

"Children, daughters, women." I didn't let go, my voice strengthening, names echoing in the great hall. "Mary Ann Holland, Annie Childs, Ada Stewart, and Elizabeth Wood—are they disposable after they've served a purpose? The morning at the stables when you believed Charlie and Violet lost to you, I saw a man destroyed. A man driven to violence for reasons personal, not political. Have you forgotten?"

Knight's backward glance was dismissive, of me, of the murdered women, and of the man he'd been that morning. He shook me off. "I've no use for sentimentality."

"Did you ever believe in the ideological fantasies Cails conjured? Or was the promise of a new life enough? Dead women a fair exchange for keeping your place in the world?"

A pitying smile, as though I didn't know what I was talking about. Then he made a grand gesture, arm sweeping to capture the great hall. "Hundreds of thousand perish in wars of plunder for the aristocracy and it is a footnote in history. Several prostitutes and actresses die in lurid circumstances and we, by the power of the presses, have a tragedy of epic proportion. The attention of politicians and the police. A first in history, Cails would say." He stopped. "He is and always has been a man of conviction, however twisted his actions appear to you now, Buchanan."

A man of conviction. But Knight no longer needed to act on those convictions. I might have lost the photographs, but I wouldn't lose this. "No one ever needs to learn the workings behind the East End killings." The words raw, not what I had planned at all. "Cails is gone. The killer with him."

"You think so?" The flatness in his eyes remained unchanged.

"Is the killer like you, in thrall to a false religion and to a powerful man who has given him an identity far superior to the one he was born with?"

"That's what you think I am?" His derision hinted at something more, something I'd missed even though it had been there all the time.

"If you have another explanation, I'm willing to hear it."

"No, you're not, Buchanan." The crowd was a tide, ebbing and flowing around us. "In your arrogance, you think you have it all sorted out and now all you're waiting for is a revelation, an admission." He stepped closer, bent his head. "Better yet," he leaned down close to my ear, "a confession."

I lifted my head slightly and said just as softly, "I would like assurances that the killings have stopped."

His breath was warm on my skin. "You think I'm the Shoreditch Savage."

Holding perfectly still, I dared myself to look into his eyes in the hope of seeing what I wanted to see. Awareness. Contrition. Regret. I held his gaze. "Cails is gone. You don't have to be the killer. And you don't have to direct the man who is."

It was unclear that he'd heard me. He pulled back, smoothing his sleeves, patting the buttons on his jacket. "You understand nothing."

The doors of the gallery were wide open to the waning daylight and to Trafalgar Square which radiated in every direction like a sundial. Red trolley cars ran like a crimson seam amid the throngs, jostling with carriages, hansoms, people on foot. Late afternoon in London.

I should go. He was right. Because we were both killers, Knight and I, and we'd journeyed from Charles I to a bronzed Horatio Nelson in the near distance with neither of us the victor. The Admiral at least had his triumph and now stared proudly into the distance amidst the pigeons and the clouds.

While I had nothing.

My eyes slipped over the square to the elongated steps of the entranceway. Crowds were dissolving, hats and capes merging with the dusk. Moving against the flow a statuesque figure, somehow remote from the throng. The redingote and movements were immediately familiar. She stared up at me with inquiring eyes from the wide sweep of the bottom stair.

Constance Knight.

CHAPTER 37

"Constance."

I called out twice before her husband pulled me back under the portico and away from the stairs. Museum attendants were beginning to shepherd people toward the exits, the big clock in the center hall clanging five o'clock. Constance startled, then threw one last look over her shoulder before melting into the crowd and away from us.

"Leave her be." Knight going against the current, moving towards the back of the atrium, taking me with him.

An umbrella jabbing my leg, people jostling for the doors. "Why leave her be? What is she doing here?"

"I've no idea." His gaze slid from the stairs towards the exits.

"You planned on meeting her here."

"No, I did not."

He turned toward a niche at the end of the great hall, motioning me to follow. He was running away, I thought. He wanted to hide. The floor seemed to tilt, as though we were unsteady on our feet, a long line of dead Greek and Roman statuary, a blur of white marble in our wake. Ghosts from another era, color stripped from their noble brows and patrician lips, peered down at us through bleached and vacant eyes. A snake writhed over the shoulder of a Medusa, a laurel wreath cut into the stern forehead of a senator like a crown of thorns. We finally stopped in an alcove. Alone and far enough away from Constance Knight for her husband's peace of mind.

"Why would your wife not acknowledge our presence? Turn away from us?" I had nothing left to lose. "Does she know about your association with Cails?" Of course she didn't. Constance Knight was the part of his existence that was calm and measured, a carefully constructed lie.

He released his breath slowly. "I'm done with this, Buchanan, and with your questions. You come to me thinking that you've the upper hand with wild speculation of Cails's disappearance, with unsound and unsubstantiated accusations that no one would ever believe, the police or the press...." His glare was granite. "And don't for a moment think you can go to my wife with your lies. Look," he moved in closer, his shoulders blocking my view, "I don't know how much clearer I can make this for you, but I will try. I am the least of your problems, nor am I your solution. Griffith is the greater threat. He has the photographs, along with an unhealthy thirst for vengeance when it comes to the daughter of the man who plundered his family's estate. That gives you two choices—either disappear from England or present yourself at Commercial Street in exchange for the damning evidence that you're so desperate to get back.

"I can't."

"For God's sake, in the greater scheme of things you could simply leave things be."

"The greater scheme of things leaves a lot of damage in its wake."

"The damage could get worse still."

From the alcove Knight looked over at the bust of Medusa where a few feet away three men had suddenly appeared in identical blue woolen overcoats with silver buttons. Close-shaven, cropped hair, narrow-eyed. My mouth dried. Detectives.

I was not sure why I held back a few moments before saying under my breath, "You told Griffith about our meeting. In addition to giving him the photographs." It felt good to say it. Yet the accusation didn't make sense, even to me. The men in a tight tangle just beyond Knight hadn't yet organized themselves, tapping each other on the shoulders, sharing terse exchanges.

I had to leave. They hadn't yet seen me in the alcove. I considered my options. The passageway to the left was already cut off, the museum attendants fussing with locks, doors slamming shut. My eyes scanned the atrium's periphery for a back door to one of the secondary passageways. Nothing.

I closed my eyes, pushed my confusion aside. It didn't matter if they were after me to bring in Tarski. It didn't matter if they were after me for the stabbing of one of their own. It didn't matter if Griffith had the Rivington photographs. It mattered that I get away. And, my eyes snapped open, the only way around them was through them.

Taking several steps backward, I expected Knight to shout out my name, give up the game, but he didn't. One of the detectives turned and with my head in profile, I barged into the remaining two men, elbows jostling. The broader of the two rammed the pedestal of the Medusa. She rocked for moment before listing and exploding across the floor. A sickening moment of silence flooded the dome.

I picked up my pace, averting my eyes. Behind me the world was coming to an end, shouts of horror, rumblings of panic, then whistles blaring as I shoved through the surging crowd, skipping down the marble steps, striding deliberately toward the main entrance, only once glancing over my shoulder. Like a force of nature, the shattered Medusa drew the crowds toward her except for one man. Pushing aggressively away from the swarm, surveying the gallery's perimeter, he was moments from spotting me. There would be others like him closing the net in Trafalgar Square.

The main entranceway was not the best idea. The clock chimed again. Half-past five, the gallery was closing but there were alternative exits, leading to Orange Street or Charing Cross where I could get lost in the crowds. A sharp left gave way to a long corridor, the backbone of the building from which smaller galleries flowed like arteries. All locked. A smaller door at the end, not of richly embossed wood. The knob rattled under my hand swinging open into a work area, deserted except for the aroma of paint and plaster and the detritus left by chisels and hammers. I raced around the counters strewn with gilded frames and pin-sized nails, skirts snagged by a row of low foot stools toward another small door. The National Gallery was built like a set of nesting dolls, it turned out, as I flew out of a small exit into another empty corridor. No closer to the street but mercifully alone.

I tried to picture the building, deciding whether to run to the end, make a right, or a left to a door leading outside. I decided first to go left then right, because my first impulse was usually wrong.

A door appeared although I couldn't remember from which direction I came. And unbelievably, a lock on the inside, one which, with shaking hands, I could slide open before launching myself outside.

CHAPTER 38

Drizzle and a glistening stone pathway wound around the side and back of the building. Rounding the corner, I stopped. In front of me, a curved drive through dense shrubs, probably spreading toward the periphery of the museum building. I imagined the detectives had all been alerted, fanning out like a contagion, heading outside using every public exit. There was no choice but to veer around the next rambling wing of the building, the windows dark, past flower beds and bushes and into the safety of the thick hedges.

The branches made a dense labyrinth, like fighting through a tightly plaited net, forcing me to bend the slippery boughs with my hands and shoulders. Stiffer branches whiplashed with my passing, scattering rainwater and leaves. I checked behind me, bent low, and where I imagined torch beams would soon be sweeping along the twisted thickets, coming in my direction.

The National Gallery faced east and I was heading west although at that point, any major corridor would have done, anything that could get me out of the maze and back to Clerkenwell. Then again, in case they'd somehow followed me, the last thing I wanted was to have Griffith's men chase me back to Alice James.

Daylight was draining, the forest of shrubs a dense, dripping green in the haze of a determined drizzle. If I didn't move soon, I realized, I wouldn't be able to manage nearly as well in the dark. Leaves and rain braided into my hair, the wind gusting in time with my pulse. I pushed forward more with my hands than with my eyes until I felt a cold coarseness rasping my palms.

A bloody tower of bricks at least a dozen feet high. Impenetrable and probably enclosing the entirety of the museum grounds. I swore under my breath. There was no choice but to turn back, before dark. The police would be gone by now, I told myself, ignoring the weakness in my legs, the pinch of my boots. Or perhaps they were searching the far corners of Trafalgar Square. Congregating under the lampposts on St Martin's Street. Shouldering their way through Charing Cross.

I tried to retrace my steps, pressing through the thick branches more with anger than any strength, conjuring in my mind's eye the entrance to the museum. Praying to a deity that I didn't believe in that the gates had yet to be locked for the night.

And then something told me that I was no longer alone.

I looked up into a haze of rain. The clouds were sailing faster now, tree branches thrashing. And then straight in front of me. Making no noise, perfectly still, a figure appeared as if he'd grown out of the shadows. Behind him, a glint of silver buttons as another man streaked from behind the shrubbery, and then another beside him. To the rear a mound of greenery laid waste, revealing their path. They moved toward me.

"Let me pass." I stepped back, retreating. "Don't come any closer."

But they did, my voice melting away in the rain.

CHAPTER 39

In his most recent manuscript, William had written much about the nature of reality and perception. Did perception create reality and, if so, how much could we trust our senses to formulate a version of the truth?

What I recalled, when I at last could, was the sky descending, the pungency of wet leaves and old wool, my arms pulled back to the point of searing pain then, impossibly, angry screams that couldn't have been my own. Clusters of clouds dropped, my eyelids battering open to absorb blackness, my body imprisoned in what felt like a funereal winding sheet. Struggling, I tried to sit up, stretching out my legs, but the enclosure held me tightly as a womb.

The nature of dreams, I told my patients, was that they always ended. We eventually woke up with torrents of relief, the rational mind flushing away the remaining dregs of unrealized fears in the birth of a new day. From death to life. I concentrated on my senses to bring me back to the living. Arms reaching out, groping for whatever around me was hard or soft, gritty or smooth. My ears ached with the effort of tracing sounds, a drumbeat that could have been the rhythm of my heart.

I didn't know how much time had passed when I first felt a prick in my arm, a blast of heat travelling over my skin. Then fresh images gusted through my head. Cails, alive and whole, his narrow face licked by flames. Sophie's eyes rolled into the back of her head, plucking out a wandering tune on the piano in my rooms on Mount Vernon Street. The Saracen Head, dark and smoky, rising up in a warped mirror. A man pushing a woman away from him almost gently before inserting a knife under her left eye and then arcing it under her nose, cutting it from her face. Charlie and Violet asleep in their tower, a widow's-walk crèche. Sentinels Constance Knight and Victoria Trevyn standing guard.

Then I heard Griffith, as if he were suddenly beside me. His voice rising and falling in streams of words I didn't understand. Photographs swam before my eyes, purplish and grey liquification. Aaron Tarski, slumping onto a bench, hands resting in his lap, water dripping from an overhead pipe. Griffith shouting over both of us, words that drowned before they could convey meaning, before he slammed a door behind him. A key grinding in a lock.

I reached out, running my hands across the smooth surface of sheets, feeling where I began and the fabric disappeared. Tracing my fingers along the texture like a blind woman, I fumbled through my own clothing that was alien to me, the rough wool not the fine silks I was accustomed to. My eyes were propped open but there were no trees or sky visible. A jolt then a prick in my arm.

This time I walked a long corridor. William came to me as he always did with long strides and his open, wanting face, staring down at me, questioning. What would he think if he knew me for the killer that I'd become? A killer, not a healer. A betrayer, not a lover. Letters scattered on a burst of wind, blue ink smearing into the yellow vellum.

Linking her arm in mine, Maggie Fisher moved into view, swampy breath, grinning, pulling a swallow of gin from a bottle.

The nature of delirium. Vivid, substantial, a painful journey to the parts of us best left alone. Maggie was leading now, prodding me along, bottle dangling in her left hand, until we reached a brick wall that she pushed against with the carelessness of a child. It yielded as though by magic and I was alone with Alice James in her bedroom in Clerkenwell. At her window—a field of waist-high grasses—where she sat weeping silently, her thin shoulders shaking. The still body of Constance Knight lay at her feet.

"I think she's dead." They were talking about me. Not Constance. Not Sophie Rivington.

"Can you hear me?" A hand on my shoulder.

My mouth opened to speak but nothing came out. I might have been lying on my side, but it was impossible to be sure. Impossible to know if I was looking at a crooked man wearing the white uniform of a hospital caretaker. Something tugged at my memory. At his side, a blurred figure, the voice raspy and female.

"I don't think she needs anymore," the caretaker said.

"She needs just enough."

"She's struggling against it."

"Some do. None prevail. We'll try again. Something different this time." The now familiar burn in my arm.

Death be not proud. Who had written those words? Death be not proud. The stanza cycled through my brain lulling me into the space between awareness and extinction.

※❦✦❦※

A strip of light, dazzling. My eyes opened and my mouth felt scorched. I tried to make sense of my surroundings. Thirst on my lips, light leaking from what appeared to be the bottom of a door. The dimensions of a room coming into focus. A pitcher of water sat in a corner as distant as a star.

I breathed, began counting the breaths, sucking on air laced with carbolic acid and lye soap. I was calm as an infant in its crib, as an infant dosed regularly and carefully with laudanum. My mind began to churn. Laudanum, *not strong enough.* Chloral hydrate, then, useful in treating everything from insomnia to anxiety and melancholia. More likely apomorphine to still mania or better still, potassium bromide.

The bitter after-taste was familiar although even the burning at the back of my throat seemed to belong to another person. I gradually became aware that my hands were clenched, fingers numb, as if the bones had been broken, refusing to loosen their grip.

This much I could tell. I lay on a cot, closed in by four walls, a door with a small, grilled window and nothing else. I took this in with the dispassion of a narcotized infant. A moaning in the background began and then stopped. All of it familiar. And then I knew.

I was alive. I was drugged. And I was being held against my will in a lunatic asylum.

CHAPTER 40

The stooped caretaker bundled me down an unending corridor like a convalescent, weak and shivering in my maid's rags. With no window in my cell to keep track of daylight, I had no way of knowing exactly how many days I'd already spent confined. An hour earlier, Pond had allowed for a rudimentary attempt at washing via a stained basin in the corner of the room. The effort had done nothing to chip away at the sediment of dirt and sweat clinging to me other than to reveal a layer of strange calm.

The trickle of what must have been a type of barbiturate still travelled through my veins, entirely too seductive. A slow and easy pull that could lead to an even easier acceptance of whatever fate Griffith had in mind. The desire to close my eyes and drift along was strong, to follow the inflamed map against my lids, the vessels charged and throbbing.

Pond was my keeper, the only human they'd allowed me to see, emptying my chamber pot, leaving trays of grey food on the floor by the cot. He said little as we dragged along, wiping at his eyes with a soiled handkerchief, while I struggled to right myself and pull away from his impartial grip. The corridor was a familiar one, stippled with iron-latched doors on either side behind which ulcerated minds festered. Waiting for the poultice of a cure or perhaps not waiting at all. I of all people knew that often what the unsound mind had to offer, its dreams and visions, was better than reality.

Unending hallways. *Bedlam was constructed with an Italianate design in mind, itself a kind of madness.*

Stumbling, I caught Pond's bony arm and imagined a flicker of recognition. Images flashed, his bustling with the keys that first night on my visit to Bethlem, the surprise at my offer of coins.

Another woman soon will die;

Unless Georgia Buchanan arrives in time.

"The patients. In the women's wing. Any unusual disturbances this past night?"

"Depends what you're meaning."

"Anything serious." Anything fatal, is what I really want to ask.

"Worst was a fit. A choking fit. Though she's one that's prone to them."

How could I have forgotten the shabby library, still empty save for the same row of books, spines cracked and worn, exposed by the weak light filtering through the grimed window. Mocking me and my professed vocation.

And where Griffith now stood, the small head with its mutton chops, hands clasped behind his back. His face dark and clenched.

Pond pulled out a chair, pushed me down. I struggled to sit upright.

"Welcome *back* to Bethlem Royal Hospital, Buchanan." Griffith moved in closer, his girth blocking my view.

I wondered which was worse, the Griffith that lived inside my head or the one outside it. "One thousand pounds," I thought I heard myself say.

Griffith crossed his arms over his chest.

"Two thousand." I was swimming up from a bottomless sea, straining toward the surface. My vision swam and I saw a blurred image of Griffith shaking his head back and forth, smile broadening to a grimace.

"You insult me," he said almost mildly before turning to Pond. "Leave us. I'll call for you to return the patient to her room when we're finished." I heard the caretaker shuffle from the library, the door closing behind him.

There were marbles in my mouth where words should have been. "I'm a patient now?"

"Look at you—tattered rags, mumbling nonsense, found wandering like a lunatic in the bushes outside the National Gallery." Griffith beamed as though each word gave him a precise joy.

"You think to bribe me, Buchanan?"

I inched my heavy head higher. "Think of the money." My lips were dry and cracked, hurting when I spoke.

Griffith barked a laugh. "The money you're offering means nothing to me and everything to you. What a change in circumstances, eh? You've discovered that unlimited resources can't solve all the problems of your own making."

In the distance the trill of a soprano practicing scales. My imagination or was the voice real? I remembered that I hated opera, the silly librettos and the quavering voices, and that my father had once underwritten a production of *The Magic Flute* in New York.

Griffith continued to speak, his voice coming from the bottom of a well. "The sins of the father, Buchanan."

The sins of *my* father. My father had made me a free woman, if that counted as a sin. Griffith's outline swam before my eyes while I tried to order the sounds coming out of his mouth. Something about his family, from Sussex, a family fallen on hard times, the phrasing genteel. *Hard times.* Griffith would not speak of indebtedness, the possibility that my father might have purchased his family's obligations. My mind wandered, taking a circuitous route, while my instincts picked up the venom in the room. "You hate me." I held myself up in the chair.

"I do, Buchanan," he said simply, "and I know hurting you will hurt your father." His statement meant to be a knife against my throat. "No one will inquire about your whereabouts for at least several months.

You've been known to disappear without much notice, then reappear in Vienna, Paris, or New York without explanation."

Griffith paused, leaning his bulk against the table, considering me. "I don't have to explain to you of all people the beneficial effects of confinement in an asylum. *Asylum as a therapeutic tool.* Those could be your words, couldn't they?" He furrowed his brow, theatrical in his concern. "Particularly if it concerns the safety of the patient. We know what happened to Sophie Rivington because you denied her the asylum as a therapeutic tool, don't we?"

My throat closed.

"*You* might benefit from such therapies, Buchanan. We wouldn't wish to see anything untoward happen to you, after all. Although it wouldn't be much of a surprise. You have been behaving erratically. Wandering about the East End at all hours."

He continued but I didn't hear, the undertow pulling me deeper again. All I knew was that he could keep me at Bedlam, drugged, forever.

He smoothed his mustache. "A familiar story. Women can become overly excited by too much education, making them incapable of reasoning, given the surplus of emotion. Allowing no room for patience, reliability or good judgment." He looked at me. "Most of your fellow mind doctors would have to agree your present collapsed state gives credence to this hypothesis."

Griffith lowered his gaze, to the water glass in my hand. I took another sip as though the drink could sharpen the dullness of my mind. Who had told Griffith about my meeting with Knight at the National Gallery? My thoughts ran like paint in the rain.

"You're calmer now. That's good."

Slowly, I nodded, finding myself in agreement, the undertow dragging me deeper.

"Thinking more clearly about what happens next. Which is entirely up to you." Griffith pulled something from inside his jacket, placing it face up on the desk in front of me.

A photograph. I knew it was Sophie Rivington, felt it like a penitent long separated from the source of her original sin.

"Would you like to keep it? Place it under your pillow?"

My mind went blank.

"You can remain here at the asylum for several more weeks, or months if that's what's required, with the accompanying *therapeutics* that ensure you remain calm and serene as nature intended. Or," Griffith raised a hand signet ring glinting, "you will conjure Aaron Tarski from wherever he's hiding or, more accurately, from wherever you're hiding him. And if you're cooperative, if you moderate your behavior, if you dispense with this willfulness, you will be weaned from your reliance on said therapeutics, in due time. And I shall decide the timing, in case you were wondering."

"He's not the killer." The words forming slowly.

He looked at me like I was the raving lunatic he was expecting. "I had the killer in my grasp, only to lose him. Because of you. We had to release him because of an unexpected alibi produced by one of his cohorts—who then disappeared into thin air. *Because of you.*"

I tried not to rock in the chair, focusing on Griffith's lips beneath the moustache, the row of snaggle teeth, sentences coming in an ugly torrent.

"Tarski is the answer to a swelling sentiment of anti-Jewry in the East End, although I have no time to dig for its source, nor the interest, knowing that to have a scapegoat, the right scapegoat in hand, would defuse the mounting social tension among the poor. And save the remnants of my reputation within the police and Whitehall. The Home Office is apoplectic. It is said even Her Royal Highness has made it clear to the Prime Minister that she wishes to see progress on the issue. All the while the streets teem with insurrection and the papers seethe with indignation."

Griffith pointed a finger at my face. "The entirety of the civilized world is concerned in bringing this man to justice. And we are no further ahead, Buchanan. What have you to say?"

I had everything to say and nothing at all.

He held up the photograph of Sophie Rivington before placing it back into the pocket of his jacket. "Don't test me further. Unfortunate accidents happen with alarming regularity in asylums. As though anyone would be surprised if you were to come to some unfortunate end, what with all your ill-advised adventures into the miseries of the diseased mind. Don't let it come to that, Buchanan." A single fly danced around his head, mesmerizing in a way, gleaming dots along his face and skin.

"Buchanan—do you understand me?"

The room flickered, the two chairs, the desk with its glass half-filled with water, the eerie serenity. Griffith edged toward the door. "It is inexplicable to me, why you would sacrifice everything for a man not worth the ground on which we stand. There is so much more at stake here than the sorry life of a foreigner."

There was much more at stake, I thought, and that was Griffith longing to see me scorched.

Griffith opened the door where Pond stood silently, head down, metal basin in one hand, tourniquet and syringe in the other.

CHAPTER 41

Medicaments—of all the things to be afraid of.
Of all the things that could destroy me. Where once tinctures and powders had served as solace to the soul, they were now instruments to be craved and feared.

The boundary between wakefulness and sleep had thinned, exhaustion piercing through the margins, one hemorrhaging into the other. The symptoms of withdrawal were textbook, familiar. The heightened states, the inflammation of the brain, bone-deep shivers that seeped to the surface of the skin like a chemical burn. Symptoms I'd witnessed in patients but never experienced myself. I had always been careful. A brief but plush encounter with morphine and a colleague in San Francisco two years earlier served as a steadfast reminder.

Charcot warned that opiates only served to magnify what was already in the mind. Cold, you would become colder. Mad, madder still.

Days and nights coalesced. Although my thoughts, disjointed and fragmented, were ready to float off into the distance. The perennial dark of my room suited my mood, I decided, perhaps the reason I'd come to London in the first place, with its perpetual canopy of low-slung skies nailed down overhead. We'd all fled to the old world, I thought, just as Alice James's image flickered suddenly in my mind's eye, wan and pallid as ever. She curled on a brocade settee in her parents' house in Boston, prepared at any moment to pull back in her shell.

My mind drifted, unmoored. At some point, it occurred to me that I'd ended up as so many of my patients had. As Alice had. Defiant and broken at the same time, tethered to an unreality that could be both liberating and imprisoning, frightening and reassuring. Alice. I floated to one of the private rooms at the sanatorium where she had been receiving hydrotherapy treatments just one year earlier. Alice wrapped in a winding sheet as though prepared for some ancient burial practice, lying on a large bed that took up most of a small box of a room, a septic stink in the air.

Her eyes half-closed, she angled her head on the pillow toward me. "And these doctors tell you that you will either die or recover. It all began when I was nineteen and I'm neither dead nor recovered."

I stood at the foot of the bed, grasping the iron rails, grasping for something I could do for her. "We can try another cure, find another way—that's why I'm here, Alice."

My head struggled with the details, straining to hold onto the images. Alice, the beneficiary of continuous bath treatments that could last from several hours to several days, oftentimes even overnight. The fantastical Bosch-like scenes. Patients immersed in specialized tubs, wrapped in packs of sheets dipped in varying temperatures.

Anxiety, agitation, neurasthenia. My tongue stumbled over the syllables. Alice James's symptoms.

Her voice echoed in my head. "And what do you suggest, Georgia?" she asked with a familiar hopelessness.

"What we'd been doing before, your coming to see me several times a week."

"I don't see how talk solves anything."

"We were making progress." Alice and I meeting regularly in Boston and then in New York. Alice was exhausted. Alice was restless. Alice only wished to sleep. She rallied and then suffered mysterious pains and fainting spells. I encouraged her to study, an outlet for her intelligence and spasmodic energy. We spoke of things, of Alice's fear that her body rebelled, betrayed her. Her thoughts of suicide.

And now I remembered her eyes like pin-holes in the white of her face, the only part of her body not swaddled in linen. A stubby oil lamp had burned on the nightstand next to a few books and a smaller diary. "I hope that the doctors here are encouraging you to continue with your writing," I said. "Expressing yourself on paper is cathartic and proof these episodes are transitory in nature. You will feel better again—because you have recovered in the past."

"They haven't taken my notebook away if that's what you mean. Not yet." Her chin trembling, eyes darting in the corner. "In the drawer, over there, something I'd like you to see." Following her gaze, to the small window over the bed and then to the white-washed table with its burning stump. "In a large envelope."

The drawer. It pulsed in my mind's eye, radiating a strange warmth. Then I'd looked down at my own hands as if they hadn't belonged to me, hovering before breaking into a vault which might be better left sealed. The shadows in the room were thickening as I'd pulled open the drawer and extracted a vellum folder held together with black string. The skin of my hands had prickled as if the paper had its own kind of conductivity. Alice had gone still, not looking at me, head turned to the wall.

William had asked me, trusted me, to treat his sister.

My head ached, suddenly heavy with dread. I thought of us together in his study in Boston, he in his cracked leather chair, with me on an upholstered foot stool playing the acolyte for as long as it amused me. *Guilt. Why do we bring such suffering and torment on ourselves?*

He hadn't answered right away but leaned over to take a book from the shelf, so close that his arm had brushed against my shoulder. *We have a need for punishment, when we judge ourselves guilty of some real or imagined crime. The punishment we seek may take on one of two forms; we either consciously suffer in having to bear guilt, or our feelings manifest in hysterical or other neurotic symptoms.*

How cool had been his words, complete in thought and degree, compared to the heat of his hand at the small of my back, later.

And so I drifted. How much of these wanderings, my fevered recollections, were accurate or the result of my own delirium at the hands of Griffith—I'd never know.

***

Pond scratched at the door out of some perverse sense of courtesy. The lock grated open while I looked for the watch pinned to my blouse when I remembered I no longer had one. Patients, I also recalled, were stripped of personal effects for fear they could be used for self-harm.

Every day the same pattern, cursory morning ablutions wherein a washbasin with grey soapy water appeared, then the charade of food a few hours later. A notebook was permitted and one dully sharpened pencil to occupy myself in the intervening hours, to make a record of my symptoms, my self-recriminations. Wasn't that what I'd recommended to my own patients?

Then every evening Pond approached with the invisibility of a well-trained butler, the tourniquet and syringe offered on a wooden tray. To tempt, to wean, to *punish*, above all, with just the right dosage, to remind me of my choices that weren't choices at all. Some days I was sharp with need while other moments a dull euphoria rushed over me in breaking waves.

I could not give up Tarski because I didn't know where he was, where Cails and Knight had hidden him. Did Maggie Fisher know his whereabouts? How could I possibly find her even if I found my way out of Bedlam? And I couldn't let myself think about Sophie

Rivington. Thoughts and doubts surged past me. The longing for a dose of Dover's powder was strong. What I would give for that rush of clarity, the ability to think clearly, to plan, to find a way out.

On the tenth day I settled on the caretaker, my only link to Griffith and the outside world.

I'd questioned him over the previous days, looking for anything that I could use, but the process had produced almost no information except for a show of meek surprise at my interest. Widowed, remarried with small children living somewhere in Shoreditch was what I had come away with. Enough reason for him to need extra coin. Although not enough that he would risk his position at Bethlem by allowing a patient—one important to the police—to walk out its doors.

In solitary confinement, one day bled into another until the days mattered not at all. Simply the scalpel-sharp pain of withdrawal and addiction purposefully applied. What was ironically named the gallery, one on either side of the asylum designed to allow patients a modicum of freedom, was *terra incognita* for the likes of me. Griffith clearly wished to keep my presence undetected so when I reappeared—if I ever did—he and I would be the only ones to know of my imprisonment. Or for the reasons behind it. My name would never have been entered into the log book kept at the registrar's station, set on what looked like an altar by the asylum's grand front doors rather than an entrance to a labyrinth for the insane.

Pond said something about the rain, his stoop even more pronounced today, then mumbled that it was the nineteenth of October. He had yet to indicate that he remembered our first meeting only six weeks previously, the fiery night I was first summoned here. Willful self-preservation on his part and I couldn't blame him. There were two kinds of caretakers for the insane. Those who did the work for food and shelter and those who craved the power over the sick and the helpless. It was difficult to say into which category Pond fell.

"May I expect another visit with Griffith soon?" I sat on the edge of the bed.

He was already backing out of the cell, towards the door. "I've no idea."

"I've yet to see a doctor."

"Entirely out of my hands, ma'am." He pretended not to know my true name.

"Tell me, Pond, then. Am I making progress? Refusing to beg for whatever you have on offer, there on your tray?" The syringe and tourniquet sat innocently by the door that Pond, diligently, fretting with the keys, kept locked at all times. The caretaker appeared vaguely alarmed at my question, not sure what to make of my tone which, in his mind at least, wandered the borders of madness and sanity.

"Not in any position to say, ma'am." Then a chastised silence. "You shouldn't cross him."

"Griffith?" I rose from the bed. "My behaviors are increasingly familiar and reliable. You're not a doctor but certainly the Assistant Commissioner is relying on your reports, Mr. Pond."

"I've not been asked to make any reports, ma'am."

"Does Griffith request an accounting from the pharmacy, inspect the used vials," I gestured toward the tray and the door, "that you bring in and out of this room every evening?"

"I can't say."

"You mean you won't say." I allowed an edge of anger in my voice.

"Your safety is my responsibility. Nothing more." Picking up the tray with the tourniquet and syringe, he turned to me again as though he'd forgotten to ask an important question. And he had. I shook my head, pulling down the stained sleeves of my blouse over my wrists. He stared at me, oddly, then reached with aged, freckled hands under the metal pan on the tray from which he produced a heavy book. A bible.

He placed it on the bed with a strange formality.

I croaked a laugh. "No need, thank you. Wouldn't you say my redemption is too late in any case?"

"You may find it of use."

I let the words settle, watching him smooth the coarse bed sheet, refold the scratchy blanket and then collect up his tray. The bible waited like an unasked-for offering while Pond fussed some more and then lumbered from the room, the key grating decisively in the lock. A sound I'd come to expect.

It was the King James bible, leather with gold detail on the cover. My childhood governesses had insisted on morning and evening prayers and studies devoted to the scriptures most school days. My father had never mentioned God unless it had been to take his name in vain, and my late mother had been Catholic, presumably. In any case, I had little recall of heavenly specifics save whenever I visited the cool recesses of churches in Italy, confronted with frescoes leaping from shadowed walls.

I thought longingly of a past summer in a small church in Sienna. I'd been surprised with Giotto's depiction of *The Kiss of Judas*, the dramatic, face-to-face confrontation between savior and traitor. The treacherous yellow cloak of the betrayer, the nocturnal lighting, the raised weaponry. And Christ's face perfectly at ease. Judas's swollen with corruption.

I sat down on the bed. The bible was heavy in my hands, the pages stained and worn. A gift from Griffith? I tried to focus, reminding myself I couldn't fight the chemistry running in rivers through my veins. At some point, the dosing would have to stop. I would then be asked to conjure Tarski, meet with the judiciary and send the Jew to the gallows. If, I thought with a sudden burst of clarity, Griffith hadn't determined in the interim that I was responsible for Cails's death and the assault on one of his men. Then I'd be the one going to the gallows.

My mouth tasted sour from the brew of drugs slowly leaching from my system. I kept my hands steady, dread keeping my mind clearer and more focused with every minute that went by. The book was heavy in my lap, burdened with parables of guilt, verses of brimstone, and the impossibilities of redemption.

The embossed cover jumped under my palms. No list of family names in the first pages, the publisher George Virtue, London 1857, prominently displayed. At one time the paper's edges had been smooth gilt but now they were rough, worn, and uneven. My fingertips played with the edges where a page seemed to have come partially loose from the seam. A short tug released a narrow piece of vellum, block letters gleamingly familiar.

To take revenge halfheartedly is to court disaster; either condemn or crown your hatred.

October 21, Bletcher Court.

Not the words of the Prophet. My finger-tips traced the letters suspended like dark, avenging ghosts before my eyes. Ghosts I'd seen before. Raising my head, I saw the room spin slowly, the cot, the wash basin, the walls unmoored.

A rush of bile blocked my throat. Another summons. Cails alive?

I closed my eyes to control the room's shifting dimensions. When I opened them again, the summons still lay on my lap. My lips moved, reading the words again, hands repetitively smoothing the thick paper flat against the bible. October 21, two days away.

Suddenly I craved whatever narcotics could wipe my mind clean.

CHAPTER 42

Footsteps in the hall, the whine of the metal door opening. I pretended to be asleep. A woman this time, not Pond, small in stature with curly red hair. She stared at me as though willing to wake the dead. Then her gaze darted around the room before she vanished back into the corridor.

Time bent and twisted and I along with it. Images of alleyways and corpses burst through my mind. Feigning illness was not difficult. There were only two things I was certain of—the 21st of October and Bletcher Court.

I dreamed of Cails, alive, standing by my bed, stethoscope dangling from his fingertips. He watched me with the precision of a scientist, eyes narrowed, Pond a shadow behind him. Then he moved through the room like a specter, touching the few items that belonged to me, thumbing through the pages of my notebook, picking up and then putting down the bible at the bottom of the bed. I wasn't sure which was worse—that I had killed Cails or that I hadn't.

Pond returned to find me sitting up, eyes glittering with fever. My face burned with sudden warmth, the pent-up desire to be rid of

Bethlem and the caretaker's unceasing focus. To find myself back in London's East End. To answer the summons placed in the bible. To solve the killings.

I complained of chills, massaged my temples, communicated my inability to sleep. Pond shuffled then paused at the door, letting out a long, ragged breath.

The next day stretched to the breaking point. I pretended to be too weak to wash, refused the filmy soup at lunchtime with a turn of my head to the wall. Then I collapsed in a heap on the bed, asking through burning lips for a tincture to help me sleep. Griffith needed me alive and well for the time being, at least. By evening, Pond appeared with the familiar tray in hand, the tourniquet and syringe and a disquieting look on his face.

Seated unsteadily on the side of the bed, I rolled up my sleeves to the elbow, ignoring the yellowing bruises scoring my skin. Pond applied the tourniquet to my arm, pulling the rubber band tightly, stooping awkwardly. He gave off the aroma of an old man and for a moment I hesitated. Holding the syringe aloft, he flicked the glass and I closed my eyes. Then the needle pricked my skin just before I raised my other hand to bring the bible, lost in my tattered skirts, down on the side of Pond's face, close enough to mine that I saw the deep folds of his skin, the lines creasing his nose.

He reacted as though I'd slapped him, dancing back when I grabbed the syringe from his grasp. I plunged it into the side of his neck, dispensing half the contents. A carotid injection site was ideal although how quickly the sedative would work was not something I was willing to consider.

He was stronger than he looked, catching me in the side of the throat before a fading look of surprise finally flashed over his face. Sinking to his knees by the bed as though asking forgiveness, he gave little resistance when I pushed him forward onto the mattress. Stunned by the blow and the sedative, he appeared paralyzed, helpless. I pulled the tourniquet from my arm and bound him, wrists behind his back, and then tore another strip from my ragged cuffs to bind his ankles to the footboard of the bed.

Rolled onto his side, the blanket covering his face, he could easily be mistaken for a slumbering patient. Me.

The room came into view, the mound on the bed, unsettling stains on the sheets, air stale and cloying. I retrieved the bible, pulled out the summons as though it carried an infection and left it prominently displayed at the bottom of the bed.

Where Griffith's men would find it. Just as I wanted them to, a road map that would lead them to the endpoint, the location of the Shoreditch Savage.

The caretaker didn't groan, didn't move, already in the thrall of what was probably the beginnings of a sleep, not too long, but just enough to allow my escape. My fingers scrambled through his pockets to find the keys which I clenched and held high over my head in a state of my own victorious delirium. Another pocket disgorged a handful of silver, probably netted by Pond in the course of his evening rounds.

I inserted first one key and then another until the door opened to one of Bedlam's devilishly long corridors. I pulled the cell door closed behind me and locked it decisively. The entranceway seemed miles away and the likelihood of encountering an orderly or caretaker at this hour was high. There were approximately two dozen keys in my hand, several of which *had to* fit into at least one of the bolts lining the corridor.

Five minutes that felt like fifty until finally one of the keys opened the third door in the corridor.

CHAPTER 43

A woman stood in the center of the room, clutching an empty bundle of rags in her arms. Crooning softly, her face was wreathed in smiles. Looking up at me, she placed a finger to her lips before resuming her low lullaby, hips swaying in time.

There were some things I wished I could forget. The patient who had succumbed to a nervous fever after the birth of her daughter; she'd drowned the infant in her bath. Not long afterwards, she'd hemorrhaged to death from eating rat poison. I retreated on silent feet, closing the door softly behind me.

I continued along the corridor, barred windows marking each cell. No one stopped my progress and if they had, they would only have seen a mad, disheveled, filthy and wide-eyed woman. A Bedlamite. Whom they would try to return to her room.

Several more doors until I found the patient I was looking for, the one who could provide me with the dose of madness I needed. It felt as though she'd been waiting for me, head held high, a moth-eaten shawl around her shoulders. Her wild eyes tilted upwards in a relieved smile.

"Mathilda, you've forgotten your wrap again." Voice soft, when she saw me standing on the threshold. "Here—please have mine as it will be chilly outside." Entering the cell, I took the shawl from her clawed, outstretched hands. "So, cheered to have some company and here you are come to take me to Hyde Park."

I had indeed. Her features were finely drawn, save for the nose eaten away by pox, skin peeled back. Who knew why her family hadn't hidden her away in one of the many private asylums that offered more wholesome surroundings. Financial troubles, or more likely, a husband who needed to hide an uncomfortable truth.

I responded to her aimless chatter, standing at a polite distance, listening to her tell me about her tumultuous day, the gardener bringing Eglantine from the greenhouse, taking dinner with her husband, theatre in Covent Gardens. I knew her reality was being swallowed by the disease that was slowly consuming her flesh. In her future lay a general paralysis, a hungry disease linked to tertiary syphilis, itself still resistant to harrowing arsenic and mercury cures.

The woman smiled vacantly, stopping her chatter, her gaze falling suddenly on a plate of food by her cot, congealed like days' old pudding. Shuddering as though at the outset of a seizure, she began shaking her head slowly at first, back and forth. Then so violently I feared she would injure herself. I moved toward her but she jerked away, snatching the plate from the floor, arms raised, flinging it at me. I twisted and dipped but the grease and shreds of meat landed like a filthy torrent on my blouse and in my hair. She was already out the door but I caught her arm, pulling her alongside with me, encouraging her wails of outrage echoing off the high ceilings.

I didn't let go, marching her toward the front of the building, a writhing, screaming creature whose cries threatened to separate my spine from my body. My thoughts were scatter-shot but I was trained in this, I reminded myself, adrenaline cutting through the opiates in my system.

An attendant in white followed by an orderly, shoes squeaking on the stone floors. Their voices boomed down the corridor toward us. Two more attendants scrambled around a corner until we were surrounded. Gaslight spat overhead throwing the entranceway with its ornate desk, elevated like an altar piece, into sharp relief behind which, I noted, pulse racing, no one was sitting. If there was enough of an uproar, a few moments of confusion, I could possibly find my way out of the asylum.

"He wants to kill me. He wants me dead!" The patient twisted my arm, the bone screaming. I bit down on my tongue. "No one believes me. You must believe me. Don't let him kill me!" Her voice simultaneously pleading and enraged, ragged with tears. A madman—or madwoman, for that matter—could take on amazing strength. I staggered back, watching, as it took two of the attendants to wrap their arms around her torso, unprepared by the wild thrashing of her legs, the scratching of her nails. One of the attendants left in the direction of the dispensary, most likely for a vial of bromide. The other hurried down the corridor to summon more help.

I took stock quickly. Thanks to Griffith's directives, no one paid me any attention. No one knew who I was, secreted away in the asylum with only Pond as my keeper. The main doors of Bedlam would be locked, I suspected, so there was no possibility of escape via the main entranceway. If I didn't move quickly, it was only a matter of time before I would be flung back into my room.

I muttered loudly enough but to no one in particular. Something about returning to the gallery to retrieve the patient's locket, something that might calm her, that I'd noticed her clutching at her waist earlier in the day. I fingered Pond's keys in my fist, the largest one on the ring that I could only hope would open the entranceway doors. I had a few moments before at least one of the attendants returned.

The cool weight of the metal in my hands was heavy as I skirted towards the front doors, knowing that the likelihood of Pond carrying entranceway keys was wildly unlikely. Desperation made fools of us all and my shaking fingers fumbled as I tried key after key. The lock and keyhole were outsized, the hasps made of hammered iron. After three trials, the largest key still hadn't rattled into place. I sagged against the wall and looked up to see two stone gargoyles staring down at me. The figures Melancholy and Raving Madness. Mocking.

Then the echo of footsteps. The entranceway was bracketed by two narrow corridors, one going in either direction. A man the size of a small wardrobe, head bowed, sloped shoulders lumbered toward the front desk. He veered from the desk toward me.

"No place for you here," he said, hand clamping on my upper arm.

The key to working with the unequal balance of power in institutions, I'd found, was to never issue challenges directly. I smiled apologetically. "The patient, the one just taken back to her cell. You must have heard the commotion." My voice shriveled at the memory. "The caretaker had carelessly left my door open and she barged in, threatening me, dragging me with her."

He studied me with eyes that had seen too much. My stained blouse, confused expression, the keys well hidden in my skirts, out of sight. "It was frightening. She was frightening." I dropped a hand to my waist, the other fanning my face. The grip on my arm tightened. "Might I have a drink of water." I put the barest emphasis on the last phrase, as though I might fall over. "I'm not certain I can make it back to my cell."

No response. The orderly was unaccustomed to making decisions. We stood in the hallway as though rooted to the spot. His eyes darted up and down the corridor, quiet again this time of night. I tried again. "I really don't feel well."

He shook his head for a moment, relenting. "Right, then, but only for a minute. Then back we goes."

There was no place to sit, unless it was behind the big desk where, I'd noticed, a low bench ran along the wall. Above the bench, a long, horizontal window. I didn't want to think of the consequences of what I was about to do. Like an experiment, the outcome might not be what I wanted.

Pushing me in front of him, the orderly propelled me up the two stairs to sit behind the ornate desk with its overview of the atrium. Sitting down on the bench, I quickly noted anything I could possibly use. Scissors, heavy paper weight, substantial clock. Nothing— except for a sheaf of papers positioned precisely in the center of the desk blotter.

Slumping further down on the bench, I rested my forehead in my palms. Out of the corner of my eye, I saw a series of doors, lintels low, cowering like the workers who made their way through them, where Pond and his like entered and exited every day. Pond's keys lay heavily in the folds of my skirt.

"Don't be fainting on me now."

"I won't," I lifted my head. "Some water, please."

The orderly knew as well as I did that every door was locked and there was no place for me to run. "Don't you be going anywhere, you hear," he said, a pure formality before lumbering down the hall away from me.

Behind me, the faint chill from the window pane. Twisting around, I seized the casement with both hands, heaving it open. No iron bars were necessary because it was almost impossible to squeeze through the twelve-inch opening. Almost impossible. I stood on the bench, then wedged my way through to the other side.

CHAPTER 44

I crept along the crenellation that wound its way across the front of the asylum. Then twisted around to bring down the casement behind me. The wind was loud in my ears and when I dared to look down, I calculated twenty feet between me and the ground.

The courtyard below flickered in a gleam of moonlight with a few remaining lights aimed at the periphery of the building.

My body felt stiff from disuse, as though every limb were wrapped in bandages. Creeping along a few more feet, my hands clutching at the building's limestone behind me, my eyes remained focused on the courtyard below. Attuned to any and every movement. I had perhaps a three-minute opportunity before the orderly or anyone else appeared in the courtyard.

I eased into a sitting position, wrapping my skirts tightly around me and tying them securely with my ragged shawl. Then I swung my legs out from the crenellation, finding a place to settle my feet. And I began to inch down in a slow slide. As controlled as I could make it. Looking straight ahead, a nose away from the wall, hands a death grip on the stones at waist level. One at a time, I put my feet lower on the wall, found the protruding stones that could give me enough purchase.

When I dared looked down, over my shoulder, I could see the tops of a scraggly shrub, perhaps five feet above the courtyard. Then the sound of footsteps on gravel. I stiffened, willing the shadows to absorb me. Legs and arms shaking, I had barely enough strength to hold my balance. I risked turning slightly to see the flare of a torch. The glow wavered, then vanished. My hands cramped, my vision blurred.

It could be guards. They might already be looking for me. I pressed the full weight of my body against the cool stone, ears straining for the slightest sound. My hands radiant with pain, I closed my eyes. Only the sound of the wind. Maybe I had fallen into a hallucinatory state.

I began to move again. Hands first, flexing. Then I slid down another foot, stepping onto a stone pane before easing myself down to the ground. Like a wild creature, I crawled underneath the shrub, breathing heavily. Counted to ten, knowing that I couldn't stay forever.

The courtyard fronting the asylum was at least two-hundred yards long, more than enough open space for someone to see me. I had to go soon.

I dropped into the night, surging into a run, my lungs opening up, until the backdrop of Bedlam's dome, lit by a glowering sky, was behind me. The massive wrought-iron entranceway of the asylum clawed at the horizon, as firmly shuttered as the gates of hell. The air was cold and layered with soot but after my imprisonment, I drank it in.

The grand gates were, in all probability, never left unlocked but there had to be a service entrance to ease the transport of supplies, somewhere at the side of the graveled yard. My body felt liberated, constraints dropping away. Running quickly now, it didn't take much to imagine the sound of footsteps in the pea stone walkway behind me. Images flickered. In the dark, it was impossible to know what I'd remembered or imagined. My attention was fixed by a shadow, a few steps away from a fluted column, movement that held my attention.

The sway of the fabric, an outline of boots, and the gait that was familiar. Where had it been—the Saracen, behind the bar? A quick glance revealed that I was alone in the courtyard. The mind played tricks. I was caught in the trap of paranoia and lingering effects of whatever Griffith had Pond pump into me.

Deep breaths of cold air bit my lungs, clearing my head with every step I took until the rounded arch of a bricked gate appeared. The latch was fixed. I cursed under my breath. Then I heard the crunch of gravel, ahead of me this time, made by a small milk wagon pulling through open gates further to the west. Hugging the shadows and before the driver took any notice, I pushed alongside in the opposite direction and onto the street.

In a few moments, I was at Lambeth Road. The glare of gaslight slicking the dark lane.

A hackney was not likely to stop for a woman in the middle of the night who looked as though she'd just escaped Bedlam.

I slowed to a walk, smoothing my hair, picking bits of food from my blouse and skirt, folding the moth-eaten shawl closer around my shoulders until I was several blocks distant from the asylum. The road was rutted and muddied from the evening's rain, but clusters of people soon appeared. Listing home from the pub, closing up shop, urging their dray horses back to the stables. It took a few moments until I secured a hackney with some of Pond's silver to take me to Bletcher Court in the East End.

CHAPTER 45

The driver had never heard of Bletcher Court, stopping instead at Dorset Street in one of the narrowest, dirtiest little alleys in the web that was London's East End. The deserted corner was littered with rows of butcher shops, hooks in the windows hanging with marbled carcasses, streaks of yellow fat marking the glass. Dozens of wagons sat ready for the morning, loaded with hides, scraps and slops.

The unnatural glow of naphtha lights lured me to the nearest alleyway in search of my bearings. A series of gabled buildings lined the south side underscored by stalls in various stages of disrepair, most of which sat empty. Signs of life at the end of the row where a grinning man with oiled curly hair held up a shrieking white rat. Several women, taking an instant from canvassing the lane for their next chance at doss money, lingered. The man, with an Italian accent and exaggerated bravado, pulled a square bit of rag from his sleeve to transform the rodent first into an old woman, a monk, and finally, a stiff, pink-nosed corpse. Then the wriggling creature was made to disappear altogether, only to be resurrected in the cap of an amazed boy standing to the side of the onlookers. I threw a coin into the cap as it was passed around. The impresario pretended not to understand when I asked for the location of Bletcher Court.

I tamped down anxiety, the fear that once again I'd be too late.

To take revenge halfheartedly is to court disaster; either condemn or crown your hatred.

Another woman soon will die;

Unless Georgia Buchanan arrives in time.

Every man is guilty of the good he did not do.

A few stalls away stood a woman in a blindingly white headdress and bedraggled skirts, presiding over a wire cage of lovebirds. She cooed to the birds with fake smiles for the benefit of passersby, waiting for the pennies that came in return for the colored paper "fortunes" neatly folded in the little box inside the cage. I told her that I didn't need my fortune told but simply the location of Bletcher Court, depositing a few pence into her hand. She threw back her head as though to think while I pressed more coins into her palm. The fussing of the birds quieted in the background. Finally, pointing behind me, over my head, she gestured in a wide arc to the left of Dorset Street.

The ground was uneven and foul. A greasy slime coated the irregular cobble stones of the narrowing channel leading to what I'd hoped was Bletcher's Court. Men with unkempt hair and pocked complexions emerged from rag shops and beer-houses. Women with sunken, red-rimmed eyes leaned in the embrace of palsied houses, rotten from chimney to cellar. Their faces appeared and vanished in the rays of an occasional gas lamp until I wondered whether I was looking at skulls and cross bones.

An arched passage appeared, low and tight, which the bird woman had told me was the entrance to Bletcher's Court. I was forced to bend my head and turn sideways to keep my shoulders from rubbing against the grubby bricks. My shawl caught on a rusted nail before I pulled into the court itself. The walls were thickly whitewashed in an attempt to smother the smell of vermin, both animal and human.

A catacomb of even smaller laneways lay beyond. Then there it was, the crooked street sign barely legible in the miasma. Bletcher's Court. Where I'd been summoned.

I stopped and I waited. The sensation again of being watched, followed, familiar now. The summoner knew my movements well. And we were expecting each other. As though whoever had been sending me these summonses was asking to be caught, asking to be stopped.

A prickling of nerves. I remembered being tethered to the ground, fighting to keep my mind from dissolving, feeling the fine mesh covering my eyes. The man in the cloak, the gash of a knife, the womb in his gloved hand. What else had I heard or seen or didn't want to remember?

Each bone and muscle in my body felt stripped bare, the withdrawal of Griffith's opiates leaving me exposed. I hoped I was thinking straight. Pond would awaken at the asylum at any moment, notify the police, my whereabouts confirmed by the summons lying by the bible at the foot of the bed. *To take revenge halfheartedly is to court disaster; either condemn or crown your hatred. October 21, Bletcher's Court.*

Cails and Knight would be stopped before they could savage one more woman. With Griffith's men as witnesses. They would have their killer. The Shoreditch Savage—not Aaron Tarski.

More images shifted through my mind. A crack, a bone splitting, Cails holding his face as I brought the metal down against his head. Going rigid before he slumped, arms falling to his side. Dying? If he was alive, he would expect to get his revenge tonight but would find coppers and truncheons waiting for him instead. Knight would be destroyed, his family along with him. I felt something splinter in my head, thinking of Constance Knight and her children. Then stopped myself, unable to go any further.

Time expanded and contracted. I pulled the shawl more closely around me. My body filled with loathing, as toxic as the drugs Griffith had put in my veins. Cold but suddenly clear-eyed, I turned around full circle in the small court, purging the pure loathing from my thoughts. Another kind of poison that would do me no good. My reckoning with Griffith and his hatred for me and my father would come another day.

Letting out a breath from my lungs, I slowed to a stop. Somehow, ahead in a crabbed corner of the court I'd missed it, a window where a single light faltered. It took under a moment to cut across toward a crooked, splintered door. I hesitated. Then the hiss of voices, male, from inside.

I knocked softly.

CHAPTER 46

A man cracked open the door, a bottle of gin in a hammed fist, face like a pudding, thin hair slicked back. He hesitated, a slow smile spreading across his face. I'd sensed I'd met his kind before with eyes above pouched skin sharp as marbles. Someone accustomed to making profitable decisions. Newspaper and rags blacked out the few windows in the room. The aroma of men, and worse, rose like a tide.

"Not makin' yer doss on a night like this?" His glance took in my moth-eaten shawl and the ripped sleeves of my blouse. "Yer must be doin' somethin' wrong with not many other girls movin' in here on the Court givin' yer the competition."

I wasn't sure what I was looking for. A prostitute, actress, the killer's next victim? Maggie Fisher?

Candles burned in the background and an old man splayed on a rotted velvet stool. He sucked on a treacle, his mouth opening and closing like a child's. Behind him was what looked like a raised mattress, two women half-sitting, half-lying in the sallow light.

The sharp-eyed man raised his bottle toward me, a welcoming toast. "'Tis a slow night but let's see what we can do fer ya." Off the side of the room there was a hallway and in its curve a door opened. A young man, a forelock of hair dipping below one eye, tumbled out, still pulling up his pants, satiation dulling his features. A furtive glance and he disappeared to the back of the house.

Calm was heavy inside me, or perhaps it was the remnants of Griffith's bromide, smothering a flicker of anger. "I'm looking for someone," I said.

"Sure yer are." He recognized something in my speech and made a mockingly low bow. "Seen better times, have ya? Why don' you come right on in." His gesture encompassed a squalid room. Leftovers from a meal, coarse bread, and straw littered the floor. A kitten, parchment thin, curled weakly on the ground. It had been scalded and had a leather collar around its neck.

The women behind him moaned, stirred. On a low table there was powder, syringe, tourniquet. I didn't need to see their arms to imagine the sores that marched up and down their pale skin, making chains binding them to the bed redundant. Nor did I need to speculate on their ages.

The sharp-eyed man shot me a glance, calculating. "A looker yer are, I can see that. Good hair, good teeth, shouldn't be no reason why not." He added something inaudible to himself as I stepped inside. One of the women sat up, blinking like a child roused from sleep. "We can make room fer yer here. I does the arranging, with the women gettin' their room and board." He laughed. "And then a little extra when they're all doin' fine. Who wouldn' want shelter from the streets these days? Each time a miserable creature is murdered, the killer has disappeared. And the police do nothin' while women shiver in bunches wonderin' whose turn will come next."

He was quite the humanitarian and I told him so. The odor coming off him overwhelming, I fought the urge to put my scarf to my nose.

Letting go of the gin bottle, he peered at my face, and then laughed again. "Can't see why you wouldna want to join us, not unless yer hidin' somethin' under those skirts I don' know."

I laughed along with him, lightheaded with a surge of emotion I didn't dare examine. "Let me make you a proposition." I took a step back. "How many women do you have staying here with you?" Eight tonight, it turned out, and I offered him an outrageous sum for their release, along with the kitten, and with the proviso that he never worked as a purveyor of flesh again.

He let out a snort, surveying me with a hand on his hip, as though I was telling him a story from a book of folk tales. While all of this was taking too much time. A spike of anxiety cut through the strange calm, warning me that I might be too late. Again.

Face slacking into distrust. "Why should I believe ye've that kind of coin?"

"Do you know Maggie Fisher?" The name came readily, dredged from some instinct and my memory of the last month.

He squinted, exaggerating the pouches under his eyes and answered too quickly. "I do. What of it?"

"She'll vouch for me." I kept the distaste from my voice. "That I'm good for the money."

He raised his hand. I stiffened. Worse still, his hand drifted away from me, to the candle burning in the window, hovering and then snuffing it out. In the near dark, the breaths of the two women on the mattress seemed louder. He pressed against me with his dirt encrusted shirt, the warm stench of gin rising.

I saw no point in wasting any more time. I stepped back, my hand pushing the door open behind me, then aimed the other hand, knuckles exposed, at the man's throat. I missed, hit too low, then turned to bring the tip of my boot into his crotch, driving air from his lungs. He buckled at the waist.

A hand wrenched my shoulder, propelling me back over the threshold and into the brume of Bletcher's Court. I stopped breathing and then something cold and sharp pressed into the base of my neck.

"I wouldn't struggle so much if I were you." I looked down to see a knife at my throat and then I looked up and into the small eyes of Maggie Fisher.

CHAPTER 47

It must have been a sign, a signal, the house plunging into darkness. No surprise. There were layers of evil here in this hovel and Maggie Fisher was part of it.

In the doorway, the man was panting heavily but he recovered enough to gather his anger together like a rabid dog on the end of a leash. "The bitch," he said, "Don' slice her neck jes yet. Would teach her a lesson first." His big hand, nails bitten to the quick, covered Maggie's and the knife's hilt, his mouth a coil of rage. I gritted my teeth against the curl of blood beginning to drip down my neck.

"Don't be so quick about it, you fool." Maggie's breath floated between us. She kept her hand on the knife and I wondered at its size. The blade could be a small thing but then again, so was a vein. "You'll get yer chance. Leave her be for the moment. We'll be back." Spoken like a dark queen of the streets.

"The bitch promised me money. She good for it?"

Maggie's voice was regal, in control. "You mean before you decide to slit her throat, Keeger?" Spoken almost in jest, as though daring him to cross her.

"Before I decide to ship her off to some pit." He spat the words.

"You're always bein' a bit hasty." Almost casually, Maggie pushed his hand off the hilt of the knife while I measured in centimeters each breath I took.

"I asked—she good for the money?" Keeger released a thick clot of phlegm at my feet.

"She is. And I'll be gettin' back to you later." The words imperious. "Now go." Maggie pulled me along with her further away from the door. Her knife guided me with amazing delicacy back into the court while I sensed the man melting into the darkness. There was a brittle strength to the older woman, but I could have possibly broken her hold. Or so I told myself. Possibly. I didn't fancy the knife finding its way across my throat, face, or elsewhere.

"You're here to take me to him, aren't you?" My mind spinning the ways I could take the weapon from her grasp. The courtyard was dimly lit but Maggie's footsteps confident and sure.

She chuckled, because she knew something that I didn't. "You could say that. You could also say that I saved you from Keeger back there, a nasty piece of work, he is. Saved you for the second time in your life."

"Why the knife, then?" I tried to keep a choking sound from my voice, wondering if she was meant to keep me intact, leaving me whole for the killer to do his bloody work.

"Jess making sure. Making sure you're alone. Can't have you screaming or worse." Practical Maggie Fisher.

"You're in Cails's employ." My fingers clenched and I wondered if I could move them fast enough to grab the blade from her grip.

Another throaty laugh. "That fancy man you keep looking for?" She stopped and it was possible that we had only moved in a circle, a gruesome dance, perhaps thirty feet from where we had started. Maggie. Clever Maggie. Then the impossible happened. The knife slipped from my throat and I exhaled. Maggie stepping away, falling into the dark behind me.

In front of me, a door above which hung the number thirteen. It was partially open, a light of a single candle burning somewhere inside.

I took a step but even on the stoop, the stink told me that I was too late.

The squat door scraped open. My vision adjusted to the dimness, shades of grey becoming readable, revealing where the walls met the floor. The room measured about ten feet from the entrance to the fireplace. There was a bed, two tables, a chair and washstand.

A rush of heat, my body drenched instantly in sweat. My arm stretched out for something to hold onto. I knew that every conceivable mutilation had been practiced on the body lying on the bed, limbs and organs strewn across the walls, the floors, the low ceiling. Intestines on the table alongside one of the woman's breasts. Large portions of the thighs cut away and the head turned to the left, mutilated beyond recognition. Gashes in all directions where the nose, cheeks, eyebrows and ears would have been. Tucked behind the head were the uterus and kidneys and the other breast. The liver between the feet. The flaps, removed from the abdomen and thighs, consecrated the table. The bed was saturated with blood. I wanted to blind myself.

A suck of air, taking the stench inside me. *Too late. I was too late.* Then something rustled in the corner, on the chair, only a whisper, at once too close and too far away. But it suddenly became clear to me all the same. The cloak, the top hat, the boots gleaming not with polish now but with bodily fluids. Victor Cails.

CHAPTER 48

The posture, the sway of the cloak as the figure stood to face me. Collar pulled high around the neck, hat low over the forehead. So familiar but in ways I didn't want it to be. Only the eyes were visible and something flashed between us. A darkening in the gaze, pulling me in, revealing something I hadn't seen before. Hadn't wanted to see. An awful secret that was revealing itself in the haze that shimmered from the gasping candle in the corner.

"You didn't divine the truth?" A laugh, low and feminine. Not Cails. Not at all. "You didn't at least guess? You, the mind doctor?"

A bright flash behind my eyes, like the explosion of a camera. Then the slow development of the daguerreotype, blurred features coalescing into a familiar face. Hair was swept off the forehead, scraped back from the face, but the bones were the same, the sharpness of the cheeks, the turn of the chin, the intensity of the gaze. "No," I said to Constance Knight. "I didn't recognize the truth."

Her voice was raspy, as though infused with sleep. "Imagine that. You failed to read my mind. Despite your pretensions otherwise. For shame, Georgia." My heart went weak. "You even lived in my household. Spent time with me, my husband and my children. Pretended you were my friend."

The corpse on the bed seemed to be laughing at me, lips blanched and cut by several incisions running obliquely down to the chin. Blood drenched the floor, glazing the air with a metallic stink.

"You know why, don't you?" Constance tightened her hold on me from across the room. I tried to back up against the threshold, but her gaze was a prison, forcing me to stand where I was.

"Why?" I tested my ability to speak, fighting the urge to double over and retch. The realization of what I'd missed was like a nail being driven through the front of my forehead, punishment for my inability to see. My refusal to understand. My obsession with Cails. My confusion over Constance Knight's own husband.

She shrugged under the voluminous cloak. "She," Constance gestured carelessly with her eyes in the direction of the intestines gleaming on the table, "Martha Cannon, I think her name is—or was, but what does it matter—is just one of many, yet one of the same. *That's why.*" Constance lowered the collar of her cloak and took the hat from her head, the light making a half moon of her face. The strong brow, wide mouth, unlike the dainty features so prized by the women of our age, I thought, defeat infusing every part of my body.

She slid, almost slipped, through the blood on the floor to stand next to the body on the bed. "They're whores and cunts. All of them." Then she fixed her glare at me. "May they all rot in hell." She pulled a hand through her hair, loosening the strands pulled back tightly, the fingers stiffening a moment before relaxing again, a tell of rage that she couldn't conceal. "And may my esteemed father rot in hell," she spat.

Her father. *The Baron didn't last long. I haven't seen such a florid case of syphilis in years. Ralston died a harrowingly painful death, a suppurating mass of pustules, howling like a dog, just eighteen months after the wedding of his daughter, Constance.*

Her mother. Syphilis contracted from Ralston, her husband. *That was the reason for her mother's illnesses, her state of collapse, losing her infants... in such a fashion. One after the other they would die during her confinement.*

Nothing inside me but a dry nausea. And Victoria Trevyn, the governess, a sleep walker. A perfect distraction that had allowed Constance Knight to launch herself into the foulest of London nights to find her children, on the nights the Shoreditch Savage was about his business. *Her business.* I recalled the aroma of crushed almonds in the nursery, Trevyn's enlarged pupils. Constance was drugging her own children and the governess. Had she sensed that Trevyn had come too close, had seen what I hadn't seen, Constance returning late at night with blood on her hands? What better way to eliminate the threat than have the governess commit suicide, given her already fragile, mental state.

"You think I'm a monster, Georgia?" Constance reading my mind, an irony I was desperately aware of. "To use my children and my cousin in the way I have? You have no idea of monstrousness until you understand my father. No, don't look at me like that. You can't possibly imagine, can't possibly know. It's not enough that he, my esteemed father, works his way through the diseased dens of actresses and whores but then he brings home the sickness to my mother. He was there enough of the time to ensure pregnancy after pregnancy, dripping and stinking with the pox." A long pull of breath, taking the air from the room leaving a suffocating void. "He was my father. And the begetter to a series of infants, babies—" Her arms rose to her sides, filling the space of the room until there was nothing but her presence and the work she had wrought. "Do you have any idea of what a poxed pregnancy looks like?" For a moment her lips trembled but nothing more came out.

I was too aware that knowledge could be powerful and useless at the same time. "The bacterium passes from the placenta to the infant from the infected mother." I was also aware of drying blood, sticky beneath my feet.

Constance was still, a storm gathering its forces. "Always so cool, always so rational. Of course, you know the science, Georgia. But do you know the reality of it? The feel of it, the smell, the suffering. What it's like to see a newborn pulled from her mother, stillborn, or worse, still alive, sunken skeleton, struggling to breathe? More reptile than human?"

Her words mesmerized, enlarging her presence even further, rendering the slaughter around us as a backdrop, a stage set to the other horrors she had witnessed.

"Have you seen a woman slowly wasting away from disease, screaming, hysterical at the thought of delivering yet another monster? Forced upon her by her husband? Because she doesn't know how to prevent the horror from happening to her or is too cowardly to finish with the pregnancy? *Have you?*"

"I haven't," I lied, my voice breaking. Abortion was a fact of life among women of all classes, biology making no distinctions, competent and willing doctors and midwives difficult to find, outcomes oftentimes too unspeakable to contemplate. I had seen the damage done in my practice, the girls and the women, desperate, wounded, lost.

Pain pulsed from Constance in waves. She closed her eyes for a moment against some recollection I was forced to imagine along with her. Only then did I start to shake. The impact of what she was, what she'd done. There was a terrible breathing in the room, hers or mine, I couldn't tell.

"You helped the doctor," I said finally and because it was the truth. "You helped your mother." Constance Knight's strong and capable hands, familiar with the tools of a surgeon. Familiar with a knife.

"I did." That recognizable confidence, sickening now. "We only had the local country doctor, my mother refusing to avail herself of a specialist, *ashamed*, if you can believe it, for sins not of her own making. While I would assist, watching, passing the cold, metallic instruments."

"Such things are never meant to be seen by someone so young. You were how old?" I asked through burning lips, clenching my hands by my side to stop the shaking.

Her eyes widened and for a moment I thought I could see the Constance Knight I'd first met, beleaguered yet strong, standing in the hallway of her house at Mayfair, worrying for her missing children. "Old enough to understand my mother's misery."

"You took care of your mother. So she wouldn't have to be alone. You gave her some control over her life, Constance. Over her body. Too often the actions we have to take are fraught with difficulty and pain and regret. You have every right to hate your father."

She didn't answer, not needing to hear anything more than that, opening a small window for me to take control. "Constance—we should go." I took a step toward her, cringing at the slide of fluids beneath my feet. "The police can't be far behind."

"You would save me." The sadness fled as suddenly as it had appeared, her skin pulled taut against her face.

"I would help you in the same spirit you strived to help your mother." I probed carefully. "What happened to you when you were young was not your fault."

When she looked up, her eyes were clear and steady, and I remembered again that at one time I'd thought we might be friends. "I am not mad." The denial sharp.

"I know you're not. Your feelings are justified." Another step closer when I saw the blade, six inches curved and shining, in her hand. "Although your actions are not."

Constance followed my gaze. "You feel that you have the right to judge me."

"Is that what you think?"

"What I think is that a woman who would have an affair with a married man is not any better than the filth we're surrounded with in this place."

She moved toward me, one long, slow stride, clearing half the room. I refused to step back. "I'm not having an affair with a married man."

"You lie."

How did she know about William? Or did she?

"I found your note to my husband," she said. "One of your many assignations, no doubt. At the National Gallery. And other times, in my home, catching you in his dressing room. Then his watching you, always so carefully and with such intensity." Her eyes fastened on mine. "That last message, your tempting him into another assignation—I asked Alice's char woman to watch you, to procure it for me."

The revelation slammed into me, almost doubling me over. Who was Alice and Katharine's char woman? I struggled to recall a face or a name, denials surging from my mouth. "There is nothing between us. Nothing. I'm not involved with your husband in any way."

Constance's expression didn't belong to a madwoman, her eyes clear, smile insinuating. "Don't insult me, Georgia, or force me to list any number of times I've seen you with Charles. He even brought you to live with us, under our roof. *My* roof. My mother may have been willfully ignorant but I'm not."

There was little I could offer her but the truth as I knew it. "Your husband loves you and the children—no one else."

Holding up the hand with the knife, she gave me a firm, polite smile. "I'm getting impatient with your lies. There are other married men as you well know. My husband is not the first of your conquests."

She couldn't possibly have known about William. Alice and the letters. I didn't move, my mind ordering me to be still. In revealing herself to me, and most importantly to herself, Constance was fanning the flames of a fury just beneath the surface. The path ahead seemed ordained.

"There is only one way to fight back and you, if anyone, should understand why I do what I do." Her voice strong with conviction.

"I'm trying to understand, Constance, if you would tell me more. That's why you sent me the summonses, isn't it? You knew you needed help, someone to stop you from hurting these women. We can talk

more about all this but here is not the place. I hear someone coming."
I raised my finger to my lips.

I'd gone too far. Whatever twisted rapport was growing between
us, it was instantly replaced by something else. "You're trying to
manipulate me. I should have killed you while I had the chance. I
could have. I noticed you following me the night I handled two more
of these sluts."

I didn't want to remember and I didn't want to acknowledge the
sickening reality of her words. "You didn't kill me then, Constance. You
stopped yourself in time because you recognized right from wrong."

"It's not only you who likes to play God, Georgia." She was growing
agitated and I should have known better. "I let you live because I
could." Standing a few feet away, she rocked on her heels as though
coming to some kind of decision. Then she threw herself against me,
her elbow glancing my jaw. The blow pitched me against the table,
slippery viscera beneath my hands as I hauled myself back to my feet.
I blinked away the sting when I saw the knife slash toward me. The tip
caught along the edge of my hand and I cried out as she slashed again,
an inch this time from my throat.

Strangulation first, I remembered. Then disembowelment. As if the
carnage around us wasn't a reminder. But unlike the other women
caught in her trap, I knew Constance for what she was, enough to
prepare myself as best I could.

The blade sculpted the air, and I sidestepped as it came down a
whisper from my ear. She wanted to see me sprawling, bleeding, quiet
at last so she could enact the ritual that calmed the acid in her veins.
Her cloak entangled her legs and mine while, gritting her teeth, she
reversed her grip on the knife with an agile sweep of her fingers.

The floor was slicked with blood, the air turning it viscous. Balance
deserting me, I fell onto my back. When I looked up, Constance was
leaning over me, straight arm pressing my chest, the knife in my face.

My breaths were shallow, paper thin. "You don't want to do this,
Constance."

"I think I do. Although I usually choke them first. Asphyxiate—isn't that the word? Believe it or not, I don't want them to suffer. And afterwards, well…" Her hand on my throat was strong, the scent of violets, incongruous, coming off her. "You really think you're so different. That's what you want me to believe. When really, you and I both know that you're just as eager to spread your legs, spread disease. To punish your own sex."

"I don't want to hurt women, Constance." I could barely speak the words, my voice no more than a hoarse breath. "My work is helping women."

"But you do—don't you see? You're like all these whores only with beauty, money, and power."

The blade caressed my cheek. I wanted desperately to imagine that I heard the slightest sound, a rustling, but that would be impossible. The police would have come with torches flaring and a drumbeat of footsteps.

"The police will be here soon, but I can get you away from this place," I tried, looking into her eyes, bright with a strange eagerness. "Back to your home, with your children, where you wish to be. Charlie and Violet. Where your heart is, Constance."

"I always ensured they were safe." Said almost with pride, a slight smile to her lips. "Asleep and out of harm's way. What mothers do for their children." Constance Knight's perversely formed maternal instincts, conflated with death and disease and shame. "And I knew you were going to rescue Trevyn. Who do you think sent off the children to fetch you?" And why the killings ceased for a time. Trevyn gone from the house, making it more difficult for Constance to resume her twisted pattern.

She nodded, arm held rigid against my breast bone. "You like to play with minds, don't you Georgia? Mine, Alice's, and that young girl, Sophie Rivington, back in Boston. The experiment that you left America to escape, the colossal failure that your father would not forgive. I returned the favor and played with yours."

Then cold steel for the second time in one night pierced my skin. A warm tear of blood rolled down my cheek. "The police will find you and they won't let you go." I was unable to keep desperation from my voice.

Her tongue slid past her lips, glistening and obscene, then a staccato sigh of sorts. The summoning of her other nature, the adjustment of her mind considering an alternative path. "Why do you want to help me?"

"Because none of this is your fault." The room was airless, my breath short.

"You think I care about such things?"

"I believe you do. Deep inside. Maybe you don't recognize it, but you do care. And that's what's made you react in such a violent, distorted manner." I continued carefully, my voice gaining strength. "You can't help what happened to you as a child, Constance. Events outside your control. The shock you witnessed and survived."

Her face blank, her hand steady.

"But you have to do the right thing, Constance. Because you can— cure yourself of this violent obsession that does nothing but hurt more women and hurt you and your family."

"What are you telling me?"

"We don't have time right now. I promise I will help you."

"You lie."

Your friend Alice James trusts me, I wanted to say, but my mind twisted around unanswered questions, long buried doubts floating to the surface. "It's what I do—and what I can do. Help you get well. Please let me try. Trust me."

The knife hovered slightly away from my face but not far enough. Suddenly there was a listlessness about her, a flattening. Or was that what I wanted to see? Hers was an unpredictable force, a coiled readiness for violence born of pain and frustration. I thought of her daughter's doll, mutilated and savaged, bearing the brunt of her anger. "For your children. For Charlie and Violet."

At that moment the door opened, and the knife came down.

CHAPTER 49

The knife came down, and it wouldn't have—if Victor Cails had not pushed his way into the room. That was the story I told myself in the years afterwards, my way of making sense of a random moment in time. The weapon missed its mark, Cails pulling Constance aside, pinning her hard against the wall, his hand clamping her wrist, the weapon clattering to the ground.

"Don't hurt her," I said, rising from the floor. I ran a palm down my neck, my fingers coming away with streaks of blood. "I nearly had her convinced to put down the blade."

Cails raised a brow. "Miss Buchanan, you never disappoint." He shook his head. Constance slumped against the wall, curling away from us. Without releasing his hold, he waited for the blankness on her face to dissolve, for the hatred and the fire to return to her eyes. The truth was bleak and I waited for Cails to see it.

"Step away from her," I said.

He ignored me, keeping his eyes trained on Constance. With his free hand, he touched her face, moving it first to the right and then to the left. Constance's gaze frozen on a point over his head.

Astounding, the human capacity for self-delusion, I thought.

"She's useless to you now," I said.

He let her go, then picked up the blade from the floor. "You think so?"

Straightening, he surveyed the atrocity around us with a measure of shock that seemed to unnerve even him. "Perhaps we should *test* your diagnosis, Miss Buchanan, whether Constance Knight is useless to me now." He reached for Constance's limp hand and closed it around the knife. She clutched it as though by instinct.

"You hate Georgia Buchanan, don't you, Constance?" he said.

Slowly, her head turned toward me, eyes clouded. My body shook but I didn't want the contagion to spread to my limbs, my arms, the tips of my fingers. A sign of weakness that Cails would spot in an instant.

Constance groaned, muttered something under her breath. A flush to her cheeks. Escalation, I thought. Blood surged to my temples. "Close your eyes, Constance. You don't need to do anything now." I was holding my breath, watching her hand clench spasmodically around the knife. "I've helped you before and I'll help you again. You have my promise." She twitched.

My glance flicked between Cails and Constance. In the awful silence, she sagged against the wall, refusing to look at us. Her mouth curled into a twist of resolve, in a fugue state of sorts. And I, pinned between them, uncertain who posed the greater threat.

I kept my voice low. "You followed me here, Cails." The statement raw and ragged. "To get to *her* first. Before the police could find us." Constance Knight, Cails's Shoreditch killer.

The dream of Cails alive came floating back. Standing by the bed in the asylum, stethoscope dangling from his fingertips, watching me with the precision of a scientist, Pond a shadow behind him. Moving through the room like a ghost, touching the few items that belonged to me, thumbing through the pages of my notebook. Picking up and then putting down the bible at the bottom of the bed. *Bletcher's Court. October 21*[st].

Not a dream, as I'd suspected.

Cails ignored me, watching Constance. My eyes riveted on the knife in her hand, I swayed towards her. Cails pivoted, placing a booted foot between me and the woman slumped against the wall. He gave me a sly smile before turning back to Constance. "You appear deep in thought, Mrs. Knight. Perhaps remembering your dear father? The Baron who cared so little for you and even less for your mother?"

Constance blinked then pulled her hand away from her side, before lifting it in front of her face as though seeing it for the first time. I fell back, my hip brushing the wall.

Cails tracked my reactions. "Surely, you're accustomed to these types of experiments, Miss Buchanan? Aren't you curious to see what happens next?"

My vision blurred until I was seeing through a scrim turned to a bloodied red. Constance straightening her shoulders, tilting her head. Staring at the remains of Martha Cannon, the victim's lower teeth crushed in, the black glistening mucosa welling from her lacerated throat. The slabs of muscle and sinew glistening in the somber light.

My lips dry. "Constance. Look away. Look at me."

The stench in the room grew stronger.

"Do you think she knows? That she's observing her handiwork? The horror of it?" Cails stood elegant and lethal even amidst the atrocity, his cane held casually in a free hand. The wound in the skull grinned wickedly, at home in the aftermath of a battlefield.

"Look at me, Constance," I said. Her eyes flickered to the blade in her hand. Something chimed in my brain, an awareness that I might not have long to live. I wiped my bloodied hands on the shawl that had slipped to my waist.

"Ah yes, the mind doctor at work," Cails said. "Did it ever occur to you that I might have another reason to follow you here?" He didn't bother with warnings, with low growls and gnashing of teeth. "You tried to kill me."

Standing unbowed, a smile split the narrow planes of his face, no doubt aware of the panic sweeping over me. "Clearly, we're not finished with each other yet. *I'm* not finished yet. I want you to understand that *you've lost.* That all your pseudo-scientific pretensions matter not at all in the greater scheme of the material world. A world that pits the poor against the rich. That's all there is, Miss Buchanan. The result of which," he pointed to Constance with his cane, "is all around us."

My breath short, I said, "Constance. Your children. Violet and Charlie." A wilting of her shoulders. A downward tilt of her chin. An eternity before she turned away from the massacre laid out in front of her. Then, compelled by some inner voice, she slanted her body towards me. Eyes still vacant, she slipped the blade against her own face, beside her cheek.

I tried to swallow. Couldn't. "I'll take you home but you must give me the knife."

"Daring of you, Miss Buchanan. If I were so cheap a thing as a mind doctor, I would say Mrs. Knight is homicidal rather than suicidal at the moment." Cails amused.

I was no longer listening, advancing slowly towards Constance, holding her gaze with my own. "If you don't want to give me the knife, just loosen your fingers, and let it drop to the ground. So easy to do, Constance. Simply relax your fingers."

She cocked her head, as though she hadn't understood my words. For a moment, there was something in her eyes, recognition, awareness, before it was gone again.

A cold beat of my heart. Then the knife dropped to the floor.

Cails gave a flinch of a smile. That hid his defeat. He swooped down to pick up the blade.

My lungs deflated, my shoulders collapsed. I held onto the silence. Constance crumpled and slid down the wall like a child, holding her head in her arms, in a strange evocation of her husband's posture that early morning in the stables. Even Cails must have known that her personae had cracked, that she would be unable to function again as either Constance Knight or as the Shoreditch Savage.

"Put down the knife," I said, only now to the man who held it t. It would be simple for Cails to kill us both, our remains mingling with Martha Cannon's.

His eyes flickered to the blade in his hand. Then back at me. "I don't think so."

For the first time, he allowed an edge of anger in his voice. I had tried to kill him, and I'd disabled his monster. And he'd never bring her back to life. "Your bourgeois efforts to identify and track a killer, diverting at best." That graveled voice that could twist and turn the truth into a lie. "Remember what I told you. If we were to eliminate poverty, inequity, and the corrupt governments in the sway of the ruling classes, we would have little need for this interest in the frontal lobes of cadavers."

The knife turned in his hand, this time pointing at Constance. "You should have listened to me the first time, when we spoke of the women you hoped to cure. You hoped to cure them of the behaviors that place them outside the realm of the peaceable and the domestic. Why? Because society requires an angel in the house. Not a devil at the hearth. When in reality," he said, "we need more devils in the service of anarchy and revolution."

My eyes still on the weapon, now gripped more tightly in his hand. "You've proven your point. You've achieved what you're after, Cails." Raising my voice. "At least for the time being. Pricking the conscience of the powerful, undermining the government, fueling social unrest. And with clean hands. No one can ever link you to these murders."

He pretended to be affronted. "Of course not. I had nothing to do with this butchery. I was not the architect of this madwoman," he turned, glancing down at Constance, a devil that had lost her fire.

"But you used her nonetheless, for your own advantage. With Knight more helpful to you than he ever imagined he could be. And with the assistance of Maggie Fisher, your eyes and ears, to keep track both of Tarski and the Shoreditch Savage."

He acknowledged neither name, eyes snapping back to me. "My own advantage? You still don't understand, a marvel given a woman of your intelligence. I do *nothing* for my own advantage."

"For the *cause*, then." I forced myself to look at Martha Cannon. "For the poor woman on the bed."

"You can barely keep the derision from your voice."

"So kill me then." I took another step toward him. "Isn't that what you really want? Kill me for having almost killed you. Kill me for taking Constance Knight away from you. Kill me for what I know and what I am. An alienist, a mind doctor, and George Buchanan's daughter." I had nothing left. We stared at each other and I saw the calculation behind his eyes.

"You know, Miss Buchanan, you're not much of a killer." His gaze flickered over my face, then dropped to the moth-eaten shawl around my shoulders. "It takes more than a poorly aimed blow to the head to finish me off."

There was only so much he could admit to himself. That much I understood. Instead, he chose to play with me, play with the weapon in his hand, turning the hilt backwards and forwards in his palm.

"And why would I kill you, Miss Buchanan? I once told you that I abhor excess of any kind." He flashed another falsely tolerant smile. Then tucked the knife into the side of his boot.

Something unlocked in my mind. I slowed my breathing. "Are you saying the murders will stop now—all of them?" At our feet, Constance Knight was muttering softly to herself, hands clasped around her waist, trying to hold herself together, tremors silently progressing the length of her body. "That you won't find another tortured soul to use to further your demented manifesto?"

"I don't know what you're talking about, Miss Buchanan." His face a polite blank. "All I know is that I have time and resources at my disposal. Opportunities always present themselves." Finally, he made me realize he was omnipresent, unstoppable, a dark horizon.

I straightened, otherwise I would have shattered.

"Don't look so devastated." Cails backed away, moving closer to the door. "Your hope that I might disappear could very well come true. If it suits my purpose."

"And you would leave an innocent man in peace," I said. "Tarski."

"He may still be collected by the police."

I checked the anger deep in my chest. "There's no evidence with which they can hold him."

"And you still refuse to give Griffith his killer, our dear Constance?"

I ignored his question. "There's no benefit—to you or the police—in the discovery that the Shoreditch Savage is a woman." I pulled the shawl taut around my shoulders. "The wife of a prominent publisher, the daughter of a peer. Someone who has managed to elude detectives and journalists with a cunning and intelligence seldom seen before. Griffith will *run* from the truth. As will his betters."

"It is a story that I could use to my advantage." Cails baiting me with now familiar deliberation. "A well-born woman seeking her revenge on the hapless lower orders. All too familiar, one might argue, except for the first time, this time, the press was paying attention."

"You would lose Charles Knight in the telling. He would never survive the scandal, and his previous lives just might come to light. A publisher in high places is a valuable thing."

"You've almost convinced me, Miss Buchanan." But I didn't believe him.

"The story ends here." The words rang in the air as I said them, exhausted and possibly mad-eyed myself.

"Ah yes, with Mrs. Knight here receiving the best of care. In some asylum devoted to catering to her malaise, her *hysteria*. Now interesting that Tarski, had he been convicted as the Shoreditch Savage, would have found himself dangling at the end of a rope, in a prison, or worming in the gutter." Cails didn't need to use the real knife against me. "You've proven my point after all, Miss Buchanan. Unless we give chase, the wealthy and the well-positioned prevail."

His victory complete, I had one more question. "Does Knight know?" I dreaded the answer.

"Know what?" A glimmer in the depth of his eyes. "That his wife is a deranged killer?"

I spoke freely now, my judgment blown to the winds. "And that you used that knowledge for your own purposes? Leveraged not just the boy you twisted into a radical but also his delusional wife?"

"You give me far too much credit."

I sagged against the wall. "I don't think I give you nearly enough."

A careless shrug. "The police can't be far behind, even with their customary inefficiency. I would suggest we depart now in the company of Mrs. Knight," Cails said. "Frankly, I could do with another series of outraged articles in the broadsheets followed by protest and anarchy in the streets."

I'd come this far. "You're not concerned that I will go with your name to the police, to Griffith?"

Cails took my wrist, as reassurance or threat, I couldn't tell. I felt my own pulse through his gloved hand. "I don't exist, Miss Buchanan, you should know that by now. And you haven't a shred of evidence to connect me to these murders."

"Maggie Fisher." I threw out the name again.

He dropped my wrist and his brows shot up. "Never met the woman before in my life."

As she would no doubt attest.

"You will have Knight go to Griffith, make the case that revealing Constance Knight as the killer serves no one in the end." I said.

Cails's smile was almost charming. "You really can read minds, Miss Buchanan, after all."

I ripped my eyes away from him to Constance who remained sitting on the floor like a child. Shoulders hunched, fingers splayed like claws, her head buried in her knees. I approached her carefully, aware of Cails behind me. I placed a hand on an ankle. Waited. Her head lifted. She sighed faintly, eyes meeting mine, refusing to look away, refusing to look at Cails looming over us. Drawing her gently to her feet, I pulled what felt like a great weight toward me.

Cails opened the door to Bletcher's Court. We all left the room behind, throbbing with the brutalized remains of Martha Cannon and the ghosts of her sisters.

CHAPTER 50

I wanted to be here. Facing Alice James. My summoner.

It was a cold January day made comfortable in Henry James's apartments with its high ceiling and walls striped in cobalt silk. Bookshelves everywhere in dark walnut, the floors varnished to a sheen in the firelight, richly fed to beat back the chill.

And yet I felt like I'd come upon a wreckage with dark corners and smoldering ashes. Alice James adrift in a curvaceous chair, the fire light flushing her cheeks. Her eyes were sharper now that her illness had given her a short reprieve.

Or perhaps she'd discovered that power, however cruel, held its own therapeutic reward.

My mouth was dry, the trickle of a cocaine lozenge dripping down the back of my throat. A sharp anger ripening with every breath I took. "You craven, evil woman," I said.

She flinched. She'd been expecting me. A part of me, the better part, warned that the woman I'd known as a patient and a friend was weak, sickly, requiring care. The better part of me lost. "You are a murderer. A manipulator."

She straightened in the chair, turning her head away from the fire. "Rather strong terms coming from you, Georgia. And what makes you think you can just come down here and accost me in such a manner." I knew she was alone, Henry returned to London from Venice but away for the evening and Katharine Loring still in her apartments in Clerkenwell.

I advanced, shutting the door behind me, bringing the damp winter cold into the sitting room. "I'm here, *accosting you*, because of what you've done." My vision tightened, focused. I wanted to lance the evil, to draw it out of her like a poison.

"What nonsense. Next, you're going to accuse me of being mad, insane." Alice let her eyes fall to her fingertips arranged on the arms of the chair.

I laughed, an empty sound. "You're not going to get away that easily. You're not insane. Cold and calculating better describes it."

"Tell me then, why didn't you go to the police?"

The fire swayed in the grate. "What should I have told them, Alice?"

"You told them nothing, of course." She came at me with surprising strength and none of the old quaver in her voice. Her expression hardened into a fixed, defiant stare. "Because no one would believe you. You have no evidence that I manipulated Constance Knight. That I primed her to gather her suppressed rage and anger—her *justified* rage and anger—"

I moved to stand over her. One hand on the back of her chair. "Was she a killer before she met you, Alice? Or did you know about her trauma and cultivate it for your own ends?"

She didn't shrink away from me. When she should have. "You should be able to answer that question yourself. What do you think, Miss Buchanan, as a *mind doctor*?"

"Answer me."

Alice blinked. "I couldn't really say." Her tone light, "whether she'd killed before." Looking down at her hands, smoothing the skin. "All I knew is that we struck a kind of accord—"

I pushed back from her chair. "An accord?" My throat raw.

She cocked her head, as though confused. "For what am I to blame? For daring to allow myself and Constance Knight a modicum of efficacy in this world? My brothers' talents are widely praised while mine are left to smolder and die. I am the sick and frail one, my feelings and desires suppressed and discounted and medicated away."

Her voice strengthening. "Constance rose above the horror of a monstrous childhood to give shape to her rage in the only way she could. Or do you believe we should have simply remained silent, compliant, paralyzed with illness and domesticity and abuse, sinned against rather than sinners ourselves. Don't you see *why* and *what* I wanted you to see?"

Suddenly I craved the lush efficiency of another lozenge, a dose of crystalline clarity.

Backing away from her slowly, I saw her watching me. Thrown off center by my silence. Watching as I moved to the drinks table in the corner, splashed a good amount of Henry's favorite brandy into a sharply etched glass. Turning my back to her, I dove into the inside pocket of my cloak, my fingers making quick work on the wrappings of a lozenge. Then brought it to my mouth. A sip of the brandy, then another one. Smoke down my throat. Before I faced her again, my body slanting against the table. "I want to hear you say it, Alice."

Behind her the fire blazed, burning away the throb behind my eyes. I shut them briefly, then opened them to bring Alice back into the frame of my vision. "*Say it.*"

For the first time, a flicker of fear in that faded gaze. "And what purpose would that serve, Georgia?"

A surge of adrenaline ripped through my veins. "I can have you committed, Alice. Not the way you'd like to spend the remainder of your short life, I shouldn't think." I felt the edges of the glass cut into my palm. "An entirely equitable outcome, when I consider it. I don't imagine you spend your time musing about what you did to your *friend,* Constance, who's now and forever institutionalized, locked away in Leicester Lunatic Asylum, unable to remember much less see her children. A specter of her former self."

Alice tipped her head to the side, her profile with its small straight nose, thin mouth.

"You manipulated a seriously ill woman, stoking her violent tendencies for your own purposes. With the result that women in the East End were preyed upon, murdered, butchered in the most hellish of ways." My voice cracked. "That's what I need to hear you say."

Alice surprised me then, getting up from the chair, her dress loose around her thinning frame. A wraith, unsteady on her feet, but with a voice deadly calm. "You dare judge me. You dare judge me? I want to hear *you* say it, Georgia, what are you to blame for? Sophie Rivington, another horrendous mistake that you didn't think I'd know about."

The fire hissed and bit through a moment of silence. "All knowing, Georgia Buchanan." Bitterness twisted her lips. "You wanted to believe you could manage Sophie Rivington on your own, with your typical arrogance. You with your singular intelligence, your beauty and your power. Your ability to go out into the world when the rest of us are locked away in ours. You didn't want to admit there was something you'd missed, content to treat the young girl with your strange, fanciful notions. Yours and Willi's." She took a breath. "Then whatever demon was terrorizing the child ripped her apart while you stood by. The way you stood by me for endless months telling me not to pay attention to the voices, to deny the yearnings that would not let me be."

I placed the glass on the table behind me with infinite care. With every step I took toward Alice, I knew I was shedding every principle I'd ever held close. About protecting and healing those who needed my help.

Alice's hands stiffened at her sides, fingers clenching the folds of her skirts.

"*I am* all knowing, Alice," I said. I knew Maggie Fisher was a friend of Katharine Loring's charwoman. I knew neither Knight nor Griffith no longer had any need for the photographs. Good enough the murders had ceased, along with the lurid headlines and the uncontrolled mobs in the streets. As for the Assistant Commissioner, I preferred to imagine his hatred for me and my father had dissipated, expiated when he'd had me under his control at the asylum. But I suspected differently. He would keep his stories to himself in an expectation that I would as well, my time spent in Bedlam my penance for the good I didn't do. It was the best a rationalization as I could claim. A way of keeping my rage stillborn.

The fire swayed on the grate, making a muted sound that pulled me from my thoughts. Alice, her gaze stranded on mine, as fierce as I'd ever seen it, the firelight flickering over what suddenly looked like tears under the hollow of her eyes.

My mind, magnetized, returned to her notes, those childish rhythms and sly quotations intended to carve out my heart. I wanted to wake with a scream, to stop the names of those women from echoing in my head. Mary Holland, Annie Childs, Ada Stewart, Elizabeth Wood, Martha Cannon, and now Constance Knight.

My words were harsh and for once I didn't care. "Tell me one thing, Alice, just one thing. Why did you send me the summonses? To put me in danger or to have me stop the Shoreditch murders?"

Leaning against the chair, as though my question might push her over. "I don't know, Georgia," she said. "A little of both, I suppose."

"You hate me so much."

"And you think I'm no more than a child. You all think I'm a child, sitting obliviously by while the rest of you get on with real life because I can't stomach what's real."

I fought the heat surging in my blood. "You're not a child, Alice, far from it."

"I saw what you did with Willi, ingratiating yourself, making yourself indispensable to him at the university. While I may not have adoring acolytes sitting at my feet at Harvard, I do have something that he could at least acknowledge."

"What would that be? Jealousy? The reason you stole the letters between William and me?" The rest of the room suddenly came into a sharp spotlight, the mantelpiece, the desk in the corner, the shelves with their books that could hide a lifetime of secrets. There was a spiking pain behind my eyes. And a sudden urge to tear the place apart.

I began with the drinks table. The wood squealed in protest as I ripped open the slim drawer meant to hold cards or letter openers. My hands shuffled through the contents before turning my attention to the mantelpiece. With one swipe, the candles and a dainty set of porcelain shepherdesses swept to the floor. My feet crunched over the broken curls and corners, my hands reaching for the books. Tossing first one and then the other to the ground. Desperate to find what I was looking for.

I didn't stop. Alice behind me, red-rimmed eyes, hands clenched at her side. "What are you doing, Georgia?" Panic in her voice, I noted with satisfaction.

"What did you do with the letters, Alice, the private letters between William and me?"

"Stop Georgia, please. You can't blame me, for knowing what was going on between the two of you. For what I felt—"

I threw a book at her feet, just missing her by an inch. "And that was the catalyst behind your monstrous actions?"

I watched as she recoiled, crumpled to the floor, like she was shedding a skin. Her head slumped on the cushion of the chair. Her words muffled against the upholstery. "You still don't understand."

I considered taking her pulse, checking her pupils when all I wanted to do was shake her. Instead, I kept my distance, not trusting myself.

She whispered, as though all the life had gone out of her. "You take it all so lightly. Sexual relations with a married man, my brother. And very probably with Charles Knight."

I was breathing hard. "This isn't about an affair, Alice." I lied to myself that I wasn't striking out in anger. That Alice needed the disinfectant that only the truth could provide. "Your love for William isn't natural. You know this. Look at me."

Lost in the cushions of the chair and the shapeless fabric of her skirts, she slowly turned to me, her eyes burning brightly as though lit by a fever. For an instant, I wondered if I'd gone too far.

"You dare judge me?" she asked for the second time that night. "Am I any worse than you? Any worse than what you were doing with my brother and with Charles Knight?"

My lips were numb. "This is insane, in the truest sense of the word. How can it be that you hate me that much? Sending the summonses to deliberately place me in the path of the Shoreditch Savage, stoking Constance's jealousy and horrific history, using William's letters to undermine me?" I had been held in an insane asylum, drugged, *because of you*, I wanted to shout.

"Get up," I said. And when she didn't respond, I kicked aside the books at my feet. My eyes stinging, watching her turn her head back into the cushions of the chair. Afraid. Diminished. Then I saw it. In the deep crease of the chair, a black ribbon, half untied, buried in the damask. In an instant, the letters were in my hands, the smooth vellum familiar and heavy at the same time. The fire spit behind me, Alice just a movement in the corner of my eye. I heard her hitch her breath. I felt her gaze burn a hole through my back.

As I fed one page at a time into the grate, watching the words curl and burn in the white-hot coals of the hearth.

"Dear God, please don't." Alice's voice a ragged whisper. "Georgia." Ignoring her hand, stretching out towards me, I thrust another letter into the fire.

A cry this time, rich with tears. The words incomprehensible. One, two and three letters at a time into the grate. Alice's choking sounds mingling with the snap of the flames. The last of the correspondence mangled in my fist then tossed onto the fire until nothing but the black ribbon remained, dangling from my fingers.

I didn't allow myself to say more. The letters were gone and with them any power Alice thought she held over me. Another ending that I could at least control.

I thought of Charcot then, not William. *If the clinician wishes to see things as they really are, he must make a* tabula rasa *of his mind and then proceed, without any preconceived notions whatsoever.*

The last of the Dover's powder pooling away, I felt weak, drained.

Turning from the fireplace, I was ready to leave. To leave Alice, a heap on the floor, an arm flung around the chair, her eyes wet turned toward me. "You don't know what you've done," she said.

I took a breath. "I think I do. These were love letters that you had no right in reading. No right in using to manipulate me. Your voyeurism only magnified your unhealthy impulses towards your brother. And only see what horrific damage that's caused."

"You're punishing me for what I feel? What I feel in my heart?" Her face beseeching. Then reading my guilt. "I will be dead in a year's time, say the doctors, and your conscience will at least be free of me, Georgia." Her old voice, frail and girlish. "In every way. You are absolved of any responsibility. The jury has already decided upon a death sentence for me minus the scaffold."

A choking in my throat as though I wanted to scream and laugh at the same time. "You feel no remorse?"

"Would it matter?" Pushing herself up, eyes suspiciously bright, holding back more tears.

"It would for reasons I can't begin to explain." Even to myself. Most of all, to myself. The room was warm, though I felt cold. My eyes on the door, not trusting myself any longer. A feeble woman at my feet.

Alice rubbed her fingers into the hallows beneath her eyes before meeting mine again. A pulse of silence. "I feel not so much remorse as regret. Why do you think those love letters meant so much to me?"

The stripes of the wallpaper rippled in time with my pulse, the unstable firelight pulling the air in the room. Pulling the air from my lungs.

"My regret is not for the hatred but for its opposite."

Her unnatural love for her brother. I might have said the words aloud.

"No," Alice shook her head; her gaze pinned to mine. "How could you not have seen it?"

Jealousy, passion, pain, madness. *How could I not have seen it?*

"My love for you, Georgia," Alice James said.

CHAPTER 51

I could be accused of arrogance, of pride and of self-indulgence. What of it? Our lives were the stories that we told ourselves, stories that I helped patients construct, making patterns and finding shapes where none existed. Playing God? Someone had to. Otherwise our time on this earth was comprised only of random events, revealing no moral arc, no heroic theme, no tragic refrain.

Playing God—I had failed spectacularly. So secure in my knowledge and my privilege. So confident in making a science my faith. Convinced that I had the power to divine the truth, tell good from evil, mad from sane, saints from sinners. Cails's cane with its empty skull wavered in and out of my consciousness. Like the empty skull, I seemed to know less about the workings of the human mind than I ever had.

I left from Liverpool for Boston aboard the Cunard Steamship Company's RMS *Britannia* on the first Monday of the following month. Back to the ghost of Sophie Rivington, whose story I had left unfinished. And away from Alice James whose story—and love—I'd failed to recognize.

I was not long for Boston and New York. Vienna, the city of spires and dreams, summoned me now. Talk of a doctor by the name of Freud, of his investigations both shocking and new. Where I would begin again, the dead women of Shoreditch and Sophie Rivington at my side.

We work in the dark, wrote Henry James, Alice and William's brother. *We do what we can. We give what we have.* And sometimes, that has to be enough.

ACKNOWLEDGMENTS

As with most compulsions, I can't say exactly when *The Women of Blackmouth Street* began unspooling in my mind's eye, visions saturated not in sepia tones but in shades of red. Impressions of a woman, a piano and the outlines of a Freudian couch. A protagonist with the genes of a Henry James heroine, I sensed, after waking one morning from a fragmented dream, except that my Georgia Buchanan was the not-so-innocent American heiress abroad. She's unapologetic, arrogant, and kind of fancy with a complicated history and a strange vocation.

The movie camera in my head followed her to the center of a monstrous crime—this time with women at the core of its bloodied heart. No room for the fainting couch, the decorative, the maternal, the wifely. Women who, despite their late 19th-century setting, had the brains, the brawn, and the daring to do the unspeakable, the unthinkable. To mastermind and to execute. All the wrong things—but for all the right reasons. A timely story that needed to be told.

There have always been strong women, whatever the era, and I want to follow where they go—out into the world where, in their complexity, they will do good and evil, leave their trace, their mark, and their stories. Georgia Buchanan and her like, going deep into what makes us flawed and what makes us human. I played with the story of the

James family—the exceptional William, Henry, and, of course, Alice. Her relationship with her brother was reported to be unusually close. She suffered from constant health problems, diagnosed at the time as hysteria. She also kept a diary, published posthumously, that was both elegant and intellectual, and gave rise to a clearer understanding of the woman she was—as much a genius as her famous brothers. Everything else in the novel concerning Alice James is simply the product of my imagination.

Because writing is a lonely sport, there's no end of people to thank for propping up the whole enterprise, supporting, coaching, bored out-of-their minds when asked to read the nth draft or offer an opinion on a tangled plot point. So, to Mary Hanley who read one of the first, embarrassing iterations and whose feedback was entirely too kind. To Jan Stephens for our walks and our talks, to Cara Lampkin, to Jenna Kalinsky, and to Lucinda Vaughan who got me over the finish line with her generous and timely insights. To Rachel Ekstrom and Scott Miller who saw the potential. And most of all to the team at Encircle, Eddie Vincent and Deirdre Wait, who offer superlative, personalized expertise and support to all their writers. A special thanks to editor Michael Piekny whose keen, frankly brilliant, and constructive insights strengthened this novel in so many ways.

Finally, much appreciation goes to my husband whose counsel and good humor I couldn't live without. He makes everything worthwhile.

ABOUT THE AUTHOR

Thea Sutton has a PhD in English literature with books and articles to her credit. She has worked in marketing and communications while dividing her time between Toronto and Southern California.

If you enjoyed reading this book,
please consider writing your honest review
and sharing it with other readers.

Many of our Authors are happy to participate in
Book Club and Reader Group discussions.
For more information, contact us at info@encirclepub.com.

Thank you,
Encircle Publications

For news about more exciting new fiction, join us at:
Facebook: www.facebook.com/encirclepub

Twitter: twitter.com/encirclepub

Instagram: www.instagram.com/encirclepublications

Sign up for Encircle Publications newsletter and specials:
eepurl.com/cs8taP